Edwin Percy Whipple

The literature of the age of Elizabeth

Edwin Percy Whipple

The literature of the age of Elizabeth

ISBN/EAN: 9783337203221

Printed in Europe, USA, Canada, Australia, Japan

Cover: Foto ©Andreas Hilbeck / pixelio.de

More available books at **www.hansebooks.com**

THE

LITERATURE

OF

THE AGE OF ELIZABETH.

BY

EDWIN P. WHIPPLE.

NINTH EDITION.

BOSTON:
HOUGHTON, MIFFLIN AND COMPANY.
The Riverside Press, Cambridge.
1884.

THESE essays on "The Literature of the Age of Elizabeth" were originally delivered as lectures before the Lowell Institute, in the spring of 1859, and were first printed in *The Atlantic Monthly* during the years 1867 and 1868.

THE phrase "literature of the age **of** Elizabeth" is **not** confined to the literature produced in the reign of Elizabeth, but is a general name for an era in literature, commencing about the middle **of** her reign, in 1580, reaching its maturity in the **reign** of James I., **between** 1603 and 1626, and perceptibly declining during the reign of his **son.** **It** is called by the name **of** Elizabeth, because it was produced in connection with influences which originated or culminated in her time, and which did not altogether cease to act after her death ; and these influences give to its great **works,** whether published in her reign or in the reign of James, certain mental and moral characteristics in common. The most glorious of all the expressions of the English mind, it is, like every other outburst of national genius, essentially inexplicable in itself. It occurred, but why **it** occurred we **can** answer **but** loosely. We can trace some of the influences which operated on Spenser, Shakespeare, Bacon, Hooker, **and** Raleigh, but the

genesis of their genius is beyond our criticism. There
was abundant reason, **in the** circumstances around them,
why they should **exercise** creative **power; but the possession of the** power **is an ultimate fact, and defies
explanation.** Still, the appearance **of so many eminent
minds in one** period indicates something in the circumstances **of the** period which aided **and** stimulated, if it
did not cause, the marvel; and **a** consideration of these
circumstances, **though it** may not enable us to penetrate
the mystery of genius, **may still shed some** light on its
character and direction.

The impulse given to the English mind in **the age of**
Elizabeth was **but one** effect of that great **movement
of the** European mind whose steps **were marked by the
revival of** letters, the invention of printing, the study
of the ancient classics, the rise of the middle class, the
discovery of America, the Reformation, the formation
of national literatures, and the general clash **and conflict of the** old with **the new, — the** old existing in de-
caying institutions, the **new in the** ardent hopes and
organizing genius **by which** institutions are created. If
the mind was not always emancipated from error during
the stir and tumult **of this** movement, it was still **stung**
into activity, and compelled **to think ; for if authority,**
whether **secular or sacerdotal, is** questioned, authority
no less **than** innovation instinctively frames reasons for

its existence. **If** power was thus driven to use the weapons of the brain, thought, in its attempt to become fact, was no less driven to use the weapons of force. Ideas and opinions were thus **all** the more directly perceived and tenaciously held, from **the** fact **that** they kindled strong passions, and frequently demanded, not merely the assent of the intellect, **but the hazard of** fortune **and** life.

At the time Elizabeth ascended the English throne, in 1558, the religious element of this movement had nearly spent its first force. There was a comparatively small band of intensely earnest Romanists, and perhaps a larger band of even more intensely earnest Puritans; but the great majority of the people, though nominally Roman Catholics, were **willing to** acquiesce in the form given to the Protestant church by the Protestant state. To Elizabeth belongs the proud distinction of having been the head of the Protestant *interest* in Europe; but the very word *interest* indicates a distinction between Protestantism as a policy and Protestantism as a faith; and she did not hesitate to put **down** with a strong hand those of her subjects whose Protestantism most nearly agreed with the Protestantism she aided in France and Holland. The Puritan Reformers, though they represented most thoroughly the doctrines and spirit of Luther **and** Calvin, were thus opposed by the English government, and were a minority of the English people. Had they succeeded in reforming the national Church, the national amusements, and the national taste, according to their ideas of reform, the history and the literature of the age of Elizabeth would have been essentially different; but they would have broken the continuity of the national life. English nature, with its basis of strong sense and strong sensuality, was hostile to their ascetic morality and to their practical belief in the all-excluding importance of religious concerns. Had they triumphed then, their very earnestness might have made them greater, though nobler, tyrants than the Tudors or the Stuarts; for they would have used the arm of power to force evangelical faith and austere morality on a reluctant and resisting people. Sir Toby Belch would have had to fight hard for his cakes and ale; and the nose of Bardolph would have been deprived of the fuel that fed its fire. The Puritans were a great force in politics, as they afterwards proved in the Parliaments of Charles and the Commonwealth; but in the time of Elizabeth they were politically but a faction, and a faction having at one time for its head the greatest scoundrel in England, the Earl of Leicester. They were a great force in literature, as they afterwards proved by Milton and Bunyan; but their position towards what is properly called the literature of the age of Elizabeth was strictly antagonistical. The spirit of that literature, in its poetry, its drama, its philosophy, its divinity, was a spirit which they disliked in some of its forms, and abhorred in others. Their energies, though mighty, are therefore to be deducted from the mass of energies by which that literature was produced.

And this brings us to the first and most marked characteristic of this literature, namely, that it is intensely human. Human nature in its appetites, passions, imperfections, vices, virtues ; in its thoughts, aspirations, imaginations ; in all the concrete forms of character in which it finds expression, in all the heights of ecstasy to which it soars, in all the depths of depravity to which it sinks,— this is what the Elizabethan literature represents or idealizes ; and the total effect of this exhibition of human life and exposition of human capacities, whether it be in the romance of Sidney, the poetry of Spenser, the drama of Shakespeare, the philosophy of Bacon, or the divinity of Hooker, is the wholesome and inspiring effect of beauty and cheer. This belief in human nature, and tacit assumption of its right to expression, could only have arisen in an age which stimulated human energies by affording fresh fields for their development, and in an age whose activity was impelled by a romantic and heroic, rather than a theological spirit.

And the peculiar **position of** Elizabeth compelled her, absolute as was her temper, to act **in harmony with her** people, and to allow individual enterprise its largest scope. Her revenue was altogether inadequate **to carry on a war** with Spain and a war with Ireland, to **assist the Protes-** tants of France and Holland, to inaugurate great schemes of American colonization, to fit out expeditions to harass the colonies **and** plunder the **commerce** of Spain, — inadequate, **in short, to make England a** power of the first class.　But the patriotism of her people, coinciding with their interests **and love of adventure,** urged them to undertake public objects as commercial speculations. They made war on her enemies for the spoils to **be ob-** tained from **her** enemies. Perhaps the **most compre-** **hensive type of the** period, representing most vividly the stimulants it presented to ambition and **avarice, to** chivalrous sentiment and greed of gain, to action and **to** **thought,** was **Sir Walter** Raleigh.　Poet, historian, courtier, statesman, military **commander,** naval com- mander, colonizer, **filibuster, he had no** talent and no accomplishment, no virtue **and no vice,** which the time **did not** tempt **into** exercise.　He participated in the widely varying ambitions **of** Spenser and Jonson, of Essex **and** Leicester, of Burleigh, Walsingham, and Sir Nicholas Bacon, of Norris and **Howard of Effingham,** of Drake, Hawkins, and **Cumberland; and in all these** he **was** thoroughly human.

The next characteristic of the higher literature of the period is its breadth and preponderance of thought, — a quality which seemed native to the time, and which was shared by the men of affairs. Indeed, no one could serve Elizabeth well whose loyalty of heart was unaccompanied by largeness **of brain.** She was so surrounded **by** foreign enemies **and** domestic factions, that **the** sagacity which makes the fewest mistakes was her **only** security against dethronement or assassination. Her statesmen, however fixed might be their convictions and energetic their wills, were, by the necessities of their position, compelled to be wary, vigilant, politic, crafty, comprehensive in their views, compromising in **their** measures. The time required minds that could observe, analyze, infer, combine, foresee, — vigorous in the grasp **of** principles, exact in the scrutiny **of facts.** Such **were** the complications of political affairs, that the difficulty, with all but the most capacious intellects, was to decide at all ; and even they sometimes found it wise to follow the drift of events which it was almost impossible to **shape** or to guide. It might be supposed, that if, in any person of the period, impetuosity of purpose or caprice of will would overbear all the restraints **of** prudence, that person was Elizabeth herself ; but she really was as indecisive in conduct **as she was** furious in passion. Proud, fierce, vain, haughty, vindictive ; a virago and a coquette; ready enough **to** box the ears **of one of her** courtiers, and threaten **with an** oath to unfrock one **of** her bishops; **despotic in** her **bearing towards** all **over whom she had** complete control; **cursed, indeed, with** every internal impulse which leads to **reckless action,** — **she** was still a thinker; and thought revealed **insecurities** in her position, in considering which even her impe**rious** will was puzzled into irresolution, and shrank from **the plain road of force to** feel its way through the crooked paths **of** hypocrisy and craft.

This comprehensiveness **of** thought did **not, in the** men of letters, interfere with loftiness of thought; but **it** connected thought with life, gave it body and form, and made **it** fertile in those weighty maxims which, while they bear directly on practical conduct, and harmoniz with the experience of men, are also characterized by that easy elevation of view and of tone which **distin**guishes philosophic wisdom from prudential moralizing. **The** Elizabethan thinkers instinctively recognized the truth that real thinking **implies** the action of the whole **nature, and not of a** single isolated faculty. They were men of large understandings; but their understandings rarely acted apart from observation and imagination, — from sentiment, passion, and character. They **not only** reasoned, but they had reason. **They looked at** things, and round things, and into things, and through things.

Though they were masters of the processes of logic, their eminent merit was their broad grasp of the premises of logic, and their ready anticipation of the results of logic. They could argue; but **they** preferred to flash the conclusions of argument **rather than** to recite its details, and their minds darted to **results** to which slower intelligences creep. From the **fact** that they had reason **in abundance,** they were somewhat chary of reasons. Their thinking, indeed, gives us the solid, nutritious, enriching substance of thought. While it comprehends the outward facts of life, it connects them with those great mental facts beheld by the inner eye **of the** mind. It thus combines massive good sense **with a** Platonic elevation of spiritual perception, and especially avoids the thinness and juicelessness which are apt **to** characterize the greatest efforts of the understanding, when understanding is divorced from character.

This equipoise and interpenetration of the faculties of the mind and the feelings of the heart, which give to these writers their largeness, dignity, sweetness, and power, are to be referred in a great degree to the imaginative element **of** their natures. They lived, indeed, in an imaginative age, — an age in which thought, feeling, aspiration, character, whether low or exalted, aimed to embody themselves in appropriate external forms, and be made visible to the eye. In the great poets and

1 *

philosophers this imagination existed both as ecstatic insight of spiritual facts **and** as shaping power, — as both the " vision and the faculty divine"; but all over the Elizabethan society, — in dress, in manners, in speech, in the badges of professions, in amusements, in pageants and spectacles, — character, class, and condition, in **all** their varieties, were directly imaged. Lamb calls all **this a** visible poetry ; **and much** which we now read as poetry was simply **the** transference into language of the common facts of **the time.**

This imaginative tendency of **the national mind ap-**peared **in a still** higher form in that chivalrous cast **of** feeling **and of** thought which we observe in **all the** **nobler men of the time.** " High-erected thoughts seated **in a heart** of courtesy," is **Sir** Philip Sidney's definition **of** the gentleman ; **and** this was the standard to which **many** aspired, **if few reached** it. This chivalry was a poetic reflection of the **feudal** age, which was departing **in** its rougher and baser realities, **but lingering** in its beautiful ideas and ideals, **especially in the** knightly love **of adventure** and the knightly reverence for woman. **It gave an air of** romance to acts, enterprises, and **amusements** which sometimes had their vulgar side. Raleigh tilted **in** silver armor before the Queen, but the silver from which the armor was made **had been** stolen from Spanish merchantmen. Sidney was eager to fight in single combat with the defamer of his uncle Leicester, though his uncle richly deserved the gibbet. Cumberland was **a** knight-errant of the seas, strangely blending the love of glory with the love of gold, the spirit of wild adventure with the spirit of commercial thrift. Something imaginative, **something** which partook of the sentiment **of the old** time, was mingled **with the** bustling practicalities of the present. If we **look at** a man like Sir Francis Drake from **the** mere understanding, we find it difficult to decide whether his enterprises were private or national, whether the patriot predominated over the pirate, or the pirate over the patriot; but if we look at him from the Elizabethan point of view, it is not difficult to discern an enthusiastic, chivalric, loyal, Protestant spirit as the presiding element of his being and the source of his pecuniary success. He did many things which, if done now, would very properly send the perpetrator of them to the gallows; yet, as a man, he was very much superior to many a modern statesman and judge, who would conscientiously order his execution. Vitally right, but formally wrong, he **in** the Elizabethan age was immensely honored.

This slight reference **to** a few of the Elizabethan men **of** action shows that literature was but one out of many expressions of the roused energies of the national heart

and brain, and that those who performed actions which
poetry celebrates were as numerous as the poets. As
the external inducements to adopt literature as a profession were not so great as in our day, — as there was no
reading public in our sense of the term, — we are at
first surprised that so much genius was diverted into
this path. But both Elizabeth and James were learned
sovereigns; both were writers; and in the courts of
both literature and learning were the fashion, and often
the avenues to distinction in Church and State. It
was recognized that literary ability was but one phase
of general ability. Buckhurst was an eminent statesman. Sidney and Spenser were men of affairs. Raleigh could do anything. Bacon was a lawyer and
jurist. Hooker, Hall, Giles and Phineas Fletcher,
and Donne were in the Church. The patronage of
educated and accomplished nobles was extended to
numerous writers like Daniel and Drayton, who could
not have subsisted by the sale of their works. None
of these can be styled authors by profession: that sad
distinction was confined to the dramatists. In the time
of Elizabeth and James the theatre was almost the only
medium of communication between writers and the people, and attracted to it all those who aimed to gain a
livelihood out of the products of their hearts and imaginations. Its literature was the popular literature of

the age. It was newspaper, magazine, novel, all in one.
It was the Elizabethan "Times," the Elizabethan
" Blackwood," the Elizabethan " Temple Bar " : it
tempted into its arena equally the Elizabethan Thack-
erays and the Elizabethan Braddons ; but the remuner-
ation it afforded to the most distinguished of the swarm
of playwrights who depended on it for bread was small.
All experienced the full bitterness of poverty, if we except Shakespeare, Jonson, and Fletcher. Shakespeare
was an excellent man of business, a part-proprietor of a
theatre, and made his fortune. Jonson was patronized
by James, and was as much a court poet as a popular
poet. Fletcher, though the most fertile of the three in
the number of his plays, and the greatest master of
theatrical effect, did not, it is supposed, altogether depend on the stage for his support. But Chapman, Dekkar, Field, Rowley, Massinger, and all the other professional playwrights, were wretchedly poor. And it
must be said, that, though we are in the custom of
affirming that the circumstances of the age of Elizabeth
were pre-eminently favorable to literature, most of the
writers, including such men as Spenser and Jonson, were
in the habit of moaning or grumbling over its degeneracy,
and of wishing that they had been born in happier times.

There were, then, three centres for the literature
of the period, — the Court, the Church, and the Theatre.

Let us consider the drama first, as it was nearer the
popular heart, was the medium through which the
grandest as well as meanest minds found expression, and
was thoroughly national, or at least thoroughly nation-
alized.

England had a drama as early as the twelfth century,
— a drama used by the priests as a mode of amusing
the people into a knowledge of religion. Its products
were called Miracle Plays. They were written, and
often acted, by ecclesiastics ; they represented the persons and events of the Scriptures, of the apocryphal
Gospels, and of the legends of saints and martyrs, and
were performed sometimes in the open air, on tempo-
rary stages and scaffolds, sometimes in churches and
chapels. The earliest play of this sort of which we
have any record was performed between the years 1100
and 1110. The general characteristic of these plays,
if we should speak after the ideas of our time, was
blasphemy, and blasphemy of the worst kind ; for the
irreverent utterance of sacred names is venial compared
with the irreverent representation of sacred persons.
The object of the writers was to bring Christianity
within popular apprehension ; and in the process they
burlesqued it. They belonged to a class of writers and
speakers, as common now as then, who vulgarize the
highest subjects in the attempt to popularize them, —

who degrade religion in the attempt to make it efficient. The writers of **the** Miracle Plays only appear worse than their Protestant successors, from the greater rudeness in the minds and manners **to** which they appealed. They did not aim to lift the people **up, but to** drag the Divinity down ; **and,** not being **in any** sense poets, they could not make what was sacred familiarly apprehended, **and at the** same time preserve that ideal remoteness **from** ordinary life which is the condition of its being reverently apprehended. Their religious dramas, accordingly, were mostly monstrous farces, full of buffoonery and indecency, though not without a certain coarse humor and power of characterization. Thus, in the play of the Deluge, Noah and his wife are close copies of contemporary character and manners, projected **on** the Bible narrative. **Mrs. Noah is a** shrew and **a** vixen ; refuses to leave her gossips and go into the ark ; scolds Noah, and is soundly whipped by him ; then wishes herself a widow, and thinks she but echoes the feeling of all the wives in the audience, in hoping for them the same good luck. Noah then takes occasion to inform all the husbands present that their proper course is to break in their wives after his fashion. By this time the water is **nearly up to** his wife's neck, and she is partly coaxed and partly forced into the ark by one **of her sons.** Again, in a play on the Adoration of the

Shepherds, the shepherds **are three** English boors, who meet with a variety of the most coarsely comical adventures in their journey to Bethlehem; who, just before the star in the east appears, get into a **quarrel** and fight, after having feasted on Lancashire jammocks and **Halton ale**; and who, when they arrive at their destination, present three gifts to the infant Saviour, namely, a bird, a tennis-ball, and a bob **of** cherries.

The Miracle **Plays** were **very popular,** and did not altogether die out before **the reign of James.** In some of them personified **abstractions came to be blended** with the persons of the drama; and in the fifteenth century a new **class of** dramatic performances **arose,** called Moral Plays, in which these personified abstractions pushed persons out of the piece, and ethics **supplanted** theology. There is, in some of these **Moral** Plays, a great deal of ingenuity displayed ·in **the** impersonation and allegorical representation **of qualities.** They took strong hold **of the** English mind. Pride, gluttony, sensuality, worldliness, meekness, temperance, faith, **in** their single and in their blended action, **were often** happily characterized; and, though they were eventually banished from the drama, they reappeared in the pageants of Elizabeth and **in the** poetry of Spenser. But their popularity **was doubtless** owing more to their fun than their **ethics;** and the two characters of the Devil and Vice, the laughable monster and the laughable buffoon, were the darlings **of the** multitude. In Ben Jonson's " Staple of News," Gossip Tattle exclaims: " My husband, Timothy Tattle, God **rest** his soul! was wont to say **that** there was no play without a fool and **a** Devil **in 't: he** was for the Devil still, **God bless** him! **The Devil** for his money, he **would say ; I** would fain see the Devil."

Nearer to the modern Play than either the Miracle **or** the Moral, was the Interlude, so called from its being acted in the intervals of a banquet. **It was a farce** in one act, and devoted to the humorous and satirical representation of contemporary manners and character, especially professional character. John **Heywood,** the jester of Henry VIII., was the best maker **of these** Interludes.

At the time that all of these three forms of the drama were more or less in esteem, Nicholas Udall, a classical scholar, produced, about the year 1540, the **first** English comedy, " Ralph Roister Doister," — very much superior, in incident and characterization, to " Gammer Gurton's Needle," written twenty years afterwards, though neither rises above the mere prosaic delineation, the first of civic, the last of country life. The poetic element, which was afterwards so conspicuous in the Elizabethan drama, did not even appear in the first English tragedy, " Gorboduc," **though it** was written by Thomas Sackville, the **author of the** Induction **to the** " Mirror **of Magistrates," and** the only great **poet** that arose between **Chaucer and** Spenser. " Gorboduc " was **acted before** Queen Elizabeth at Whitehall, **by** the Gentlemen **of the** Inner Temple, in January, **1562. It was** received with great applause ; but it appears, as read now, **singularly** frigid and unimpassioned, with not even, as Campbell **says, " the unities of space and** time to circumscribe its **dulness." It has all the** author's justness, weight, and fertility **of thought, but little** of his imagination ; and **though** celebrated as the first English play written in blank verse, the measure, in Sackville's hands, is wearisomely monotonous, and conveys no notion **of** the elasticity and variety of which it was afterwards found **capable,** when used by Marlowe and Shakespeare. The tragedy is not deficient in terrible events, **but even** its murders make us yawn.

It is probable that **the** fifty-two plays performed at court between 1568 and **1580, and of** which nothing is **preserved but the** names, **contained** little to make us **regret their loss.** Neither at the Royal Palace, nor the **Inns of Court, nor the** Universities, — at all of which plays were performed, — could a free and original national drama be built up. This required **a public theatre, and an** audience composed of all classes of the people. Ac-

cordingly, the most important incident in the history of
the English stage was the patent granted by the crown,
in 1574, to James Burbage and his associates, players
under the protection of the Earl of Leicester, to perform in the City and Liberties of London, and in all
other parts of the kingdom ; "as well," the phraseology
runs, "for the recreation of our loving subjects, as for
our own solace and pleasure, when we shall think fit to
see them."

But the Corporation of London, thorough Puritans,
were determined, as far as their power extended, to
prevent the Queen's subjects from having any such
" recreation," and her Majesty herself from enjoying
any such "solace and pleasure." "Forasmuch as the
playing of interludes, and the resort to the same, are
very dangerous for the infection of the plague, whereby
infinite burdens and losses to the city may increase ; and
are very hurtful in corruption of youth with inconti-
nence and lewdness ; and also great wasting both of the
time and thrift of many poor people ; and great provoking of the wrath of God, the ground of all plagues ;
great withdrawing of the people from public prayer,
and from the service of God ; and daily cried out against
by all preachers of the word of God ; — therefore," the
Corporation ordered, "all such interludes in public
places, and the resort to the same, shall wholly be pro-

hibited as ungodly, and humble suit made to the Lords, that like prohibition be in places near the city."

The players, thus expelled the city, withdrew to the nearest point outside the Lord Mayor's jurisdiction, and, in 1576, erected their theatre in Blackfriars. Two theatres, "The Curtain" and "The Theatre," were erected by other companies in Shoreditch. Before the end of the century there were at least eleven. To these round wooden buildings, open to the sky, with only a thatched roof over the stage, the people flocked daily for mental excitement. There was no movable scenery; the female characters were played by boys; and the lowest theatres of our day are richer in appointments than were the finest of the age of Elizabeth. "Such," says Malone, " was the poverty of the old stage, that the same person played two or three parts; and battles on which the fate of an empire was supposed to depend were decided by three combatants on a side." It is difficult for us to conceive of the popularity of the stage in those days. One of the spies of Secretary Walsingham, writing to his employer in 1586, thus groans over the taste of the people: "The daily abuse of stage plays is such an offence to the godly, and so great a hindrance to the Gospel, as the Papists do exceedingly rejoice at the blemish thereof, and not without cause; for every day in the week the player's bills are set up in sundry places of the city; . . . . so that, when the bells toll to the lecturer, the trumpets sound to the stages. Whereat the wicked faction of Rome laugheth for joy, while the godly weep for sorrow. . . . . It is a woful sight to see two hundred proud players jet in their silks, while five hundred poor people starve in the streets. . . . . Woe is me! the play-houses are pestered when the churches are naked. At the one, it is not possible to get a place; at the other, void seats are plenty." It may here be said, that the mutual hostility of the players and the Puritans continued until the suppression of the theatres under the Commonwealth; and for fifty or sixty years the Puritans were only mentioned by the dramatists to be mercilessly satirized. Even Shakespeare's catholic mind was not broad enough to include them in the range of its sympathies.

That this opposition to the stage by the staid and sober citizens was not without cause, soon became manifest. The characteristic of the drama, before Shakespeare, was intellectual and moral lawlessness; and most of the dramatists were men as destitute of eminent genius as of common principle. Stephen Gosson, a Puritan, in a tract published in 1581, attacks them on grounds equally of taste and morals; and five years afterwards Sir Philip Sidney speaks of the popular plays as against all "rules of honest civility and skilful poetry." But Gosson indicates also the sources of their plots. Painter's " Palace of Pleasure," a series of not over-modest tales from the Italian ; " The Golden Ass "; " The Ethiopian History "; " Amadis of France "; "The Round Table ";—all the licentious comedies in Latin, French, Italian, and Spanish were thoroughly ran-sacked, he tells us, " to furnish the play-houses of London." The result, of course, was a chaos ; but a chaos whose materials were wide and various, indicating that the English mind was in contact with, and attempting roughly to reproduce, the genius of Greece and Rome, of France, Spain, and Italy, the chronicles and ro-mances of the Middle Ages, and was hospitable to intel-lectual influences from all quarters. What was needed was the powerful personality and shaping imagination of genius, to fuse these seemingly heterogeneous materials into new and original forms. " The Faerie Queene " of Spenser, and the drama of Shakespeare, evince the same assimilation of incongruous elements which Gosson derides and denounces as it appeared in the shapeless works of mediocrity. There was not merely to be a new drama, but a new art, and new principles of criticism to legitimate its creative audacities. The materials were rich and various. The difficulty was, that to combine them into original forms required genius, and genius higher, broader, more energetic, more imagi-

native, and more humane than had ever before been
directed to dramatic composition.

The immediate predecessors of Shakespeare—Greene,
Lodge, Kyd, Peele, Marlowe — were all educated at
the Universities, and were naturally prejudiced in favor
of the classics. But they were, at the same time, wild
Bohemian youths, thrown upon the world of London to
turn their talents and accomplishments into the means
of livelihood or the means of debauch. They depended
principally on the popular theatres, and of course addressed the popular mind. Why, indeed, should they
write according to the rules of the classic drama? The
classic drama was a growth from the life of the times in
which it appeared. Its rules were simply generalizations from the practice of classic dramatists. A drama
suited to the tastes and wants of the people of Greece
or Rome was evidently not suited to the tastes and
wants of the people of England. The whole frame-
work of society, — customs, manners, feelings, aspirations, traditions, superstitions, religion, — had changed;
and, as the drama is a reflection of life, either as actually existing or ideally existing, it is evident that both
the experience and the sentiments of the English audiences demanded that it should be the reflection of a
new life. These dramatists, however, in emancipating
themselves from the literary jurisprudence of Greece

and **Rome, put little** but individual caprice in its place. **Released from formal** rules, they did not rise **into the artistic region** of principles, but **fell into the pit of anarchy and** mere lawlessness. Lacking **the** higher imagination which conceives living ideas **and** organizes living works, their dramas evince no coherence, no subordination of parts, no grasp of the subject as a whole. There **is a** German play in which Adam is represented as passing across the stage, "**going to** be created." The drama **of the age of Elizabeth, in the** persons of Greene, **Peele, Kyd,** and **others,** indicates, **in** some such rude way, that it is "going to be created."

That this dramatic shapelessness was not inconsistent **with single** poetic conceptions of the greatest force and fineness, might be proved by abundant quotations. Lodge, for example, **was** a poor dramatist ; but what living poet would not be proud to own this exquisite description, in his lyric **of** " Rosaline," **of the** person **and influence of beauty ?**

> " **Like to the clear in highest sphere,**
> **Where all imperial** glory shines,
> **Of selfsame** color is her hair,
> Whether unfolded or in twines.

> " Her eyes are sapphires set in **snow,**
> Refining heaven by every wink;
> The gods do fear whenas **they glow,**
> **And I do** tremble when I think.

> "Her cheeks are like the blushing cloud
>   That beautifies Aurora's face;
> Or like the silver-crimson shroud,
>   That Phœbus' smiling looks doth grace

> "Her lips are like two **budded roses,**
>   Whom ranks of lilies neighbor nigh,
> Within which bounds she **balm encloses,**
>   Apt to entice a deity.

> "Her neck like to a stately tower,
>   Where Love himself imprisoned lies,
> To watch for glances every hour
>   From her divine and sacred eyes.

> "With orient pearl, with ruby red,
>   With marble white, with sapphire blue,
> Her body everyway is fed,
>   **Yet soft in touch, and** sweet in view.

> "Nature herself her **shape admires;**
>   The gods are wounded **in** her sight;
> And Love forsakes his heavenly fires,
>   And at her eyes his brand doth light."

But a more potent spirit than any **we** have men-
tioned, and the greatest of Shakespeare's predecessors,
was Christopher Marlowe, a man of humble parentage,
but **with Norman blood** in his brains, if not in his veins.
He was, indeed, **the proudest** and fiercest of intellectual
aristocrats. The son of a shoemaker, and born in 1564,
his unmistakable genius seems to have gained him

2

friends, who looked after his early education, and sent
him, at the age of seventeen, to the University of Cambridge. He was intended for the Church, but the
Church had evidently no attractions for him. The study
of theology appears to have resulted in making him an
enemy of religion. There was, indeed, hardly a Christian element in his untamable nature ; and, though he
was called a sceptic, infidelity in him took the form of
blasphemy rather than of denial. He was made up
of vehement passions, vivid imagination, and lawless
self-will; and what Hazlitt calls "a hunger and thirst
after unrighteousness" assumed the place of conscience
in his haughty and fiery spirit. Before the age of
twenty-three we find him in London, an actor and a
writer for the stage, and the author of the "great sensation work" of his time, — the tragedy of "Tamburlaine." This portentous melodrama, a strange compound of inspiration and desperation, has the mark of
power equally on its absurdities and its sublimities. The
first play written in blank verse for the popular stage,
its verse has an elasticity, freedom, and variety of movement which makes it as much the product of Marlowe's
mind as the thoughts and passions it conveys. It had
no precedent in the verse of preceding writers, and is
constructed, not on mechanical rules, but on vital principles. It is the effort of a glowing mind, disdaining to

creep along paths previously made, and opening **a new** path for itself. This scornful intellectual **daring, the** source **of Marlowe's** originality, **is** also the source **of his** defects. **In** the **tragedy of** " Tamburlaine " he selects for his hero a character through whom he can express his own extravagant impatience **of** physical obstacles and moral restraints. No regard is paid to reality, even **in** the dramatic sense of the word : **a** shaggy and savage **force** dominates over everything. The writer seems to say, with his truculent hero, " This **is** my mind, and **I** will have it so." This self-asserting intellectual insolence is accompanied by an unwearied energy, **which** half redeems the bombast **into which it runs, or rather** rushes ; and strange gleams of the purest splendors **of** poetry are continually transfiguring **the** bully into **the** bard.

Thus, in the celebrated scene in which Tamburlaine is represented in a chariot drawn by captive kings, and berating them for their slowness in words which so captivated Ancient Pistol, there is a glorious stroke of impassioned imagination, which makes us almost forgive **the** swaggering fustian which precedes and follows **it :—**

> " Hallo ! ye pampered jades **of** Asia !
> What, can ye draw but twenty miles a **day ? —**
>
> .   .   .   .   .
>
> The horse that guide the golden eye of heaven,

> And blow the morning from their nostrils,
> Making their fiery gait above the clouds,
> Are not so honored in their governor
> As you, ye slaves, in mighty Tamburlaine."

"Faustus," "The Jew of Malta," "Edward the Second," "The Massacre of Paris," "Dido, Queen of Carthage," are the names of Marlowe's remaining plays. They all, more or less, exhibit the eager creativeness of his mind, and the furious arrogance of his disposition. "They abound," says Hunt, "in wilful and self-worshipping speeches, and every one of them turns upon some kind of ascendency at the expense of other people." His "Edward the Second" is the best historical play written before Shakespeare's, and exhibits more discrimination in delineating character than any of Marlowe's other efforts. His "Jew of Malta" is a powerful conception, marred in the process of embodiment. His "Faustus" perhaps best reflects his whole genius and experience. The subject must have taken strong hold of his nature, for, like Faustus, he had himself doubtless held intimate business relations with the great enemy of mankind, and was personally conscious of the struggle in the soul between the diabolical and the divine. The characters of Faustus and Mephistopheles are both conceived with great depth and strength of imagination ; and the last scene of the play, exhibiting

the agony of supernatural terror in which Faustus
awaits the coming of the fiend who has bought and
paid for his soul, is not without touches of sublimity.
There is one line, especially, which is loaded with
meaning and suggestiveness, — that in which harbor-
ing for a moment the possibility of salvation amid the
gathering horrors of his doom, Faustus exclaims, —

" See where Christ's blood streams in the firmament! "

Marlowe's life, though short and reckless, was fertile in
works. Besides the plays we have mentioned, he probably wrote many which have been lost ; and his translations from Ovid, and his unfinished poem of " Hero
and Leander," would alone give him a position among
the poets of his period. He was killed in a tavern
brawl, in the year 1593, at the early age of twenty-nine.[*]

---

[*] Beard, in his " Theatre of God's Judgments " (1597), makes his
death the occasion to point a ferocious moral. He speaks of him as
" by practice a play-maker and a poet of scurrilitie, who, by giuing
too large a swing to his owne wit, and suffering his lust to haue the
full reines," at last " denied God and his sonne Christ, and not onely
in word blasphemed the Trinitie, but also (as it is credibly reported)
wrote bookes against it, affirming our Sauiour to be but a deceiuer,
and Moses to be but a coniurer and seducer of the people, and the
Holy Bible to bee but vaine and idle stories, and all religion but a
deuice of policie. But see what a hooke the Lord put in the nostrils
of this barking dogge! So it fell out, that, as he purposed to stab
one whom he ought a grudge vnto, with his dagger, the other party

Though Marlowe's **poetical** contemporaries and followers could **say little or** nothing in defence of his life, when it was mercilessly assailed **by** Puritan pamphleteers, there was **no** lack **of** testimonials **to his genius.** Ben Jonson celebrated "his mighty **line"**; Drayton described **his** raptures as "all fire **and air," and** testified **to his** possession of those " brave, sublunary things that the **first poets had "; and** Chapman, **with a** yet closer perception **of his** unwithholding self-committal **to the Muse, said that**

" He stood

Up to the chin in the Pierian flood."

A still higher **tribute to** his eminence **comes from** Shakespeare himself, who, in his **" As You Like It,"** quotes **with** approval a line from Marlowe's poem **of " Hero and Leander," —** the only case in which Shakespeare has publicly recognized the genius **of an Elizabethan writer.**

perceiuing so anoyded the stroke, **that withall- catching** hold of his **wrist, hee stabbed his owne dagger into his owne** head, in such sort **that, notwithstanding all the meanes of** surgerie that could bee **wrought, hee shortly after died thereof ;** the manner of his death being so terrible (for he euen cursed and blasphemed to his last gape, and together with **his** breath an oath flew out of his mouth), that it was not only a manifeste signe of God's judgement, but also an horrible and fearefull terror to all that beheld him. **But herein did the** justice of God most noteably appeare, in that hee compelled his owne hand, which had written these blasphemies, to bee the instrument **to punish** him, and that in **his braine which** had deuised **the** same."

But this stormy, irregular genius, compound **of Alsa**tian ruffian and Arcadian singer, whose sudden death, in the height of his glory **and** his pride, seemed to threaten the early English drama with irreparable loss, was **to be** succeeded **in** his **own walk** by **the** greatest Englishman, **by the** greatest **man, that ever made the** theatre or literature his medium of communication with the world. To some thoughts on this man — need we **say it is** Shakespeare? — we shall invite the attention **of** the reader in the next chapter.

SHAKESPEARE.

I.

THE biography of Shakespeare, if we merely look at the bulk of the books which assume to record it, is both minute and extensive; but when we subject the octavo or quarto to examination, we find a great deal that is interesting about his times, and some shrewd and some dull guessing about his probable actions and motives, but little about himself except a few dates. He was born in Stratford-on-Avon, in April, 1564, and was the son of John Shakespeare, tradesman, of that place. In 1582, in his nineteenth year, he married Anne Hathaway, aged twenty-six. About the year 1586 he went to London and became a player. In 1589 he was one of the proprietors of the Blackfriars Theatre, and in 1595 was a prominent shareholder in a larger theatre, built by the same company, called the Globe. As a playwright he seems to have served an apprenticeship; for he altered, amended, and added to the dramas of others before he produced any himself. Between the year 1591, or thereabouts, and the year 1613, or thereabouts, he wrote over thirty plays, the precise date of whose composition it is hardly possible to **fix. He** seems to have made yearly visits to Stratford, where **his** wife and children resided, and **to** have invested money there **as** he increased in wealth. Mr. Emerson has noted, that about the time he **was writing** Macbeth, per- **haps the** greatest tragedy of ancient or modern times, " **he sued** Philip Rogers, in **the** borough-court of Strat- ford, for thirty-five shillings tenpence, for corn delivered to him at various times." In 1608, Mr. Collier esti- mates his income at four hundred pounds a year, which, allowing for the decreased value of money, is equal to eight **or nine** thousand dollars **at** the present **time. About the year 1610, he retired** permanently to Strat- **ford, though he** continued to write plays for the **com-** pany with which **he was** connected. **He** died **on the** 23d of April, 1616.

Such is essentially the meagre result of a century of research into the external life of Shakespeare. As there is hardly a page in his writings which does not **shed** more light upon the biography of his mind, and **bring** us nearer to the individuality **of** the man, the an- **tiquaries** in **despair** have been compelled to abandon him to the psychologists ; and the moment the transition from external to **internal** facts is made, the most obscure of men passes into the most notorious. For this person- ality and soul we call Shakespeare, the recorded inci-

dents of whose outward career were so few and trifling,
lived a more various life — a life more crowded with
ideas, passions, volitions, and *events* — than any potentate the world has ever seen. Compared with his experience, the experience of Alexander or Hannibal, of
Cæsar or Napoleon, was narrow and one-sided. He
had projected himself into almost all the varieties of
human character, and, in imagination, had intensely
realized and *lived* the life of each. From the throne
of the monarch to the bench of the village alehouse,
there were few positions in which he had not placed
himself, and which he had not for a time identified with
his own. No other man had ever seen nature and human life from so many points of view ; for he had looked
upon them through the eyes of Master Slender and
Hamlet, of Caliban and Othello, of Dogberry and Mark
Antony, of Ancient Pistol and Julius Cæsar, of Mistress
Tearsheet and Imogen, of Dame Quickly and Lady Macbeth, of Robin Goodfellow and Titania, of Hecate and
Ariel. No king or queen of his time had so completely
felt the cares and enjoyed the dignity of the regal state
as this playwright, who usurped it by his thought alone ;
and the freshest and simplest maiden in Europe had no
innocent heart-experience which this man could not
share, — escaping, in an instant, from the shattered brain
of Lear, or the hag-haunted imagination of Macbeth, in

order to feel the tender flutter of her soul in his **own.**
And none of these forms, though mightier or more **ex**-
quisite than the ordinary forms of humanity, could hold
or imprison him a moment longer **than** he chose to abide
in it. He was **on an** excursion through the world of
thought and action, to seize the essence of all the excitements of human nature, — terrible, painful, criminal,
rapturous, or humorous; and to do this in a short
earthly career, he was compelled to condense ages into
days, and lives into minutes. He exhausts, in **a** short
time, all the glory and all the agony there is on the
throne or on the couch of Henry IV., and then, wearied
with royalty, is **off** to the Boar's Head to have a rouse
with Sir John. He feels all the flaming pride and scorn
of the aristocrat Coriolanus; his brain widens with **the**
imperial ideas, and his heart beats with the measureless
ambition, of **the** autocrat Cæsar; and anon he has
donned a greasy apron, plunged into the roaring Roman
mob, and is yelling against aristocrat and autocrat with
all the gusto of democratic rage. He is now a prattling
child, and in a second he is the murderer with the knife
at its throat. Capable of *being* all that he actually or
imaginatively *sees*, **he enters into at will,** and abandons
at will, the passions that **brand** or blast other natures.
Avarice, malice, envy, jealousy, hatred, revenge, remorse,
neither in their separate nor mutual action are strong

enough to fasten **him** ; and the same may be said of love and pity and friendship and joy and ecstasy ; for behind and within this multiform personality is **the person** Shakespeare, — serene, self-conscious, vigilant, individualizing the facts of his consciousness, and pouring his own soul into each creation, without ever parting wîth the personal identity which is at the heart **of all, which disposes and co-ordinates all, and which** dictates the impression **to be left by all:**

And this **fact conducts us to the** question of Shakespeare's individuality. **We are prone** to place him **as a** man below other great men, because we make a distinction between the man and his genius. We gather **our** notion of Shakespeare from the meagre details of **his** biography, and in his biography he appears little **and** commonplace, — not by any means so striking a person as Kit Marlowe or Ben Jonson. To this individuality we tack on a universal genius, — which **is about as** reasonable as it would be **to** take the controlling power of gravity from the sun **and attach** it to one of the asteroids. Shakespeare's genius is not something distinct *from* the **man ; it is** the expression *of* the man, just as the sun's attraction is the result of its immense **mass.** The measure of a man's individuality **is his creative** power ; and all that Shakespeare created **he individually** included. We must, therefore, if we desire to grasp his

greatness, discard from our minds all associations connected with **the pet** epithets which other authors **have**
condescended to shower upon him, such as " Sweet
Will," **and** " Gentle Shakespeare," and " Fancy's child,"
—fond but belittling phrases, **as** little appropriate **as**
would be the patronizing chatter **of** the planet Venus
about the dear, darling little Sun ;—we must discard
all these from our conceptions, and consider him prima
rily as a vast, comprehensive, personal soul and force,
that passed from eternity into time, with all **the wide**
aptitudes and affinities for the world he entered bound
up in his individual being from the beginning. These
aptitudes and affinities, **these** quick, deep, and **varied**
sympathies, were so many inlets of the world without
him ; and facts pouring into **such a** nature were swiftly
organized into faculties. Nothing, indeed, amazes us **so**
much, in the biography of Shakespeare's mind, as the
preternatural rapidity with which **he** assimilated knowledge into power, and experience into insight. The
might of his personality is indicated by its resistance to,
as much as its breadth is evinced by its receptivity of,
objects ; for his force was never overwhelmed or submerged by **the** multiplicity of impressions that **unceas**
ingly rushed in **upon it.** **His soul** lay genially open **to**
the world of nature and human life, to receive the objects **that** went streaming into it, but never parted with

the power of **reacting upon** all it received. This would
not be so marvellous had he merely taken in **the forms**
and outside appearances of **things. All his perceptions,**
however, were vital ; and the life **and force of the ob-**
jects he drew into his consciousness tugged with his
own life and force for the mastery, and ended in simply
enriching the spirit they strove to subdue. This inde-
structible spiritual energy, which becomes mightier with
every exercise of might ; which plucks **out the** heart
and absorbs the vitality of everything it touches ; which
daringly commits itself to the fiercest, and joyously to
the softest passions, without losing its moral and mental
sanity ; which in the most terrible excitements is **as**
" the blue dome **of** air " to the tempest that rages **be-**
neath it ; which, aiming to include everything, refuses
to be **included** by anything, and in **the sweep of its**
creativeness acts with a confident audacity, **as if in it**
Nature were humanized and humanity individualized ;—
in short, this unexampled energy of blended sensibility,
intelligence, and will, is what constitutes the man Shakespeare ; **and this man is no mere** name for an impersonal,
unconscious genius, that did its marvels by instinct, no
name for a careless playwright who blundered into mir-
acles, but is essentially a person, creating strictly within
the limitations of his individuality, — within those limitations appearing to be impersonal only because **he is**

comprehensive enough to cover a wide variety of special natures, — and, above all, a person individually as **great,** at least, as the **sum of** his whole works.

In regard to the real mystery **of** this man's power, both criticism and philosophy are mute. His appearance **is** simply a fact in the world's intellectual history, **which can be** connected with no preceding fact nor with the spirit of his **age.** "It is the nature of poetry," **says** Emerson, "to spring, like the rainbow daughter of Wonder, from the invisible, to abolish **the past, and to** refuse all **history."** **All** that we know **is, that** the **capacities** and splendors of Shakespeare's mind existed potentially in the vital germ of the spiritual nature born with him into the world; and that his works are **the** result of the unfolding of **this.** The glory of the Elizabethan **age,** it is absurd **to call him its product, for the** puzzle is not so much the peculiarities of what he assim**ilated as** his powers of assimiliation, and in any age these powers would probably have worked equal, if different **effects.** Take, for instance, single thoughts **and** imaginations of his, such **as** the following, and see if you can account for them by any knowledge you have of the manners **and** customs of the England of Elizabeth : —

> " The morning steals upon the night,
> Melting the darkness."

"**How sweet** the moonlight sleeps upon this bank!"

"The benediction of these covering heavens
Fall on their heads like dew."

Things evil "are our outward **consciences.**"

A substitute shines brightly **as a king,**
Until a king **be by;** and then his state
Empties itself, as doth an inland brook
Into the main of waters."

**O Westmoreland! thou art a summer bird,
Which ever in the haunch of winter sings
The lifting up of day.**"

"**Cheer your heart:**
Be you not troubled with the time, which **drives**
O'er your content these strong necessities;
But let determined things to Destiny
Hold unbewailed their way."

But single passages like these, though **they hint of**
the inmost essence of the poet, and drop upon the mind,
as Carlyle says, "like a splendor out of heaven," —
though they demonstrate the independence of time and
place of the imagination whence they come, — are still
no adequate measure of Shakespeare's power. If, however, we pass from these to what is a more decisive
test of his self-conscious, self-directed **creative energy,**
namely, **to** his mode of organizing a whole drama, **we**
shall find that his method, processes, and results are

different **from those of** the dramatists of his own age **or** of any other age. The materials he uses are as nothing when compared with his transformation of them into works of art. Let us, in illustration, glance at his method **of** creation, as successfully **exerted in any one of** his great dramas, say Hamlet, **or** King Lear, or Macbeth, or Othello.

He takes **a** story or a history, **with** which the people **are** familiar, the whole interest **of** which **is narrative.** He finds it a mere succession of incidents ; he leaves it a combination of events. He finds the persons named in it mere commonplace sketches of humanity ; **he leaves** them self-subsisting, individual characters, more real to the mind than the men and women we daily meet.

Now the first fact that strikes us when we compare the original story with Shakespeare's magical transform- **ation of** it is, that everything is **raised** from the actual world into a Shakespearian world. He alters, enlarges, expands, enriches, enlivens, informs, *recreates* every- **thing,** lifting sentiment, passion, humor, thought, action, **to the level of** his own nature. Through incidents and through characters **is** shot Shakespeare's soul, — a soul that yields itself **to every** mould of being, from the clown to the monarch, endows every class of character it animates with the Shakespearian felicity and certainty **of speech,** and, being in *all* as well as in *each*, so connects **and** relates the society he has called into life, that they unite to form a whole, while existing with perfect distinctness **as** parts. The characters are not developed by isolation, but by sympathy or collision, and the closer they come together the less they run together. They **are** independent of each other, and yet necessitate each **other.** None of them could appear **in any** other play without exciting disorder ; **yet in** this play their discord conduces to the general harmony. And so tough is the hold on existence of these beings that, though thousands of millions of men **and** women have been born, have died, and **have** been forgotten since they were created, and though the actual world has strangely changed, these men and women of Shakespeare's are still alive, **and Shakespeare's** world still remains untouched **by time.**

This drama, thus made self-existent in the **free heaven** of art, implies, in its conception and execution, processes analogous to those which **are** followed **by** Nature herself in the production of **her works;** and modern critics **have** not hesitated to award to Shakespeare the distinction **of** being an organizer after her pattern. The drama which we have been describing is, like her works, not simple, but complex. It has unity, it has the widest variety, it has unity in variety. The most diverse and seemingly heterogeneous materials all aid to form a whole, "vital in every part"; and the organization is strictly an addition **to** the world, with nothing in literature and nothing in nature which exactly matches it. And it is alive, and refuses to die. Nature herself is compelled to adopt it into her race,

> "And give to it an equal date
> With Andes and with Ararat."

You can gaze at it as you can gaze **at a** natural landscape, where hills, rocks, woods, stubble, grass, clouds, sky, atmosphere, each separate, each related, combine to form one impressive effect of beauty and power.

Perhaps, however, it would be more proper to call this Shakespearian drama an approximation to an **organic** product, rather than a realization of one. The processes of nature are followed, but the perfection of nature is the ideal it aims at rather than reaches. Still, if we allow for human defects and imperfections, and take into view the fact that Shakespeare had to submit **to** conditions imposed by his audience as well as conditions imposed by his genius, his work measurably fulfils the requirements of Kant's concise definition of an organic creation, namely, "that thing in which all the parts are mutually ends and means."

Admitting, then, that the drama we are considering has organic form, and not merely mechanical regularity, the question arises, What is the inner law, the central

idea, the principle of life, by which, and in obedience to
which, it was organized? Perhaps the new school of
philosophic critics have done almost as much injury to
Shakespeare's fame, in their attempt to answer this
question, as they have done good in rescuing his dramas
from the old school of sciolists and commentators, who
were pecking at him with their formal rules of taste.
The philosophic critics very properly insisted that he
should be judged by principles deduced from his own
method, and not by rules generalized from the method
of the Greek dramatists; that the laws by which he
should be tried were the laws which he acknowledged
and obeyed, the laws of his own creative imagination;
and that the very originality of his dramas freed them
from tests which are applicable only to the products
of imitation. They thus raised Shakespeare from a
breaker of the laws into a lawgiver; and the brilliant
vagabond, whom every catchpole of criticism thought he
could hustle about and reprimand, was all at once lifted
into a dictator of law to the bench.

Having relieved Shakespeare from these policemen
of letters, and substituted some reach of human vision
for their rat's eyes, the new school of philosophic critics
proceeded to state what *were* the ideas which formed
the ground-plans and organizing principles of his works;
but in doing this, they brought Shakespeare down to

their own level, and made him their spokesman. **Intel-**
lectual egotism supplanted intellectual interpretation.
Read Schlegel, **Ulrici,** even Gervinus, and you are delighted as long as they confine themselves **to the busi-**
ness of exposing the folly of the critics they supplanted;
but when they come to **the** real problem, and attempt to
state the meaning and purpose of Shakespeare in any
given play, you are apt to be as much surprised as was
that philanthropist, who was confidentially informed that
the ultimate object Napoleon **had** in view in his numerous wars was the establishment of Sunday schools.
They find in Shakespeare's plays certain ethical, political, or social generalities, which, **it seems, they were**
written to illustrate, **or** rather from which **the** plays
grow, as from **so** many roots. But causes are **to be**
measured by effects; the effects here are marvellous
structures of genius; and these **do** not shoot up from
the withered roots of barren truisms. A whole must be
greater than any of its parts; and yet the philosophic
idea of a Shakespearian drama, as eliminated by the
German professors, is less than the least of its parts.
A single magical word in Shakespeare is often greater,
and has more reach of application, than the professorial
bit of wisdom which they present as the grand total of
the play, and which is often too obvious in itself to make
a resort to Shakespeare necessary for a perception of

its truth. Their " ground ideas" of the dramas are not worth any minor Shakespearian ideas they are assumed to include.

Indeed, before we claim to understand a Shakespearian whole, we must first see if we are competent to take in one of its parts. It is evident that the most important parts are the characters, and in respect to these, and to Shakespeare's method of characterization, there is much misconception. What are these characters? Are they copies of men and women, as we see them in the world, — slightly idealized portraits of persons, witty, passionate, thoughtful, or criminal? Are they such people as Shakespeare might have seen in the streets of London in the time of Elizabeth? No, for they are plainly Shakespearian, and not merely Elizabethan. Even the court-fools are endowed with the Shakespearian quality, are perfect of their kind, and are such court-fools as Shakespeare might have conceived himself to be one of, if he had, in Mr. Weller's phrase, "been born in that station of life."

Yet these characters are certainly not individualized qualities and passions, for they are eminently natural. If their naturalness does not come from their being portraits, slightly varied and heightened, of individuals, in what does their naturalness consist?

In answer to this question, it is first to be said, that

these characters prove that Shakespeare had a conception of *human nature*, abstracted from all *individuals*. He not only looked *at* individuals, **and** *into* individuals, but *through* individuals to **their** common basis in humanity. **But** he did not rest here. **This** imaginative analysis, this vital generalization, this glance into the sources of things, evinces, of course, his possession of the profoundest philososophical genius as the foundation **of his** dramatic genius; but it is not the genius itself, for he also surveyed human nature in action, human nature as modified by human life, by manners, customs, institutions, and beliefs, and by that primitive personality which separates men, as humanity unites them.

These characters, then, are individual natures rooted in human nature. **The** question then arises, Is **their** individuality particular or representative? The **least** observation shows, we think, that they stand for more than individuals. We are continually saying that this **or** that person of our acquaintance resembles one of Shakespeare's characters; we may even learn much about him by studying the character he resembles; but we never thoroughly identify him with the character; for the character **is** more powerful, more perfectly developed, acts out the law of his being with more **freedom**, than the actual person with whom he is compared.

Further than this, — if we are accustomed to classify

the persons we know, so as to include many individuals under one type, we shall find that we can include scores of our acquaintances in one of Shakespeare's characters, and then not exhaust its full application. It is not, therefore, his mere variety of characterization, but something peculiar in each of the varieties, which makes him pre-eminently the poet of human nature. Why, for example, is not Charles Dickens as great a novelist as Shakespeare is a dramatist? Dickens has delineated as wide a variety of persons as Shakespeare, if by variety we mean the absence of repetition. There is no reason but the shortness of life why he should not people literature with new individuals, until his characters are numbered by the thousand, all in a certain sense original, all discriminated from each other, but few or none *representative*. The single character of Hamlet represents more individuals than do all the individuals Dickens has delineated.

Again, Jane Austen is placed by Macaulay next to Shakespeare for the felicity, certainty, and nicety of her portraitures of character. The most evanescent lines of distinction between persons who appear alike she seizes with wonderful tact, and indicates these differences without the least resort to caricature. If the best characterization means simply the best portrait-painting, there is no reason why Elizabeth, in " Pride and Prejudice," should not be **placed side** by side with Juliet **and Cordelia.**

But everybody feels that neither Dickens, with his range of observation, nor **Jane** Austen, with her subtilty of observation, makes **any** approach **to Shakespeare.** What is the reason?

The reason is, that Shakespeare does not paint individuals, but individualizes classes. **In** his great nature, **the** processes of reason and imagination, of philosophic insight and poetic insight, worked harmoniously together. His observation of persons only supplied him with hints for his creations. He did not take up at **haphazard this** man and that woman, and, because of their oddity or beauty, reproduce them in **his** story; **but he distin-**guished in each actual person the signs of a class **na-**ture, midway between his general **nature** and his individual peculiarities. He classified men as the naturalist classifies the Animal Kingdom. Agassiz is not confused by the perplexing spectacle of the myriads of animals which form the materials of his science; for the moment **his** eye lights upon them, they fall into certain great **natural divisions,** distinguished by recognized marks of structure. Under **each of** a few grand divisions he includes innumerable individuals. Now the difference between Agassiz and a mere observer and describer of animals **is** the difference between Shakespeare and

Dickens, only that Shakespeare works on phenomena more complicated, and presenting more obstacles to classification, than Agassiz deals with.

In his deep, wide, and searching observation of mankind, Shakespeare detects bodies of men who agree in the general tendencies of their characters, who strive after a common ideal of good or evil, and who all fail to reach it. Through these indications and hints he seizes, by his philosophical genius, the law of the class; by his dramatic genius, he gathers up in one conception the whole multitude of individuals comprehended in the law, and embodies it in a character; and by his poetical genius he lifts this character into an ideal region of life, where all hindrances to the free and full development of its nature are removed. The character seems all the more natural because it is *perfect of its kind,* whereas the actual persons included in the conception are imperfect of their kind. Thus there are many men of the type of Falstaff, but Shakespeare's Falstaff is not an actual Falstaff. Falstaff is the ideal head of the family, the possibility which they dimly strive to realize, the person they would be if they could. Again, there are many *Iagoish* men, but only one Iago, the ideal type of them all; and by studying him we learn what they would all become if circumstances were propitious, and their loose malignant tendencies were firmly knit to-

gether in positive will and diabolically alert intelligence.
And it is the **same with** the rest **of** Shakespeare's great
creations. The immense domain of human nature they
cover is due to the fact, not merely that they are not
repetitions of individuals, but **that** they are not repeti-
tions of the same types or classes of individuals.
The moment we analyze them, the moment we break
them up into their constituent elements, we are amazed
at the wealth of wisdom and knowledge which formed
the materials of each individual embodiment, and the
inexhaustible interest and fulness of meaning and application revealed in the analytic scrutiny of each. Compare, for example, Shakespeare's Timon of Athens —
by no means one of Shakespeare's mightiest efforts **of**
characterization — with Lord Byron, both **as man and
poet,** and we shall find that Timon is the highest logical
result of the Byronic tendency, **and** that **in him,** rather
than in Byron, the essential misanthrope is impersonated.
The number of poems which Byron wrote does not af-
fect the matter at all, because the poems are all expansions and variations of one view of life, from which
Byron could not escape. Shakespeare, had he pleased,
might have filled **volumes** with Timon's poetic misanthropy ; but, **being a** condenser, he was contented with
concentrating the idea of the whole class in one grand
character, and of putting into his mouth the truest, most

splendid, most terrible things which have ever been uttered from the misanthropic point of view ; and then, victoriously freeing himself from the dreadful mood of mind he had imaginatively realized, he passed on to occupy other and different natures. Shakespeare is superior to Byron on Byron's own ground, because Shakespeare grasped misanthropy from its first faint beginnings in the soul to its final result on character, — clutched its inmost essence, — discerned it as one out of a hundred subjective conditions of mind, — tried it thoroughly, and found it was too weak and narrow to hold *him*. Byron was *in* it, could not escape *from* it, and never, therefore, thoroughly mastered the philosophy *of* it. Here, then, in one corner of Shakespeare's mind, we find more than ample space for so great a poet as Byron to house himself.

But Shakespeare not only in one conception thus individualizes a whole class of men, but he communicates to each character, be it little or colossal, good or evil, that peculiar Shakespearian quality which distinguishes it as his creation. This he does by being and living for the time the person he conceives. What Macaulay says of Bacon is more applicable to Shakespeare, namely, that his mind resembles the tent which the fairy gave to Prince Ahmed. " Fold it, and it seemed a toy for the hand of a lady. Spread it, and the armies of powerful sultans might repose beneath its shade." **Shakespeare** could run his sentiment, passion, reason, imagination, into any mould **of** personality **he** was capable of **shaping,** and think and speak from that. The result is that every character **is** a denizen of **the Shakespearian** World ; **every** character, from Master Slender to Ariel, is in some sense a poet, that is, is gifted with imagination **to** express his whole nature, and make himself inwardly known ; yet we feel throughout that the " thousand-souled " Shakespeare is still but one soul, **capable of** shifting into a thousand **forms, but leaving its peculiar** birth-mark on every individual **it informs.**

Now it is difficult, perhaps impossible, for **a critic to** reproduce synthetically **in** his own consciousness, **or** thoroughly to analyze into all its elements, **any single** prominent character that Shakespeare **has drawn.** His characters, however, **are not** represented apart **from** each other, but as acting on each other **; and,** great as they separately are as conceptions, they **are** but integral portions of a still mightier conception, which in**cludes the** whole drama in which they appear. The value of **what we** call the incidents of such a drama consists in their being such incidents as would most naturally spring from **the** mutual action of such persons, or as would best develop their natures. The plot is **of** **small** account as disconnected from the characters, but of great moment as vitally inwrought with them, and giving coherence to the living organism which results from the combination. It is for this reason that we pay little heed to improbable incidents in the story, provided the incidents serve to bring out the persons. It is very improbable that a bond should have been given payable in a pound of flesh, and still more so that any court in Christendom could have recognized its validity; but who thinks of this in the Shakespearian society of "The Merchant of Venice"?

Now it is doubtless true that a drama of Shakespeare thus organized, with characters comprehending an immense range of human character, and yielding to analysis laws of human nature which radiate light into whole departments of human life, produces on our minds, as we read, the effect of unity in variety. We perceive it as a whole, and think therefore we perceive the whole of it. But is it true that we really receive the colossal conception of Shakespeare himself? Shakespeare, it is plain, can only convey to us what we are capable of taking in; the mind that perceives reduces greatness to its own mental stature; and persons, according to their taste, culture, experience, height of intelligence, capacity of approaching Shakespeare himself, obtain different impressions, varying in depth and breadth, of each of his great plays. Who, for instance, has stated

the general conception of the play of " Hamlet"? **The**
idea of that drama, as given by different critics, is only
so much of the idea as could be got into the heads of
the critics. Their interpretation **at** best belongs **to the**
class of *Mémoires pour servir ;* — the rounded whole **is**
described by minds that are angular ; and Shakespeare's
conception is measuring them, while they are felicitating
themselves that they are measuring it.

Even Goethe, the most comprehensive intelligence
since Shakespeare, failed to "pluck out the heart" of
Hamlet's mystery. Indeed, it is beginning to be considered, that his remarks on the character, though delicate and profound in themselves, do not touch the essential individuality of Hamlet ; that his ingenuity was
exercised in the wrong direction ; and that, in his criticism, he resembled the sturdy and rapid walker, who
checked his pace to ask a boy how far it was to Taun-
ton. "If you go on in the way you 're now going," was the reply, " it 's twenty-four thousand miles ;
if you turn back, it 's only five." But though some
critics since Goethe have not been so elaborately wrong
as he, Hamlet **is** still outside of the largest thought in
the right direction. **A** distinguished thinker has said
that there are moods of the mind in which Hamlet appears little, for what he suggests is infinitely more than
what he is. This is true as to Shakespeare, but not true

as to other minds; for until we have grasped the conception that Shakespeare has embodied, we have no right to suppose ourselves capable of going beyond it into that vastness of contemplation of which, from Shakespeare's height of vision, the character was an inadequate expression. Again, it is a common remark, that the school of philosophic critics, especially in their attempts to dive into the meaning of Hamlet, are continually giving Shakespeare the credit of their own thoughts. Giving Shakespeare the credit! Well might he reply, if such were the case, " Beggar that I am, I am even poor in thanks !"

Shakespeare, then, as regards his most gigantic conceptions, has probably never been adequately conceived. He must be tried by his peers; and where are his peers? We know that he grows in mental stature as our minds enlarge, and as we increase in our knowledge of him; but he has never been included by criticism as other poets have been included. The greatest and most interpretative minds which have made him their study, though they may have commenced with wielding the rod, soon found themselves seduced into taking seats on the benches, anxious to learn instead of impatient to teach; and have been compelled to admit that the poet who is the delight of the rudest urchin in the pit of the playhouse, is also the poet whose works defy the highest faculties of the philosopher thoroughly to comprehend.

SHAKESPEARE.

II.

IN the last chapter we spoke of Shakespeare's **general** comprehensiveness and creativeness, of his method **of** characterization, and of the identity of his genius with **his** individuality. **We** purpose now to treat of some particular topics included in the general theme ; **and, as** criticism on him is like coasting along a continent, **we** shall **make little** pretension **to** system **in the order of taking them up.**

The first of these topics is the succession **of Shake-**speare's **works,** considered as **steps in the growth and** development **of his** powers, — a subject which **has al-**ready been ably handled by Mr. **Verplanck. The facts, as** far as they can be ascertained, are these. **Shake-speare** went to London about the **year** 1586, in **his** twenty-second year, and found some humble employ-**ment in one of** the theatrical companies. Three years afterwards, in **1589, he had** risen to be one of the share-holders of the Blackfriars Theatre. **In** 1592 he had ac-**quired** sufficient reputation **as a** dramatist, **or at least as a recaster** of the plays of others, **to excite the jealousy** of the leading playwrights, whose crude dramas he condescended to rewrite or retouch. That graceless vagabond, Robert Greene, addressing from his penitent death-bed his old friends Lodge, Peele, and Marlowe, and trying to dissuade them from "spending their wits" any longer in "making plays," spitefully asserts: "There is an upstart crow beautified with our feathers, that, with his tiger's heart wrapped in a player's hide, supposes he is as able to bombast out a blank verse as the best of you; and, being an absolute Johannes Factotum, is, in his own conceit, the only Shake-scene in the country." Doubtless this charge of adopting and adapting the productions of others includes some dramas which have not been preserved, as the company to which Shakespeare was attached owned the manuscripts of a great number of plays which were never printed, and it was a custom, when a play had popular elements in it, for other dramatists to be employed in making such additions as would give continual novelty to the old favorite. But of the plays published in our editions of Shakespeare's writings, it is probable that the Comedy of Errors, and the three parts of King Henry VI., are only partially his, and should be classed among his adaptations, and not among his early creations. The play of Pericles bears no marks of his mind, except in some scenes of transcendent power and beauty, which start **up from the rest** of the work **like towers** of gold from **a plain of** sand ; **but** these scenes **are in** his latest manner. **In** regard to the tragedy of Titus Andronicus, **we are so** constituted **as to resist** all **the** external evidence by which such a shapeless mass **of** horrors and absurdities **is fastened** on Shakespeare. **Mr.** Verplanck thinks it one of Shakespeare's **first at-** tempts at dramatic composition ; but first attempts must **reflect** the mental condition of the author **at the** time they were made ; and we know the mental condition of Shakespeare in his early manhood **by** his poem of Venus and **Adonis,** which he expressly styles " the first heir of his invention." **Now** leaving out of view the fact **that Titus** Andronicus stamps the impression, not of youthful, but of matured depravity of taste, its **execrable** enormities of feeling and incident could **not** have proceeded from the sweet and comely nature **in** which the poem had **its** birth. The best criticism on Titus Andronicus was made by Robert Burns, when **he was** nine years old. His schoolmaster was reading the play aloud in his father's cottage, and when he came to the scene where Lavinia enters with her hands cut off and her tongue **cut** out, little Robert fell a-crying, and threatened, in **case** the play was left in the cottage, to burn it. It is hard to believe that what Burns de- spised and detested at the age of nine could have been

written by Shakespeare at the age of twenty-five.
Taking, then, Venus and Adonis as the point of departure, we find Shakespeare at the age of twenty-two
endowed with all the faculties, but relatively deficient in
the passions, of the poet. The poem is a throng of
thoughts, fancies, and imaginations, somewhat cramped
in the utterance. Coleridge says that " in his poems
the creative power and the intellectual energy wrestle
as in a war embrace. Each in its excess of strength
seems to threaten the extinction of the other. At
length in the drama they were reconciled, and fought
each with its shield before the breast of the other."
Fine as this is, it would perhaps be more exact to say
that in his earlier poems his intellect, acting in some
degree apart from his sensibility, and playing with its
own ingenuities of fancy and meditation, condensed its
thoughts in crystals. . Afterwards, when his whole nature became liquid, he gave us his thoughts in a state
of fusion, and his intellect flowed in streams of fire.

Take, for example, that passage in the poem where
Venus represents the loveliness of Adonis as sending
thrills of passion into the earth on which he treads, and
as making the bashful moon hide herself from the sight
of his bewildering beauty : —

" But if thou fall, O, then imagine this!
The earth, in love with thee, thy footing trips.

> And all is but **to rob** thee of a kiss.
>
>> Rich preys make true men thieves; so do thy lips
> Make modest **Dian** cloudy **and forlorn,**
> **Lest she** should steal a kiss and **die** forsworn.

> " **Now** of this dark night I perceive the reason:
>> Cynthia for shame obscures her silver shrine,
> Till forging Nature be condemned **of treason,**
>> For stealing moulds from heaven that were divine,
> Wherein she framed thee, in high heaven's despite,
> To shame the sun by day and her by night."

This is reflected and reflecting passion, or, **at least,** imagination awakening **passion,** rather **than passion** penetrating imagination.

Now mark, by contrast, **the gush of the heart into the** brain, dissolving **thought, imagination, and expres-**sion, so that **they run molten, in** the delirious ecstasy **of** Pericles on recovering his long-lost child : —

> " O Helicanus! strike me, honour'd sir,
>> Give me a gash, put me to present pain,
> Lest this great sea of joys, rushing upon me,
> O'erbear the shores of my mortality,
> And drown me with their sweetness."

If, as is probable, Venus **and** Adonis was written as early as 1586, **we may** suppose that the plays which represent the immaturity of his genius, and which are strongly marked **with the** characteristics of that poem, namely, The Two Gentlemen of Verona, the first draft

of Love's Labor's Lost, and the original Romeo and
Juliet, were produced before the year 1592.   Following
these came King Richard III., King Richard II., A
Midsummer Night's Dream, King John, The Merchant
of Venice, and King Henry IV., all of which we know
were written before 1598, when Shakespeare was in
his thirty-fourth year.   During the next eight years he
produced King Henry V., The Merry Wives of Wind-
sor, As You Like it, Hamlet, Twelfth Night, Measure
for Measure, Othello, Macbeth, and King Lear.   In
this list are the four great tragedies in which his genius
culminated.   Then came Troilus and Cressida, Timon
of Athens, Julius Cæsar, Antony and Cleopatra, Cym-
beline, King Henry VIII., The Tempest, The Winter's
Tale, and Coriolanus.   If heed be paid to this order
of the plays, it will be seen at once that a quotation
from Shakespeare carries with it a very different degree
of authority, according as it refers to the youth or the
maturity of his mind.

Indeed, when we reflect that between the production
of The Two Gentlemen of Verona and King Lear
there is only a space of fifteen years, we must admit
that the history of the human intellect presents no other
example of such marvellous progress; and if we note
the giant strides by which it was made, we shall find
that they all imply a progressive widening and deepen-

i... of soul, a positive growth of the nature of the man, until in Lear **the** power became supreme and became amazing. **Mr.** Verplanck considers the period when he produced his four great tragedies to be the period of his intellectual grandeur, as distinguished from **an** earlier **period** which he thinks shows the perfection of his merely poetic and imaginative power; but the **fact** would seem to be that his increasing greatness as a philosopher was fully matched by his increasing greatness as a poet, and that, in the devouring swiftness of his onward and upward movement, imagination kept abreast of reason. His imagination was never more vivid, all-informing, and creative, — never penetrated with more unerring certainty to the inmost spiritual essence of whatever it touched, — never forced words and rhythm into more supple instruments of thought and feeling, — than when it miracled into form the terror and pity and beauty of Lear.

Indeed, the coequal growth of his reason and imagination was owing to the wider scope and increased energy of the great moving forces of his being. It relates primarily **to** the heart rather than the head. It is the immense fiery force behind his mental powers, kindling them into white heat, and urging them to efforts almost preternatural, — it is this which impels the daring thought beyond the limits of positive knowledge, and prompts the starts of ecstasy in whose unexpected radiance nature and human life are transfigured, and for an instant shine with celestial light. In truth he is, relatively, more intellectual in his early than in his later plays, for in his later plays his intellect is thoroughly impassioned, and though it has really grown in strength and massiveness, it is so fused with imagination and emotion as to be less independently prominent.

The sources of individuality lie below the intellect; and as Shakespeare went deeper into the soul of man, he more and more represented the brain as the organ and instrument of the heart, as the channel through which sentiment, passion, and character found an intelligible outlet. His own mind was singularly objective; that is, he saw things as they are in themselves. The minds of his prominent characters are all subjective, and see things as they are modified by the peculiarities of their individual moods and emotions. The very objectivity of his own mind enables him to assume the subjective conditions of less-emancipated natures. Macbeth peoples the innocent air with menacing shapes, projected from his own fiend-haunted imagination; but the same air is sweet and wholesome to the poet who gave being to Macbeth. The meridian of Shakespeare's power was reached when he created Othello, Macbeth, and Lear, — complex personalities, representing the conflict and

complication of the mightiest passions in colossal forms of human character, and whose understandings and **im**aginations, whose perceptions of nature and human life, and whose weightiest utterances of moral wisdom, are **all** thoroughly subjective **and** individualized. **The** greatness of these characters, as compared with his earlier creations, consists in the greater intensity and amplitude of their natures, and the wider variety of faculties and passions included in the strict unity of their natures. Richard III., for example, is one of his earlier characters, and, though excellent of its kind, its excellence has been approached **by** other dramatists, as, for instance, Massinger, in **Sir** Giles Overreach. But no other dramatist has been able to grasp and represent a **char**acter similar in kind to Macbeth, and the reason is that Richard is comparatively a simple conception, **while** Macbeth is a complex one. There is unity and versatility in Richard; there is unity and variety in Macbeth. Richard is capable of being developed with almost logical accuracy; for, though there is versatility in the play **of** his intellect, there is little variety in the motives which direct his intellect. His wickedness is not exhibited in the making. He is so completely and gleefully a villain from the first, that he is not restrained from convenient crime by any scruples or relentings. The vigor of his will is due to his poverty of feeling and conscience. He is a brilliant and efficient criminal because he is shorn of the noblest attributes of man. Put, if you could, Macbeth's heart and imagination into him, and his will would be smitten with impotence, and his wit be turned to wailing. The intellect of Macbeth is richer and grander than Richard's, yet Richard is relatively a more intellectual character; for the intellect of Macbeth is rooted in his moral nature, and is secondary in our thoughts to the contending motives and emotions it obeys and reveals. In crime, as in virtue, what a man overcomes should enter into our estimate of the power exhibited in what he does.

The question now comes up, — and we suppose it must be met, though we should like to evade it, — How, amid the individualities that Shakespeare has created, are we to detect the individuality of Shakespeare himself? In answer it may be said, that, if we survey his dramas in the mass, we find three degrees of unity; — first, the unity of the individual characters; second, the unity of the separate plays in which they appear; and third, the unity of Shakespeare's own nature, — a nature which, as it developed, deepened, expanded, and increased in might, but did not essentially change, and which is felt as a potent presence throughout his works, binding them together as the product of one mind. He did not literally go out of himself to inform other natures, but he included these natures in himself; and, though he does not infuse his individuality into his characters, he does infuse it into the general conceptions which the characters illustrate. His opinions, purposes, theory of life, are to be gathered, not from what his characters say and do, but from the results of what they say and do; and in each play he so combines and disposes the events and persons that the cumulative impression expresses his own judgment, indicates his own design, and conveys his own feeling. His individuality is so vast, so purified from eccentricity, and we grasp it so imperfectly, that we are apt to deny it altogether, and conceive his mind as impersonal. In view of the multiplicity of his creations, and the range of thought, emotion, and character they include, it is **a common** hyperbole of criticism to designate him as universal. But, in truth, his mind was restricted, in its creative action, like other minds, within the limits of its personal sympathies, though these sympathies in him were keener, quicker, and more general than in other men of genius. He was a great-hearted, broad-brained person, but still a person, and not what Coleridge calls him, an " omnipresent creativeness." Whatever he could sympathize with he could embody and vitally represent; but his sympathies, though wide, were far from being universal, and, when he was indifferent or hostile, the dramatist was partially suspended in the satirist and caricaturist, and oversight took the place of insight. **Indeed, his** limitations are more easily indicated than his enlargements. We know **what** he has not done more surely than we know what he has done ; for if **we** attempt to follow his genius in any of the numerous lines of direction along which it sweeps with such victorious ease, we soon come to the end of our tether, and **are confused with** a throng of thoughts and imaginations, which, **as** Emerson exquisitely says, " sweetly **torment us with** invitations to their own *inaccessible* **homes."** But there were some directions which **his** genius did not take, — not so much from lack **of mental** power as from lack of disposition or from positive antipathy. Let us consider some of these.

And first, Shakespeare's religious instincts and sentiments were comparatively weak, for **they were not creative.** He has exercised his genius in the creation of **no** character in which religious **sentiment** or religious passion is dominant. He could not, of course, — he, the poet of feudalism, — overlook religion as an element of the social organization of Europe, but he did not seize Christian ideas in their essence, or look at the **human** soul in its direct relations with God. And just **think of** the field of humanity closed to him ! For sixteen hundred years, remarkable men and women had appeared, representing all classes of religious character, from the ecstasy of the saint to the gloom of the fanatic ; yet his intellectual curiosity was not enough excited to explore and reproduce their experience. Do you say that the subject was foreign to the purpose **of** an Elizabethan playwright ? The answer is, that Dekkar and Massin-**ger** attempted it, for a popular audience, in "The Virgin Martyr "; and though **the** tragedy of "The Virgin Mar-tyr " is a huddled mass of beauties and deformities, its materials of incident and characters, could Shakespeare have been attracted to them, might have been organized into as great a drama as Othello. Again, Marlowe, in his play of " Doctor Faustus," has imperfectly **treated a** subject which in Shakespeare's hands would have been made into a tragedy sublimer than Lear, could he have thrown himself into it with equal earnestness. Mar-lowe, from the fact that he **was a** brawling atheist, had evidently at some time directed his whole heart and imagination to the consideration of religious questions, and had resolutely faced facts from which Shakespeare turned away.

Shakespeare, also, in common with the other dram-atists of the time, looked at the Puritans as objects of satire, laughing *at* them instead of gazing *into* them. They were doubtless grotesque enough in external **ap**-pearance ; but the poet of human nature should have

penetrated through the appearance to the substance, and
recognized in them, not merely the possibility of Cromwell, but **of** the ideal of character which Cromwell but
imperfectly represented. You may say that Shakespeare's nature was too sunny and genial to admit the
Puritan. It was not too sunny or genial to admit Rich-
ards, and Iagos, and Gonerils, and " secret, black, and
midnight hags."

It may be doubted also if Shakespeare's affinities extended to those numerous classes of human character
that stand for the reforming and philanthropic sentiments of humanity. We doubt if he was hopeful for
the race. He was too profoundly impressed with **its**
disturbing passions to have faith in its continuous **progress.** Though immensely greater than **Bacon, it** may
be questioned if he could thoroughly have appreciated
Bacon's intellectual character. He could have delineated him to perfection in everything but in that peculiar
philanthropy of the mind, that spiritual benignity, that
belief in man and confidence in his future, which both
atone and account for so **many of Bacon's** moral defects.
There is no character in his plays that covers the elements of such a man as Hildebrand or Luther, or either
of the two Williams of Orange, or Hampden, or **Howard,** or Clarkson, or scores of other representative men
whom history celebrates. Though the broadest individ-

nal nature which human nature has produced, human
nature is immensely broader than he.

It would be easy to quote passages from Shakespeare's works which would seem to indicate that his
genius was not limited in any of the directions which
have been pointed out; but these passages are thoughts
and observations, not men and women. Hamlet's
soliloquy, and Portia's address to Shylock, might be adduced as proofs that he comprehended the religious element; but then who would take Hamlet or Portia as
representative of the religious character in any of its
numerous historical forms? There is a remark in one
of his plays to this effect : —

> " It is an heretic that makes the fire,
> Not she which burns in 't."

This might be taken as a beautiful expression of Christian toleration, and is certainly admirable as a general
thought; but it indicates Shakespeare's indifference to
religious passions in indicating his superiority to them.
It would have been a much greater achievement of
genius to have passed into the mind and heart of the
conscientious burner of heretics, seized the essence of
the bigot's character, and embodied in one great ideal
individual a class of men whom we now both execrate
and misconceive. If he could follow the dramatic process of his genius for Sir Toby Welch, why could he not
do it for **St.** Dominic ?

Indeed, toleration, in the sense that Shakespeare has given to the word, is not expressed in maxims directed against intolerance, but in the exercise of charity towards intolerant men ; and it is thus necessary to indicate the limitations of his sympathy with his race, in order to appreciate its real quality and extent. His unapproached greatness consists, not in including human nature, but in taking the point of view of those large classes of human nature he did include. His sympathetic insight was both serious and humorous ; and he thus equally escaped the intolerance of taste and the intolerance of intelligence. What we would call the worst criminals and the most stupid fools were, as mirrored in his mind, fairly dealt with ; every opportunity was afforded them to justify their right to exist ; their words, thoughts, and acts were viewed in relation to their circumstances and character, so that he made them inwardly known, as well as outwardly perceived. The wonder of all this would be increased, if we supposed, for the sake of illustration, that the persons and events of all Shakespeare's plays were historical, and that, instead of being represented by Shakespeare, they were criticised by Macaulay. The result would be that the impression received from the historian of every incident and every person would be different, and would be wrong. The external facts might not be altered ; but the falsehood would proceed from the incapacity or indisposition of the historian to pierce to the heart of the facts by sympathy and imagination. There would be abundant information, abundant eloquence, abundant invective against crime, abundant scorn of stupidity and folly, perhaps much sagacious reflection and judicial scrutiny of evidence ; but the inward and essential truth would be wanting. What external statement of the acts and probable motives of Macbeth and Othello could convey the idea we have of them from being witnesses of the conflict of their thoughts and passions ? How wicked and shallow and feeble and foolish would Hamlet appear, if represented, not in the light of Shakespeare's imagination, but in the light of Macaulay's epigrams ! **How the historian** would display the dazzling fence of his rhetoric on the indecision of the prince, his brutality to Ophelia, his cowardice, his impotence between contending motives, and the chaos of blunders and crimes in which he sinks from view ! The subject would be even a better **one for** him than that of James the Second ; yet the **very** supposition of such a mode of treatment makes us feel the pathos **of the** real Hamlet's injunction to the friend who strives to be his companion in death : —

> " Absent thee from felicity awhile,
> And in this harsh world draw thy breath in pain,
> *To tell my story.*"

4

If the historian would thus deal with the heroes, such "small deer" as Bardolph and Master Slender would of course be puffed out of existence with one hiss of lordly contempt. Yet Macaulay has a more vivid historical imagination, more power of placing himself in the age about which he writes, than historians like Hume and Hallam, whose judgments of men are summaries of qualities, and imply no inwardness of vision, no discerning of spirits. In the whole class, the point of view is the historian's, and not the point of view of the persons the historian describes. The curse which clings to celebrity is, that it commonly enters history only to be puffed or lampooned.

The truth is, that most men, the intelligent and the virtuous as well as the ignorant and the vicious, are intolerant of other individualities. They are uncharitable by defect of sympathy and defect of insight. Society, even the best, is apt to be made up of people who are engaged in the agreeable occupation of despising each other; for one association for mutual admiration there are twenty for mutual contempt; yet while conversation is thus mostly made up of strictures on individuals, it rarely evinces any just perception of individualities. James is indignant or jocose at the absence of James in John, and John is horror-stricken at the impudence of James in refusing to be John. Each person feels himself to be misunderstood, though he never questions his power to understand his neighbor. Egotism, vanity, prejudice, pride of opinion, conceit of excellence, a mean delight in recognizing inferiority in others, a meaner delight in refusing to recognize the superiority of others, all the honest and all the base forms of self-assertion, cloud and distort the vision when one mind directs its glance at another. For one person who is mentally conscientious there are thousands who are morally honest. The result is a vast massacre of character, which would move the observer's compassion were it not that the victims are also the culprits, and that pity at the spectacle of the arrow quivering in the sufferer's breast is checked by the sight of the bow bent in the sufferer's hands. This depreciation of others is the most approved method of exalting ourselves. It educates us in self-esteem, if **not** in knowledge. The savage conceives **that the** power of the enemy he kills is added to his own. Shakespeare more justly conceived that the power of **the** human being with whom he sympathized was added to his own.

This toleration, without which an internal knowledge of other natures is impossible, Shakespeare possessed beyond any other man recorded in literature or history. It is a moral as well as mental trait, and belongs to the highest class of virtues. It is a virtue which, if generally exercised, would remove mutual hostility **by en-lightening** mutual ignorance. And in Shakespeare we have, for once, a man great enough to be modest and charitable ; who has the giant's power, but, far from **using it** like a giant, trampling **on** weaker creatures, **prefers to** feel them in his arms rather than feel them under his feet ; and whose toleration **of others is the** exercise of humility, veracity, beneficence, and justice, **as well as** the exercise of reason, imagination, and hu-**mor. We shall never** appreciate Shakespeare's genius until we recognize in him the exercise of the most difficult virtues, **as well as** the exercise of the most wide-reaching intelligence.

It is, of course, not **so** wonderful that he should take the point of view of characters in themselves beautiful and noble, though even these might appear very differ-ent under the glance **of** a less soul-searching eye. **For** such aspects of life, however, all genius has **a** natural **affinity.** But the marvel of his comprehensiveness is **his mode of** dealing with the vulgar, the vicious, and the low, — with persons who are commonly spurned as dolts **and knaves.** His serene benevolence did not pause at what are called " deserving objects of charity," but extended to the undeserving, who are, in truth, **the** proper objects of charity. If we compare him, in this respect, with poets like **Dante** and **Milton,** in whom elevation is the predominant characteristic, we shall find that they tolerate humanity only in its exceptional examples of beauty and might. They are aristocrats of intellect and conscience, — the noblest aristocracy, but also the haughtiest and most exclusive. They can sympathize with great energies, whether celestial or diabolic, but their attitude towards the feeble and the low is apt to be that of indifference or contempt. Milton can do justice to the Devil, though not, like Shakespeare, to "poor devils." But it may be doubted if the wise and good have the right to cut the Providential bond which connects them with the foolish and the bad, and set up an aristocratic humanity of their own, ten times **more** supercilious than the aristocracy of blood. Divorce **the** loftiest qualities from humility and geniality, and they quickly contract a pharisaic taint; and if there is anything which makes the wretched more wretched, it is the insolent condescension of patronizing benevolence, — if there is anything which makes the vicious more vicious, it is the " I-am-better-than-thou " expression on the face of conscious virtue. Now Shakespeare had none of this pride of superiority, either in its noble or ignoble form. Consider that, if his gigantic powers had been directed by antipathies instead of sympathies, he would have left few classes **of** human character untouched by his terrible scorn. Even if his antipathies had been those of taste and morals, he would have done so much to make men hate and misunderstand each other, — so much to destroy the very sentiment of humanity, — that he would have earned the distinction of being the greatest satirist and the worst man that ever lived. But instead, how humanely he clings to the most unpromising forms of human nature, insists on their right to speak for themselves as much as if they were passionate Romeos and high-aspiring Bucking- hams, and does for them what he might have desired should be done for himself had he been Dogberry, or Bottom, or Abhorson, or Bardolph, or any of the rest ! The low characters, the clowns and vagabonds, of Ben Jonson's plays, excite only contempt or disgust. Shakespeare takes the same materials as Ben, passes them through the medium of his imaginative humor, and changes them into subjects of the most soul-enriching mirth. Their actual prototypes would not be tolerated ; but when his genius shines on them, they " lie in light " before our humorous vision. It must be admitted that in his explorations of the lower levels of human nature he sometimes touches the mud deposits ; still, he never hisses or jeers at the poor relations through Adam he there discovers, but magnanimously gives them the wink of consanguinity.

This is one extreme of his genius, — the poetic com-

prehension and embodiment of the low. What was the
other extreme? How high did he mount in the ideal
region, and what class of his characters represents his
loftiest flight? It is commonly asserted that his supernatural beings, — his ghosts, spectres, witches, fairies, and
the like, — exhibiting his command of the dark side and
the bright side, the terror and the grace, of the supernatural world, indicate his rarest **quality; for** in these,
it is said, he went out of human nature itself, and
created beings that never existed. Wonderful as these
are, we must recollect that in them he worked on a
basis of popular superstitions, on a mythology as definite
as that of Greece and Rome, and though he recreated
instead of copying his materials, though he Shakespear-
ianized them, he followed the same **process of his**
genius in delineating Hecate and Titania as in delineating Dame Quickly and Anne Page. All his characters, from the rogue Autolycus to the heavenly Cordelia,
are in a certain sense ideal; but the question now relates to the rarity of the elements, and the height of the
mood, and not merely to the action of his mind; and
we think that the characters technically called supernatural which appear in his works are much nearer the
earth than others which, though they lack the name,
have more of the spiritual quality **of** the thing. The
highest form of the supernatural **is to** be found in the
purest, highest, most beautiful souls.

Did it never strike you, in reading The Tempest, that Ariel is not so supernatural as Miranda? We may be sure that Ferdinand so thought, in that rapture of wonder when her soul first shone on him through her innocent eyes ; and afterwards, when he asks,

> " I do beseech you
> (Chiefly that I might set it in my prayers)
> What is your name ? "

And doubtless there was a more marvellous melody in **her voice than in the mysterious** magical music

> " That crept by him upon the waters,
> Allaying both their fury and his passion
> With its sweet air."

Shakespeare, indeed, in his transcendently beautiful embodiments of feminine excellence, the most exquisite creations in literature, passed into a region of sentiment and thought, of ideals and of ideas, altogether higher and more supernatural than that region in which he shaped his delicate Ariels and his fairy Titanias. The **question has been** raised whether sex extends to soul. However this may be decided, here is a soul, with its records in literature, who is at once the manliest of men, and the most womanly of women ; who can **not only** recognize the feminine element in existing individuals, **but** discern the **idea,** the pattern, the radiant **genius,** of

womanhood itself, as it hovers, unseen by other **eyes,**
over the living representatives of the sex. Literature
boasts many eminent female poets and novelists; but
not one has ever approached Shakespeare in the purity,
the sweetness, the refinement, the elevation, of his perceptions of feminine character, — much less approached
him in the power of embodying these perceptions in persons. These characters are so thoroughly domesticated
on the earth, that we are tempted to forget the heaven
of invention from which he brought them. The most
beautiful of spirits, they are the most tender of daugh-
ters, lovers, and wives. They are "airy shapes," but
they "syllable men's names." Rosalind, Juliet, Ophelia, Viola, Perdita, Miranda, Desdemona, Hermione,
Portia, Isabella, Imogen, Cordelia, — if their names **do**
not call up their natures, the most elaborate **analysis**
of criticism will be of no avail. Do you say that these
women are slightly idealized portraits of actual women?
Was Cordelia, for example, simply a good, affectionate
daughter of a foolish old king? To Shakespeare himself she evidently " partook of divineness " ; and he hints
of the still ecstasy of contemplation in which her nature
first **rose** upon his imagination, when, speaking through
the lips of a witness of her tears, he hallows them as
they fall : —

> " She shook
> The holy water from her heavenly eyes."

4 *

And these Shakespearian women, though all radiations from one great ideal of womanhood, are at the same
time intensely individualized. Each has a separate soul,
and the processes of intellect as well as emotion are
different in each. Each, for example, is endowed with
the faculty, and is steeped in the atmosphere, of imagination ; but who could mistake the imagination of
Ophelia for the imagination of Imogen ? — the loitering,
lingering movement of the one, softly consecrating
whatever it touches, for the irradiating, smiting efficiency,
the flash and the bolt, of the other ? Imogen is perhaps
the most completely expressed of Shakespeare's women ;
for in her every faculty and affection is fused with
imagination, and the most exquisite tenderness is combined with vigor and velocity of nature. Her mind
darts in an instant to the ultimate of everything. After
she has parted with her husband, she does not merely
say that she will pray for him. Her affection is winged,
and in a moment she is enskied. Slie does not look up,
she goes up: she would have charged him, she says,

> " At the sixth hour of morn, at noon, at midnight,
> T' encounter me with orisons, for then
> *I am in heaven for him.*"

When she hears of her husband's inconstancy, the possible object of his sensual whim is at once consumed in
the fire that leaps from her impassioned lips : —

> " Some jay of Italy,
> Whose mother is her painting, hath betrayed him."

Mr. Collier, ludicrously misconceiving the instinctive action of Imogen's mind, thinks the true reading is, " who smothers her with painting." Now Imogen's wrath first reduces the light woman to the most contemptible of birds and the most infamous of symbols, the jay, and then, not willing to leave her any substance at all, annihilates her very being with the swift thought that the paint on her cheeks is her mother, — that she is nothing but the mere creation of painting, a phantom born of a color, without real body or soul. It would be easy to show that **the mental** processes of all Shakespeare's **women** are as individual as their dispositions.

And now think of the amplitude of this **man's soul !** Within the immense space which stretches between **Dog**berry **or** Launcelot Gobbo and Imogen **or** Cordelia, lies the Shakespearian world. No other **man ever** exhibited such philosophic comprehensiveness ; but philosophic comprehensiveness is often displayed apart from creative comprehensiveness, and along the whole vast line of facts, laws, analogies, and relations over which Shakespeare's intellect extended, his perceptions **were** vital, his insight was creative, his thoughts flowed **in** forms. And now, was he proud of his **transcendent** superiorities ? Did he think that **he** had exhausted all that

can appear before the sight of the eye and the sight of
the soul ? No. The immeasurable opulence of the undiscovered and undiscerned regions of existence was never
felt with more reverent humility than by this discoverer,
who had seen in rapturous visions so many new worlds
open on his view. In the play which perhaps best exhibits the ecstatic action of his mind, and which is alive
in every part with that fiery sense of unlimited power
which the mood of ecstasy gives, — in the play of Antony and Cleopatra, — he has put into the mouth of the
Soothsayer what seems to have been his own modest
judgment of the extent of his glance into the universe of matter and mind : —

> " In nature's infinite book of secrecy
>   A little I can read ! "

BEN JONSON.

AUTHORS are apt to be popularly considered as physically a feeble folk, — as timid, nervous, dyspeptic rhymers or prosers, unfitted to grapple with the rough realities of life. We shall endeavor here to present the image of one calculated to reverse this impression, — the image of a stalwart man of letters, who lived two centuries and a half ago, in the greatest age of English literature, who undeniably had brawny fists as well as forgetive faculties, who could handle a club as readily as a pen, hit his mark with a bullet as surely as with a word, and — a sort of cross between the bully and the bard — could shoulder his way through a crowd of prize-fighters to take his seat among the tuneful company of immortal poets. This man, Ben Jonson, commonly stands next to Shakespeare in a consideration of the dramatic literature of the age of Elizabeth ; and certainly, if the " thousand-souled " Shakespeare may be said to represent mankind, Ben as unmistakably stands for English-kind. He is " Saxon " England in epitome, — John Bull passing from a name into a man, — a proud, strong, tough, solid, domineering individual, whose intellect and personality cannot be severed, even in thought, from his body and personal appearance. Ben's mind, indeed, was rooted in Ben's character ; and his character took symbolic form in his physical frame. He seemed built up, mentally as well as bodily, out of beef and sack, mutton and Canary ; or, to say the least, was a joint product of the English mind and the English larder, of the fat as well as the thought of the land, of the soil as well as the soul of England. The moment we attempt to estimate his eminence as a dramatist, he disturbs the equanimity of our judgment by tumbling head-foremost into the imagination as a big, bluff, burly, and quarrelsome man, with "a mountain belly and a rocky face." He is a very pleasant boon companion as long as we make our idea of his importance agree with his own ; but the instant we attempt to dissect his intellectual pretensions, the living animal becomes a dangerous subject, — his countenance flames, his great hands double up, his thick lips begin to twitch with impending invective, and, while the critic's impression of him is thus all the more vivid, he is checked in its expression by a very natural fear of the consequences. There is no safety but in taking this rowdy leviathan of letters at his own valuation ; and the relation of critics towards him is as perilous as that of the jurymen towards the Irish advocate, who had an unpleasant habit of sending them the challenge of the **duellist whenever** they brought in a verdict against any of his clients. There is, in fact, such a vast animal force in old Ben's self-assertion, that he bullies posterity as he bullied his contemporaries; and, while we admit his claim to rank **next** to Shakespeare among the dramatists of his age, we beg our readers to understand that we do it under intimidation.

The qualities of this bold, racy, and brawny egotist can be best conveyed in a biographical form. He was born in 1574, the grandson of a gentleman who, for his religion, lost his estate, and for a time his liberty, in Queen Mary's reign, and the son of a clergyman in humble circumstances, who died about a month before his "rare" offspring was born. His mother, shortly after the death of her husband, married a master-bricklayer. Ben, who as a boy doubtless exhibited brightness of intellect and audacity of spirit, seems to have attracted the attention of Camden, who placed him in Westminster School, of which he was master. Ben there displayed so warm a love of learning, and so much capacity in rapidly acquiring it, that at the age of sixteen he is said to have been removed to the University of Cambridge, though he stated to Drummond, long afterwards, that he was "master of arts in both the Universities, by their favor, not his studie." His **ambition** at this time, if we may believe some of his biographers, was to be a clergyman ; and had it been gratified, he would probably have blustered his way to a bishopric, and proved himself one of the most arrogant, learned, and pugnacious disputants of the English Church Militant, — perhaps have furnished the type of that peculiar religionist, compounded of bully, pedant, and bigot, whom Warburton was afterwards, from the lack of models, compelled to originate.　But after residing a few months at the University, Ben, deserted by his friends and destitute of money, found it impossible to carry out his design ; and he returned disappointed to his mother's house.　As she could not support him in idleness, the stout-hearted student adopted the most obvious means of earning his daily bread, and for a short time followed the occupation of his father-in-law, going to the work of bricklaying, according to the tradition, with a trowel in one hand, but with a Horace in the other.　His enemies among the dramatists did not forget this when he became famous, but meanly sneered at him as "the lime-and-mortar poet."　When we reflect that in the aristocratic age of good Queen Bess, play-writing, even the writing of Hamlets and Alchymists, was, if we may trust Dr. Farmer, hardly considered " a creditable employ," we may form some judgment of the position of the working classes, when a mechanic was thus deemed to have no rights which a playwright "was bound to respect."

We have no means of deciding whether or not Ben was foolish enough to look upon his trade as degrading; that it was distasteful we know from the fact that he soon exchanged the trowel for the sword; and we hear no more of his dealing with bricks, if we may except his questionable habit of sometimes carrying too many of them in his hat. At the age of eighteen he ran away to the Continent, and enlisted as a volunteer in the English army in Flanders, fully intending, doubtless, as fate seemed against his being a Homer or an Aristotle, to try if fortune would not make him an Alexander or a Hannibal. As ill-luck would have it, however, his abundant vitality had little scope in martial exercise. He does not appear to have been in any general engagement, though he signalized his personal prowess in a manner which he was determined should not be forgotten through any diffidence of his own. Boastful as he was brave, he was never weary of bragging how he had encountered one of the enemy, fought with him in presence of both armies, killed him, and triumphantly "taken *opima spolia* from him."

After serving one campaign, our Ajax-Thersites returned, at the age of nineteen, to England, bringing with him, according to Gifford, "the reputation of a brave

man, a smattering of Dutch, and an empty purse." To
these efficiencies and deficiencies he probably added
the infirmity of drinking; for, as " our army in
Flanders " ever drank terribly as well as " swore
terribly," it may be supposed that Ben there laid,
deep and wide, the foundation of his bacchanalian
habits. ' Arrived in London, and thrown on his own
resources for support, he turned naturally to the stage,
and became an actor in a minor playhouse, called
the Green Curtain. Though he was through life
a good reader, and though at this time he was not
afflicted with the scurvy, which eventually so punched
his face as to make one of his satirists compare it, with
witty malice, to the cover of a warming-pan, he still
never rose to any eminence as an actor. He had not
been long at the Green Curtain when a quarrel with
one of his fellow-performers led to a duel, in which Jonson killed his antagonist, was arrested on a charge of
murder, and, in his own phrase, was brought "almost at
the gallowes," — an unpleasant proximity, which he
hastened to increase by relieving the weariness of imprisonment in discussions on religion with a Popish
priest, also a prisoner, and by becoming a convert to
Romanism. As the zealous professors of the old faith
had passed, in Elizabeth's time, from persecutors into
martyrs, Ben, the descendant of one of Queen Mary's

victims, evinced more **than** his usual worldly prudence in seizing this occasion to join their company, **as he** could reasonably **hope** that, if he escaped hanging on the **charge of** homicide, he still might contrive **to be** beheaded **and** disembowelled on **a** charge of treason. **In** regard, however, to the original cause of his imprisonment, it would seem that, on investigation, it was found the duel had been forced upon him, that his antagonist had taken the precaution of bringing into the field a sword ten inches longer than his own, and thus, far from expecting **to** be the victim **of** murder, had not unsagaciously counted on committing it. Jonson was released ; but, apparently vexed at this propitious **turn** of his fortunes, instead of casting about for some means of subsistence, he almost immediately married a woman as poor as himself, — a wife **whom he** afterwards curtly described as " **a** shrew, yet honest." **A shrew, indeed !** **As** if Mrs. Jonson must not often have had just occasion **to use** her tongue tartly ! — as if her redoubtable Ben **did not** often need its acrid admonitions ! They seem **to have** lived together until 1613, when they separated.

Absolute necessity drove Jonson again to the stage, probably both **as actor** and writer. He began his dramatic career, **as** Shakespeare had begun his, by doing job-work for the managers, — that is, by altering, recasting, and making additions to, old plays. At last, in

1596, in his twenty-second year, he placed himself at a bound among the famous dramatists of the time, by the production, at the Rose Theatre, of his comedy of Every Man in his Humor. Two years afterwards, having in the mean time been altered and improved, it was, through the influence of Shakespeare, accepted by the players of the Blackfriars Theatre, Shakespeare himself acting the characterless part of the Elder Knowell.

Among the writers of the Elizabethan age, — an age in which, for a wonder, there seemed to be a glut of genius, — Ben is prominent more for racy originality of personal character, weight of understanding, and quickness of fancy, than for creativeness of imagination. His first play, Every Man in his Humor, indicates, to a great extent, the quality and the kind of power with which he was endowed. His prominent characteristic was will, — will carried to self-will, and sometimes to self-exaggeration almost furious. His understanding was solid, strong, penetrating, even broad, and it was well furnished with matter derived both from experience and books; but, dominated by a personality so fretful and fierce, it was impelled to look at men and things, not in their relations to each other, but in their relations to Ben. He had reached that ideal of stormy conceit in which, according to Emerson, the egotist declares, "Difference from me is the measure of absurdity."

Even the imaginary characters he delineated as a dramatist were all bound, as by tough cords, to the will that gave them being, lacked that joyous freedom and careless grace of movement which rightfully belonged to **them** as denizens of an ideal world, and had to obey their master Ben, as puppets obey the **showman.** **His** power of external observation was pitilessly keen and searching, and it was accompanied by a rich, though somewhat coarse and insolent vein of humor; but his egotism commonly directed his observation to what was below, rather than above himself, and gave to his humor a scornful, rather than a genial tone. **He** huffs even in his hilarity; his fun is never infectious; and his very laughter is an assertion of superior wisdom. He has none of that humanizing humor, which, in Shakespeare, makes us like the vagabonds we laugh at, and which insures for Dogberry and Nick Bottom, Autolychus and Falstaff, warmer friends among readers than many great historic dignities of the state and the camp can command.

In regard to the materials of the dramatist, Jonson, **in** his vagrant career, had seen human nature under many aspects; but he had surveyed it neither with the eye of reason nor **the eye of** imagination. His mind fastened on the hard actualities of observation, without passing to what they implied or suggested. Deficient, thus, in philosophic insight and poetic insight, his shrewd,

contemptuous glance rarely penetrated beneath the manners and eccentricities of men. His attention was
arrested, not by character, but by prominent peculiarities
of character, — peculiarities which almost transformed
character into caricature. To use his own phrase, he
delineated " humors " rather than persons, that is, individuals under the influence of some dominant affectation,
or whim, or conceit, or passion, that drew into itself,
colored, and mastered the whole nature, — "an acorn,"
as Sir Thomas Browne phrases it, "in their young
brows, which grew to an oak in their old heads." He
thus inverts the true process of characterization. Instead of seeing the trait as an offshoot of the individual,
he individualizes the trait. Every man is *in* his humor,
instead of every humor being in its man. In order that
there should be no misconception of his purpose, he
named his chief characters after their predominant
qualities, as Morose, Surly, Sir Amorous La Fool, Sir
Politic Would Be, Sir Epicure Mammon, and the like ;
and, apprehensive even then that his whole precious
meaning would not be taken in, he appended to his
dramatis personæ further explanations of their respective
natures.

This distrust of the power of language to lodge a
notion in another brain is especially English ; but Ben,
of all writers, seems to have been most impressed with

the necessity of pounding an idea into the perceptions of his countrymen. His mode resembles the attempt of that honest Briton who thus delivered his judgment on the French nation: "I hate a Frenchman, sir. Every Frenchman is either a puppy or a rascal, sir." And then, fearful that he had not been sufficiently explicit, he added, "Do you take my idea?"

With all abatements, however, the comedy of Every Man in his Humor is a remarkable effort, considered as the production of a young man of twenty-two. The two most striking characters are Kitely and Captain Bobadil. Give Jonson, indeed, a peculiarity to start with, and he worked it out with logical exactness. So intense was his conception of it, that he clothed it in flesh and blood, gave it a substantial existence, and sometimes succeeded in forcing it into literature as a permanent character.

Bobadil, especially, is one of Ben's masterpieces. He is the most colossal coward and braggart of the comic stage. He can swear by nothing less terrible than "by the body of Cæsar," or "by the foot of Pharaoh," when his oath is not something more terrific still, namely, "by my valor"! Every school-boy knows the celebrated passage in which the boasting Captain offers to settle the affairs of Europe by associating with himself twenty other Bobadils, as "cunning i' the fence" as himself, and challenging an army of forty thousand men, twenty at a time, and killing the whole in a certain number of days. Leaving out the cowardice, we may say there was something of Bobadil in Jonson himself; and it may be shrewdly suspected that his conceit of destroying an army in this fashion came into his head in the exultation of feeling which followed his own successful exploit, in the presence of both armies, when he was a soldier in Flanders. Old John Dennis described genius " as a furious joy and pride of soul at the conception of an extraordinary hint." Ben had this "furious joy and pride," not only in the conception of extraordinary hints, but in the doing of extraordinary things.

Jonson followed up his success by producing the plays of Every Man out of his Humor and Cynthia's Revels, — dramatic satires on the manners, follies, affectations, and vices, of the city and the court. One good result of Jonson's egotism was, that it made him afraid of nothing. He openly appeared among the dramatists of his day as a reformer, and, poor as he was, refused to pander to popular tastes, whether those tastes took the direction of ribaldry, or blasphemy, or bombast. He had courage, morality, earnestness ; but then his courage was so blustering, his morality so irascible, and his devotion to his own ideas of art so exclusive, that he

was constantly defying and insulting the persons he proposed to teach. Other dramatists said to the audience,
" Please to applaud this " ; but Ben said, " Now, you
fools, we shall see if you have sense enough to applaud
this ! " **The** stage, to be sure, was to **be** exalted **and**
improved, but it was to be done by his own works, and
the glory of literature was to be associated with the
glory of Master Benjamin. This conceit, by making
him insensible to Shakespeare's influence, made him,
next to Shakespeare, perhaps **the** most original dramatist of the time. He differed from his brother dramatists not in degree, but in kind. He felt it was not for
him to imitate, but to produce models for imitation, — not
for him to catch the spirit of the age, but **to** originate a
better. In short, he felt and taught belief in Ben ; and,
high as posterity rates the literature of the age of Elizabeth, it would be supposed from his prologues **and** epi-
logues that he conceived his fat body to have fallen on
evil days.

In every Man out of his Humor and Cynthia's Revels,
he is in a raging passion throughout. His verse groans
with the weight of **his** wrath. " My soul," he exclaims,

> " Was never ground into such oily colors
> To flatter vice and daub iniquity.
> **But** with an arméd and resolvéd hand
> I 'll strip the ragged follies of the time
> Naked as **at** their birth,

5 o

> . . . . and with a whip of steel
> Print wounding lashes on their iron ribs."

But though he exhausts the whole rhetoric of railing, invective, contempt, and scorn, we yet find it difficult to feel any of the indignation he labors to excite. Admiration, however, cannot be refused to Jonson's prose style in these as in his other plays. It is terse, sharp, swift, biting, — every word a die that stamps a definite image. Occasionally the author's veins, to use his own apt expression, seem to "run quicksilver," and "every phrase comes forth steeped in the very brine of conceit, and sparkles like salt in fire." Yet, though we have scenes in which there is brightness in every sentence, the result of the whole is something like dulness, as the object of the whole is to exalt himself and depress others. But in these plays, in strange contrast with their general character, we have a few specimens of that sweetness of sentiment, refinement of fancy, and indefinite beauty of imagination, which, occupying some secluded corner of his large brain, seemed to exist apart from his ordinary powers and passions. Among these, the most exquisite is this Hymn to Diana, which partakes of the serenity of the moonlight, whose goddess it invokes : —

> " Queen and huntress chaste and fair,
>   Now the sun is laid to sleep,
> Seated in thy silver chair,

State in wonted manner keep.
Hesperus entreats thy light,
Goddess excellently bright!

" Earth, let not thy envious shade
Dare itself to interpose;
Cynthia's shining orb was made
Heaven to clear when day did close.
Bless us, then, with wishéd sight,
Goddess excellently bright.

" Lay thy bow of pearl apart
And thy crystal-gleaming quiver;
Give unto the flying hart
Space to breathe how short soever, —
Thou that mak'st a day of night,
Goddess excellently bright."

If, as Jonson's adversaries maliciously asserted, " **every** line of his poetry cost him a cup of sack," we must, **even** in our more temperate days, **pardon** him the eighteen **cups** which, in this melodious lyric, went into his mouth **as sack,** but, by some precious chemistry, came out through his pen as pearls.

It was inevitable **that the** imperious attitude Jonson assumed, **and** the **insolent** pungency of his satire, should rouse the wrath **of the** classes he lampooned and **the** enmity **of** the poets he ridiculed **and** decried.   **Among** those who conceived themselves assailed, or who felt insulted by his arrogant tone, **were two** dramatists,

Thomas Dekkar and John Marston. They soon recriminated; and, as Ben was better fitted by nature to dispense than to endure scorn and derision, he, in 1601, produced The Poetaster, the object of which was to silence forever, not only Dekkar and Marston, but all other impudent doubters of his infallibility. The humor of the thing is, that, in this elaborate attempt to convict his adversaries of calumny in taxing him with self-love and arrogance, he ostentatiously exhibits the very qualities he disclaims. He keeps no terms with those who profess disbelief in Ben. They are "play-dressers and plagiaries," "fools or jerking pedants," "buffoon barking wits," tickling "base vulgar ears with beggarly and barren trash," while his are

> " The high raptures of a happy Muse,
> Borne on the wings of her immortal thought,
> That kicks at earth with a disdainful heel,
> And beats at heaven's gate with her bright hoofs."

Dekkar retorted in a play called Satiromastrix; or, the Untrussing of the Humorous Poet; but, though the scurrility is brilliantly bitter, it is less efficient and "hearted" than Jonson's. This literary controversy, conducted in acted plays, had to the public of that day a zest similar to that we should enjoy if the editors of two opposing political newspapers should meet in a hall filled with their subscribers, and fling their thundering edito-

rials in person at each other's heads. The theatre-goers
seem to have declared for Dekkar and Marston ; **and**
Ben, disgusted **with** such **a proof of** their incapacity of
right judgment, sulked and growled in his den, and for
two years gave nothing to the stage. He had, however,
found a patron, who enabled him to do this without undergoing the famine of insufficient meat, and the still more
dreadful drought of insufficient drink ; for, in a gossip-
ing diary of the period, covering these two years, we
are informed, " B. J. now lives with one Townsend, and
scorns the world." While, however, pleasantly engaged
in this characteristic occupation, for which he had a natural genius, **he was** meditating a play which he thought
would **demonstrate** to all judging spirits his possession
equally of the acquirements of the scholar and **the tal-**
ents of the dramatist. In the conclusion of the **Apolo-**
getic Dialogue which accompanies **The** Poetaster, he
had hinted his purpose in these energetic lines : —

> " Once I 'll say, —
> To strike the ears of Time in these fresh strains,
> As shall, beside the cunning of their ground,
> Give cause to some of wonder, some despite,
> And more despair to imitate their sound.
> I that spend half my nights and **all** my days
> Here in **a** cell, to get a dark, pale face,
> To come forth with the ivy and the bays,
> And in this age can hope no better grace, —

> Leave me! There's something come into my thought,
> That must and shall be sung high and aloof,
> Safe from the wolf's black jaw, and the dull ass's hoof! "

Accordingly, in 1603, he produced his weighty tragedy of Sejanus, at Shakespeare's theatre, The Globe, — Shakespeare himself acting one of the inferior parts. Think of Shakespeare laboriously committing to memory the blank verse of Jonson!

Though Sejanus failed of theatrical success, its wealth of knowledge and solid thought made it the best of all answers to his opponents. It was as if they had questioned his capacity to build a ship, and he had confuted them with a man-of-war. To be sure, they might reiterate their old charge of " filching by translation," for the text of Sejanus is a mosaic; but it was one of Jonson's maxims that he deserved as much honor for what he reproduced from' the classics as for what he originated. Indeed, in his dealings with the great poets and historians of Rome, whose language and much of whose spirit he had patiently mastered, he acted the part, not of the pickpocket, but of the conqueror. He did not meanly crib and pilfer in the territories of the ancients: he rather pillaged, or, in our American phrase, " annexed " them. " He has done his robberies so openly," says Dryden, " that one sees he fears not to be taxed by any law. He invades authors like a

monarch, and what would be theft in any other poet **is**
only victory in him."

One incident connected with the bringing out of Sejanus should not be omitted. Jonson told Drummond
that **the** Earl of Northampton had a mortal enmity to
him "for beating, on a St. George's day, one of his at-
tenders"; and he adds, that Northampton had him
"called before the Councell for his Sejanus," and accused him there both of " Poperie and treason."

Jonson's relations with Shakespeare seem always to
have been friendly; and about this time we hear of
them as associate members of the greatest of literary
and of convivial clubs, — the club instituted by Sir
Walter Raleigh, and known to all after-times **as the**
" Mermaid," being so called from **the tavern in which**
the meetings were held. Various, however, as were the
genius and accomplishments it included, it lacked one
phase of ability which has deprived us of all participa-
tion in its wit and wisdom. It could boast of Shakespeare, and Jonson, and Raleigh, and Camden, and
Beaumont, and Selden; but, alas! it had no Boswell to
record its words,

" So nimble, and so full of subtile flame."

There are traditions of " wit-combats " between Shakespeare and Jonson; and doubtless there was many a
discussion between them touching the different principles

on which their dramas were composed; and then Ben, astride his high horse of the classics, probably blustered and harangued, and graciously informed the world's greatest poet that he sometimes wanted art and sometimes sense, and candidly advised him to check the fatal rapidity and perilous combinations of his imagination, — while Shakespeare smilingly listened, and occasionally put in an ironic word, deprecating such austere criticism of a playwright like himself, who accommodated his art to the humors of the mob that crowded the "round O" of the Globe. There can be no question that Shakespeare saw Ben through and through, but he was not a man to be intolerant of foibles, and probably enjoyed the hectoring egotism of his friend as much as he appreciated his real merits. As for Ben, the transcendent genius of his brother dramatist pierced through even the thick hide of his self-sufficiency. "I did honor him," he finely says, "this side of idolatry, as much as any other man."

On the accession of James of Scotland to the English throne, Jonson was employed by the court and city to design a splendid pageant for the monarch's reception; and, with that absence of vindictiveness which somewhat atoned for his arrogance, he gave his recent enemy, Dekkar, three fifths of the job. About the same time he was reconciled to Marston; and in 1605 assisted

him and Chapman in a comedy called " Eastward Hoe !"
One passage in this, reflecting on the Scotch, gave mortal offence to James's greedy countrymen, who invaded
England in his-train, and were ravenous and clamorous
for the spoils of office. Captain Seagul, in the play,
praises what was then the new settlement of Virginia,
as " a place without sergeants, or courtiers, or lawyers,
or intelligencers, only a few industrious Scots perhaps,
who indeed are dispersed over the whole earth. But as
for them, there are no greater friends to Englishmen
and England, when they are out on 't, in the world, than
they are ; and, for my own part, I would a hundred
thousand of them were there, for we are all one countrymen now, ye know, and we should find ten times
more comfort of them there than we **do** here." This
bitter taunt, which probably made the theatre roar with
applause, was so represented to the king, that Marston
and Chapman were arrested and imprisoned. Jonson
nobly insisted on sharing their fate ; and as he had
powerful friends at court, and was esteemed by James
himself, his course may have saved his friends from disgraceful mutilations. A report was circulated that the
noses and ears of all three were to be slit ; and Jonson
tells us that, in an entertainment he gave to Camden,
Selden, and other friends, after his liberation, his old
mother exhibited a paper full of " lustie strong poison,"

5 *

which she said she had intended to mix *in his drink*, in case the threat of such a shameful punishment were officially announced. The phrase, " his drink," is very characteristic; and, whatever liquid was meant, we may be sure that it was not water, and that the good lady would have daily had numerous opportunities to mix the poison with it.

The five years which succeeded his imprisonment carried Jonson to the height of his prosperity and glory. During this period he produced the three great comedies on which his fame as a dramatist rests, — The Fox, The Silent Woman, and The Alchymist, — and also many of the most beautiful of those Masques, performed at court, in which the ingenuity, delicacy, richness, and elevation of his fancy found fittest expression. His social position was probably superior to Shakespeare's. He was really the Court Poet long before 1616, when he received the office, with a pension of a hundred marks. We have Clarendon's testimony to the fact that " his conversation was very good, and with men of the best note." Among his friends occurs the great name of Bacon.

In 1618, when " Ben Jonson " had come to be a familiar name on the lips of all educated men in the island, he made his celebrated journey on foot to Scotland, and was hospitably entertained by the nobility and gentry around Edinburgh. Taylor, the water poet, in his " Pennylesse Pilgrimage " to Scotland, has this amiable reference to him. "At Leith," he says, " I found my long approved and assured good friend, Master Benjamin Jonson, at **one** Master John Stuart's house. I thank him for his great kindness ; for, at my taking leave of him, he gave me a piece of gold of two-and-twenty shillings' value, **to** drink his health in England." One object of Jonson's journey was to visit the poet Drummond. He passed three or four weeks with Drummond at Hawthornden, and poured out his mind to him without reserve or stint. The finical and fastidious poet was somewhat startled **at this** irruption of his burly guest into **his dainty** solitude, took notes of his free conversation, especially when he decried his contemporaries, and further performed the rites of hospitality by adding a caustic, though keen, summary of his qualities of character. Thus, according to his dear friend's charitable analysis, Ben " was a great lover and praiser of himself ; a contemner and scorner of others ; given rather to losse a friend than a jest ; jealous of every word and action of those about him (especiallie after drink, which is one of the elements in which he liveth) ; **a** dissembler of ill parts which raigne in him, a bragger of some good that **he** wanteth ; thinketh nothing well bot what either he himself or some of his friends and countrymen have said or done; he is passionately kynde and angry; careless either to gaine or keep; vindictive, but, if he be well answered, at himself." It is not much to the credit of Jonson's insight, that, after flooding his pensively taciturn host with his boisterous and dogmatic talk, he parted with him under the impression that he was leaving an assured friend. Ah! your demure listeners to your unguarded conversation, — they are the ones that give the fatal stabs!

A literal transcript of Drummond's original notes of Jonson's conversations, made by Sir Robert Sibbald about the year 1710, has been published in the collections of the Shakespeare Society. This is a more extended report than that included in Drummond's works, though still not so full as the reader might desire. The stoutness of Ben's character is felt in every utterance. Thus he tells Drummond that "he never esteemed of a man for the name of a lord," — a sentiment which he had expressed more impressively in his published epigram on Burleigh : —

> " Cecil, the grave, the wise, the great, the good,
>   What is there more that can ennoble blood ? "

He had, it seems, "a minde to be a churchman, and, so he might have favor to make one sermon to the King, he careth not what thereafter sould befall him ; for he

would not flatter though he saw Death."   Queen Elizabeth is the mark of a most scandalous imputation, **and**
the mildest of Ben's remarks respecting her is that she
" never saw herself, after she became old, in a true glass ;
they painted her, *and sometymes would vermilion* her
nose."   " Of all styles," he said, " he most loved to be
named Honest, and hath of that one hundred letters
so naming him."   His judgments on other poets were
insolently magisterial.   " Spenser's stanzas pleased him
not, nor his matter " ;   Samuel Daniel was a good honest
man, but no poet ;   Donne, though " the first poet in the
world in some things," for " not keeping of accent, deserved hanging " ;   Abram Fraunce, " in his English
hexameters, **was** a foole " ;   Sharpham, Day, and Dekkar
were all rogues ;   Francis Beaumont " loved too much
himself and his own verses."   Some biographical **items**
in the record of these conversations are of interest.   It
seems that the first day of every new year the Earl of
Pembroke sent him twenty pounds " to buy bookes."
By all his plays he never gained two hundred pounds.
" Sundry tymes he hath devoured his bookes," that is,
sold them to supply himself with necessaries.   When he
was imprisoned for killing his brother actor in a duel, in
the Queen's time, " his judges could get nothing of him
to all their demands but I and No.   They placed two
damn'd villains, to catch advantage of him, with him,

but he was advertised by his keeper "; and he added, as
if the revenge was as terrible as the offence, " of the
spies he hath ane epigrame." He told a few personal
stories to Drummond, calculated to moderate our wonder that Mrs. Jonson was a shrew ; and, as they were
boastingly told, we must suppose that his manners were
not so austere as his verse. But perhaps the most
characteristic image he has left of himself, through these
conversations, is this : " He hath consumed a whole
night in lying looking to his great toe, about which he
hath seen Tartars and Turks, Romans and Carthagin-
ians, feight in his imagination."

Jonson's fortunes seem to have suffered little abate-
ment until the death of King James, in 1625. Then
declining popularity and declining health combined
their malice to break the veteran down; and the remaining twelve years of his life were passed in doing
battle with those relentless enemies of poets, — want
and disease. The orange — or rather the lemon — was
squeezed, and both court and public seemed disposed to
throw away the peel. In the epilogue to his play of
The New Inn, brought out in 1630, the old tone of de-
fiance is gone. He touchingly appeals to the audience
as one who is " sick and sad "; but, with a noble humility, he begs they will refer none of the defects of the
work to mental decay.

> " All that his weak and faltering tongue doth crave
>   Is **that you not refer it** to his brain;
>   **That 's yet** unhurt, although set round with pain."

The audience were insensible to this appeal. **They found the** play dull, and hooted it from the stage. Perhaps, after having been bullied **so** long, **they took delight** in having Ben " on the hip." Charles the First, however, who up to this time seems to have neglected his father's favorite, now generously sent him **a** hundred pounds to cheer him in his misfortunes ; and shortly after he raised his salary, as Court Poet, from **a** hundred marks to a hundred pounds, adding, in compliment to Jonson's known tastes, a tierce of Canary, — a wine of which **he** was so fond as to be nicknamed, **in** ironical reference to a corpulence which rather assimilated him to **the ox,** " a Canary bird." It is to this period, we **suppose, we** must refer his **testimony to his** own obesity in his Epistle to my Lady Coventry.

> " So you have gained a Servant and a Muse:
>   The first of which I fear you will refuse,
>   And you may justly: being a tardy, cold,
>   Unprofitable chattle, fat and old,
>   Laden with belly, and doth hardly approach
>   His friends, but to break chairs or crack a coach.
>   His weight is twenty stone, within two pound ;
>   And that 's made up, as doth the purse abound."

As his life declined, it does not appear that his disposition was essentially modified. There are two characteristic references to him in his old age, which prove that Ben, attacked by palsy and dropsy, with a reputation perceptibly waning, was Ben still. One is from Sir John Suckling's pleasantly malicious " Session of the Poets " : —

> " The first that broke silence was good old Ben,
>   Prepared before with Canary wine,
>   And he told them plainly he deserved the bays,
>   For his were called works where others were but plays.
>
>   .   .   .   .   .
>
> " Apollo stopped him there, and bade him not go on;
>   'T was merit, he said, and not presumption,
>   Must carry 't; at which Ben turned about,
>   And in great choler offered to go out."

That is a saucy touch, — that of Ben's rage when he is told that presumption is not, before Apollo, to take the place of merit, or even to back it !

The other notice is in a letter from Howell to Sir Thomas Hawk, written the year before Jonson's death : —

" I was invited yesternight to a solemn supper by B. J., where you were deeply remembered. There was good company, excellent cheer, choice wines, and jovial welcome. One thing intervened, which almost spoiled the relish of the rest, — that B. began to engross all the discourse, to vapor extremely by himself, and, by vilifying others, to magnify his own **Muse.** For **my part, I** am content to dispense with the Roman infirmity **of** Ben, now that time has snowed upon his pericranium."

But this snow of time, however it may have begun **to cover up** the **massive** qualities of **his** mind, **seems** to have left untouched his strictly poetic faculty. **That** shone out in his last hours, with more than usual splendor, in the beautiful pastoral drama of The Sad Shepherd; and it may be doubted if in the whole of his works any other passage can be found so exquisite in sentiment, fancy, and expression as the opening lines **of** this charming product of his old age.

> " Here she was wont to go! and here! **and here!**
> Just where those daisies, pinks, and violets grow :
> The world may find the Spring by following her ;
> For other print her airy steps ne'er left :
> Her treading would not bend a blade of grass,
> Or shake the downy blow-ball from his stalk !
> But like the soft west-wind she shot along,
> And where she went the flowers took thickest root,
> As she had sowed them with her odorous foot ! "

Before he could complete The Sad Shepherd he was struck with mortal illness ; and the brave old man prepared **to** meet his last enemy, and, if possible, convert him into a friend. As early as 1606 he had returned to the English Church, after having been for twelve years a Romanist ; and his penitent death-bed was attended by the Bishop of Winchester. He died in August, 1637, in his sixty-fourth year, and was buried in Westminster Abbey. The inscription on the common pavement stone which was laid over his grave,

"O RARE BEN JONSON!"

still expresses, after a lapse of two hundred years, the feelings of all readers of the English race.

It must be admitted, however, that this epithet is sufficiently indefinite to allow widely differing estimates of the value of his works. In a critical view, the most obvious characteristic of his mind is its bulk; but its creativeness bears no proportion to its massiveness. His faculties, ranged according to their relative strength, would fall into this rank:— first, BEN; next, understanding; next, memory; next, humor; next, fancy; and last and least, imagination. Thus, in the strictly poetic action of his mind, his fancy and imagination being subordinated to his other faculties, and not co-ordinated with them, his whole nature is not kindled, and his best masques and sweetest lyrics give no idea of the general largeness of the man. In them the burly giant becomes gracefully *petite;* it is Fletcher's Omphale "smiling the club" out of the hand of Hercules, and making him, for the time, "spin her smocks." Now the greatest poetical creations of Shakespeare are those in which he is **greatest** in reason, and greatest in passion, and greatest **in** knowledge, as well as greatest in imagination, — his poetic power being

> "Like to the fabled Cytherea's zone,
> Binding all things with beauty."

His mind is "one entire and perfect chrysolite," while Jonson's rather suggests the pudding-stone. The poet *in* **Ben** being thus but a comparatively small portion *of* Ben, works by effort, rather than inspiration, and leaves the impression of ingenuity rather than inventiveness. But in his tragedies of Sejanus and Catiline, and especially in his three great comedies of The Fox, The Alchymist, and The Silent Woman, the whole man is thrust forward, with his towering individuality, his massive understanding, his wide knowledge of the baser side of life, his relentless scorn of weakness and wickedness, his vivid memory of facts and ideas derived from books. They seem written with his fist. But, though **they** convey a powerful impression of his collective ability, they do not convey a poetic impression, and hardly an agreeable one. His strongest characters, as might be expected, are not heroes or martyrs, but cheats or dupes. **His most** magnificent cheat is Volpone, in The Fox; his most magnificent dupe is Sir Epicure Mammon, in The Alchymist; but in their **most** gorgeous mental rioting in imaginary objects of **sense, the** effect is produced by a dogged accumulation of successive images, which are linked by no train of strictly imaginative association, and are not fused into unity of purpose by the fire of passion-penetrated imagination.

Indeed, it is a curious psychological study to watch the laborious process by which Jonson drags his thoughts and fancies from the reluctant and resisting soil of his mind, and then lays them, one after the other, with a deep-drawn breath, on his page. Each is forced into form by main strength, as we sometimes see a pillar of granite wearily drawn through the street by a score of straining oxen. Take, for example, Sir Epicure Mammon's detail of the luxuries he will revel in when his possession of the philosopher's stone shall have given him boundless wealth. The first cup of Canary and the first tug of invention bring up this enormous piece of humor : —

> "My flatterers
> Shall be the pure and gravest of divines
> That I can get for money."

Then another wrench of the mind, and, it is to be feared, another swallow of the liquid, and we have this : —

> "My meat shall all come in in Indian shells,
> Dishes of agate, set in gold, and studded
> With emeralds, sapphires, hyacinths, and rubies."

Glue that on, and now for another tug : —

> "**My** shirts
> I 'll **have of** taffeta-sarsnet, soft and light
> As **cobwebs; and** for all my other raiment,
> It **shall be such as** might provoke the Persian,
> **Were** he to teach the world riot anew."

And then, a little heated, his imagination **is stung into** action, and this refinement of sensation flashes out: —

> " My gloves of fishes' and birds' skins perfumed
> *With gums of Paradise and Eastern air.*"

And now we have an extravagance jerked violently out from his logical fancy : —

> " I will have all my beds blown up, not stuffed;
> Down is **too hard.**"

But all this **patient** accumulation of particulars, each **costing a mighty** effort of memory or analogy, produces no cumulative effect. Certainly, the word " strains," **as** employed to designate the effusions of poetry, has a peculiar significance as applied to Jonson's verse. No hewer of wood or drawer of water ever earned his daily wages by a more conscientious putting forth of **daily** labor. Critics — and among the critics Ben is the most clamorous — call upon us to admire and praise the construction of **his plays.** But his plots, admirable of their kind, are **still** but elaborate contrivances **of the** understanding, all distinctly thought out beforehand **by the method** of logic, not the method of imagination ;

regular in external form, but animated by no living internal principle; artful, but not artistic; ingenious schemes, not organic growths; and conveying the same kind of pleasure we experience in inspecting other mechanical contrivances. His method is neither the method of nature nor the method of art, but the method of artifice. A drama of Shakespeare may be compared to an oak; a drama by Jonson to a cunningly fashioned box, made of oak-wood, with some living plants growing in it. Jonson is big; Shakespeare is great.

Still we say, "O rare Ben Jonson!" A large, rude, clumsy, English force, irritable, egotistic, dogmatic, and quarrelsome, but brave, generous, and placable; with no taint of a malignant vice in his boisterous foibles; with a good deal of the bulldog in him, but nothing of the spaniel, and one whose growl was ever worse than his bite; — he, the bricklayer's apprentice, fighting his way to eminence through the roughest obstacles, capable of wrath, but incapable of falsehood, willing to boast, but scorning to creep, still sturdily keeps his hard-won position among the Elizabethan worthies as poet, playwright, scholar, man of letters, man of muscle and brawn; as friend of Beaumont and Fletcher and Chapman and Bacon and Shakespeare; and as ever ready, in all places and at all times, to assert the manhood of Ben by tongue and pen and sword.

MINOR ELIZABETHAN DRAMATISTS.

IN the present chapter we propose to consider six
dramatists who were more immediately the contemporaries of Shakespeare and Jonson, and who have the
precedence in time, — and three of them, if we may believe some critics, not altogether without claim to the
precedence in merit, — of Beaumont and Fletcher, Massinger, and Ford. These are Heywood, Middleton,
Marston, Dekkar, Webster, and Chapman.

They belong to **the** school of dramatists of which
Shakespeare was the head, and which is distinguished
from the school of Jonson by essential differences of
principle. Jonson constructed his plays on definite external rules, and could appeal confidently to the critical
understanding, in case the regularity of his plot and the
keeping of his characters were called in question.
Shakespeare constructed his, not according to any rules
which could be drawn from the practice of other dramatists, but according **to** those interior laws which the
mind, in its creative action, instinctively divines and
spontaneously obeys. In his case, **the appeal is not to**
the understanding alone, but to the feelings and faculties

which were concerned in producing the work itself; and the symmetry of the whole is felt by hundreds who could not frame an argument to sustain it. The laws to which his genius submitted were different from those to which other dramatists had submitted, because the time, the circumstances, the materials, the purpose aimed at, were different. The time demanded a drama which should represent human life in all its diversity, and in which the tragic and comic, the high and the low, should be in juxtaposition, if not in combination. The dramatists of whom we are about to speak represented them in juxtaposition, and rarely succeeded in vitally combining them so as to produce symmetrical works. Their comedy and tragedy, their humor and passion, move in parallel rather than in converging lines. They have diversity; but as their diversity neither springs from, nor tends to, a central principle of organization or of order, the result is often a splendid anarchy of detached scenes, more effective as detached than as related. Shakespeare alone had the comprehensive energy of impassioned imagination to fuse into unity the almost unmanageable materials of his drama, to organize this anarchy into a new and most complex order, and to make a world-wide variety of character and incident consistent with oneness of impression. Jonson, not pretending to give his work this organic form, put forth his whole strength to give it mechanical regularity, every line in his **solidest** plays costing him, as the wits **said,** "a cup of sack." But the force implied in a Shakespearian drama, a force that crushes and dissolves the resisting materials into **their** elements, and recombines or fuses them into a new substance, is a force so different in kind from Jonson's, **that** it would, of course, be idle to attempt an estimate of its superiority in degree. And in regard to those minor dramatists who will be the subjects of the present essay, if they fall below Jonson in general ability, they nearly **all afford** scenes and passages superior **to his** best in depth of passion, vigor of imagination, and audacious self-committal to the primitive instincts of the heart.

The most profuse, but perhaps the least **poetic of** these dramatists, was Thomas Heywood, of whom **little** is known, except that he was one of the most prolific writers the world has ever seen. **In** 1598 he became an actor, or, as Henslowe, who employed him, phrases **it,** "came and hired himself to me as a covenanted servant for two years." The date of his first published **drama** is 1601 ; that of his last published work, a General History of Women, is 1657. As early as 1633 he represents himself as having had an " entire hand, **or at** least a main finger," in two hundred and twenty plays, of which only twenty-three were printed. True it is, he says, " that my plays are not exposed **to the world in** volumes, to bear the title of Works, as others : one reason is, that many of them, by shifting and change of companies, have been negligently lost ; others of them are still retained in the hands of some actors, who think it against their peculiar profit to have them come in print ; and a third, that it was never any great ambition in me to be in this kind voluminously read." It was said of him, by a contemporary, that " he not only acted every day, but also obliged himself to write a sheet every day for several years ; but many of his plays being composed loosely in taverns, occasions them to be so mean." Besides his labors as a playwright, he worked as translator, versifier, and general maker of books. Late in life he conceived the design of writing the lives of all the poets of the world, including his contemporaries. Had this project been carried out, we should have known something about the external life of Shakespeare ; for Heywood must have carried in his brain many of those facts which we of this age are most curious to know.

Heywood's best plays evince large observation, considerable dramatic skill, a sweet and humane spirit, and an easy command of language. His style, indeed, is singularly simple, pure, clear, and straightforward ; but it conveys the impression of a mind so diffused as almost to be characterless, and incapable of flashing its thoughts through the images of imaginative passion. He is more prosaic, closer to ordinary life and character, than his contemporaries. Two of his plays, and the best of them all, A Woman Killed with Kindness, and **The** English Traveller, are thoroughly domestic dramas, the first, and not the worst, of their class. **The** plot of The English Traveller is specially good ; and in reading few works of fiction do we receive a greater shock of surprise than in Geraldine's discovery of the infidelity of Wincott's wife, whom he loves with a Platonic devotion. It is as unanticipated as the discovery, in Jonson's Silent Woman, that Epicœne is no woman at all, while at the same time it has less the appearance of artifice, and is more the result of natural causes.

With less fluency of diction, less skill in fastening **the** reader's interest to his **fable,** harsher in versification, and generally clumsier in construction, the best **plays** of Thomas Middleton are still superior to Heywood's in force of imagination, depth of passion, and fulness of matter. It must, however, be admitted that the sentiments which direct his powers are not so fine as Heywood's. He depresses the mind, rather than invigorates it. The eye he cast on human life was not the eye of a sympathizing poet, but rather that of a sagacious cynic. His observation, though sharp, close, and vigilant, is somewhat ironic and unfeeling. His penetrating, incisive intellect cuts its way to the heart of a character

as with a knife ; and if he lays bare its throbs of guilt
and weakness, and lets you into the secrets of its
organization, he conceives his whole work is performed.
This criticism applies even to his tragedy of Women
Beware Women, a drama which shows a deep study of
the sources of human frailty, considerable skill in exhibiting the passions in their consecutive, if not in their
conflicting action, and a firm hold upon character ; but
it lacks pathos, tenderness, and humanity ; its power is
out of all proportion to its geniality ; the characters,
while they stand definitely out to the eye, are seen
through no visionary medium of sentiment and fancy ;
and the reader feels the force of Leantio's own agoniz-
ing complaint, that his affliction is

> " Of greater weight than youth was made to bear,
>   As if a punishment of after-life
>   Were fall'n upon man here, so new it is
>   To flesh and blood, so strange, so insupportable."

There is, indeed, no atmosphere to Middleton's mind ;
and the hard, bald caustic peculiarity of his genius,
which is unpleasingly felt in reading any one of his
plays, becomes a source of painful weariness as we plod
doggedly through the five thick volumes of his works.
Like the incantations of his own witches, it " casts a
thick scurf over life."   It is most powerfully felt in his
tragedy of The Changeling, at once the most oppress-

ive and impressive effort of his genius. The character of De Flores in this play has in it a strangeness **of** iniquity, such **as** we think is hardly paralleled in the whole range of the Elizabethan drama. The passions of this brute-imp are not human. They **are** such as might be conceived of as springing from the union of animal with fiendish impulses, in a nature which knew ·no law outside of its own lust, **and was** as incapable **of a** scruple as of a sympathy.

But of all the dramatists of the time, the most disagreeable in disposition, though by no means the least powerful in mind, was John Marston. The time of his birth is not known; his name is entangled in contemporary records with that of another John Marston; **and** we may **be** sure that his mischief-loving spirit **would** have been delighted could **he have** anticipated that **the** antiquaries, a century after his death, would be driven to despair by the difficulty of discriminating one from the other. It is more than probable, however, that he was **the** John Marston who was of a respectable family in Shropshire, who took his bachelor's degree at Oxford in 1592, and who was afterwards married to a daughter of a chaplain **of** James the First. Whatever **may** have been Marston's antecedents, they were such **as to** gratify his tastes as a cynical observer of the crimes and follies of men, — an observer whose hatred of **evil**

sprang from no love of good, but to whom the sight of depravity and baseness was welcome, inasmuch as it afforded him the occasion to indulge his own scorn and pride. His ambition was to be the English Juvenal ; and it must be conceded that he had the true Iago-like disposition " to spy out abuses." Accordingly, in 1598, he published a series of venomous satires called The Scourge of Villanie, rough in versification, condensed in thought, tainted in matter, evincing a cankered more than a caustic spirit, and producing an effect at once indecent and inhuman. To prove that this scourging of villany, which would have put Mephistopheles to the blush, was inspired by no respect for virtue, he soon followed it up with a poem so licentious that, before it was circulated to any extent, it was suppressed by order of Archbishop Whitgift, and nearly all the copies destroyed. A writer could not be thus dishonored without being brought prominently into notice, and old Henslowe, the manager, was after him at once to secure his libellous ability for the Rose. Accordingly, we learn from Henslowe's diary, under date of September 28, 1599, that he had lent to William Borne, " to lend unto John Mastone," " the new poete," " the sum of forty shillings," in earnest of some work not named. There is an undated letter of Marston to Henslowe, written probably in reference to this matter, which is characteristic in its disdainfully confident tone. Thus it runs : —

"Mr. Henslowe, at the Rose on the Bankside.

"If you like my playe of Columbus, it is verie well, and you shall give me noe more than twentie poundes for it, but **If** nott, lett me have it by the Bearer againe, as I know the kinges men will freelie give me as much for it, and the profitts of the third daye moreover.

"Soe I rest yours,

"John Marston."

He seems not to have been popular among the band of dramatists he now joined, and it is probable that his insulting manners were not sustained by corresponding **courage**. **Ben Jonson** had many quarrels **with him,** both literary and personal, and mentions one occasion on which he **beat** him and took away his pistol. **His** temper was Italian, rather than English, and one would **conceive of** him as quicker with the stiletto than the fist. His connection with the stage ceased, in 1613, after he had produced a number of dramas, of which nine have **been** preserved. He died about twenty years afterwards, in 1634, seemingly in comfortable circumstances.

Marston's plays, whether comedies or tragedies, all bear the mark of his bitter and misanthropic spirit, — a spirit that seemed cursed by the companionship of its own thoughts, and forced them out through a well-grounded fear that they would fester if left within. His comedies of The Malcontent, The Fawn, and What You Will, have no genuine mirth, though an abundance of scornful wit, — of wit which, in his own words, "stings, blisters, galls off the skin, with the acrimony of its sharp quickness." The baser its objects, the brighter its gleam. It is stimulated by the desire to give pain, rather than the wish to communicate pleasure. Marston is not without sprightliness, but his sprightliness is never the sprightliness of the kid, though it is sometimes that of the hyena, and sometimes that of the polecat. In his Malcontent he probably drew a flattering likeness of his inner self: yet the most compassionate reader of the play would experience little pity in seeing the Malcontent hanged. So much, indeed, of Marston's satire is directed at depravity, that Ben Jonson used to say that " Marston wrote his father-in-law's preachings, and his father-in-law his comedies." It is to be hoped, however, that the spirit of the chaplain's tirades against sins was not, like his son-in-law's, worse than the sins themselves.

If Marston's comic vein is thus, to use one of Dekkar's phrases, that of " a thorny-toothed rascal," it may be supposed that his tragic is a still fiercer libel on humanity. His tragedies, indeed, though not without a gloomy power, are extravagant and horrible in conception and conduct. Even when he copies, he makes the thing his own by caricaturing it. Thus the **plot** of Antonio's Revenge is plainly taken from Hamlet, but it is **Hamlet** passed through Marston's intellect and imagination, **and so** debased **as to look** original. Still, the intellect in Marston's tragedies strikes the reader as forcible in itself, and as capable of achieving excellence, **if** it could only be divorced from the bad disposition and deformed conscience which direct its exercise. He has fancy, and he frequently stutters into imagination ; but **the** imp that controls his heart corrupts his taste and taints his sense of beauty, and the result is that he has **a** malicious satisfaction in deliberately choosing words whose uncouthness finds no extenuation in their **expressiveness, and** in forging elaborate metaphors which **disgust** rather than delight. His description of a storm **at** sea is among the least unfavorable specimens **of this** perversion of **his** poetical powers : —

> " The sea grew mad;
>
> .   .   .   .   .
>
> Strait swarthy darkness *popt out* Phœbus' eye,
> And blurred the jocund face of bright-cheek'd day;
> Whilst cruddled fogs masked even darkness' brow;
> Heaven bade 's good night, and the rocks groaned
> At the intestine uproar of **the main.**"

It must be **allowed** that both his tragedies and comedies are full of strong and striking thoughts, which show a searching inquisition into the worst parts of human nature.   Occasionally he expresses a general **truth** with great felicity, as when he says,

> " Pygmy cares
> Can shelter under patience' shield; but giant griefs
> Will burst all covert."

His imagination is sometimes stimulated into unusual power in expressing the fiercer and darker passions ; as, for example, in this image : —

> " O, my soul 's enthroned
> In the triumphant chariot of revenge ! "

And in this : —

> " Ghastly Amazement, with upstarted hair,
>   Shall hurry on before, and usher us,
>   Whilst trumpets clamor with a sound of death."

He has three descriptions of morning, which seem to have been written in emulation of Shakespeare's in Hamlet; two of them being found in the tragedy which Hamlet suggested.

> " Is not yon gleam the shuddering morn that flakes
>   With silver tincture the east verge of heaven ?
>   .   .   .   .   .
>   For see the dapple-gray coursers of the morn
>   Beat up the light with their bright silver hoofs,
>   And chase it through the sky.
>   .   .   .   .   .
>   Darkness is fled; look, infant morn hath drawn

> Bright silver curtains 'bout the couch of night;
> And now **Aurora's horse** trots azure rings,
> **Breathing fair** light about the firmament."

These last two lines appear feeble enough as **contrasted with the** beautiful intensity **of** imagination **in** Emerson's picturing of the same **scene : —**

> " O, tenderly the haughty Day
> *Fills his blue urn with fire.*"

The most beautiful passage in Marston's plays is the lament **of** a father over the dead body of his son, who has been defamed. It is so apart from his usual style, as to breed the suspicion that the worthy chaplain's daughter, whom he made Mrs. Marston, **must have given it to** him from her purer imagination : —

> "**Look on** those **lips,**
> Those now lawn pillows, on **whose tender softness**
> Chaste modest speech, stealing from **out his breast,**
> Had wont to rest itself, as loath to post
> From out so fair an inn: look, look, they seem
> To stir,
> And breathe defiance to black obloquy."

If among **the** dramatists of **the** period any person could be selected **who** in disposition **was** the opposite **of** Marston, **it** would be Thomas Dekkar, — a man whose inborn sweetness **and** gleefulness of soul carried him **through** vexations and miseries **which** would **have**

crushed a spirit less hopeful, cheerful, and humane. He was probably born about the year 1575 ; commenced his career as player and playwright before 1598 ; and for forty years was an author by profession, that is, was occupied in fighting famine with his pen. The first intelligence we have of him is characteristic of his whole life. It is from Henslowe's diary, under date of February, 1598 : " Lent unto the company, to discharge Mr. Decker out of the counter in the powltry, the sum of 40 shillings." Oldys tells us that " he was in King's Bench Prison from 1613 to 1616 "; and the antiquary adds ominously, " how much longer I know not." Indeed, Dr. Johnson's celebrated enumeration of the scholar's experiences would stand for a biography of Dekkar : —

"Toil, envy, want, the patron, and the jail."

This forced familiarity with poverty and distress does not seem to have imbittered his feelings or weakened the force and elasticity of his mind. He turned his calamities into commodities. If indigence threw him into the society of the ignorant, the wretched, and the depraved, he made the knowledge of low life he thus obtained, serve his purpose as dramatist or pamphleteer. Whatever may have been the effect of his vagabond habits on his principles, they did not stain the sweetness and purity of his sentiments. There is an innocency in

his very coarseness, **and** a brisk, bright good-nature chirps in his **very** scurrility. In the midst of distresses of all **kinds,** he still seems, **like his** own Fortunatus, **"all** felicity up to the brims"; **but that** his content with Fortune is not owing to an unthinking ignorance of her caprice and injustice is proved by the words he puts into **her** mouth : —

> " This world is Fortune's ball wherewith she sports.
> Sometimes I strike it up into the air,
> And then create I emperors and kings;
> Sometimes I spurn it, at which spurn crawls out
> The wild beast multitude: curse on, you fools,
> 'T is I that tumble princes from their thrones,
> And gild false brows with glittering diadems;
> 'T is I that tread on necks of conquerors,
> And when like semi-gods they have been drawn
> In ivory chariots to the Capitol,
> Circled about with wonder of all eyes,
> The shouts of every tongue, love of all hearts,
> Being swoln with their own greatness, I have pricked
> The bladder of their pride, and made them die
> As water-bubbles (without memory):
> I thrust base cowards into honor's chair,
> Whilst the true-spirited soldier stands by
> Bareheaded, and all bare, whilst at his scars
> They scoff, that ne'er durst view the face of wars.
> I set an idiot's cap on virtue's head,
> **Turn** learning out of doors, clothe wit in rags,
> And paint ten thousand images of loam
> In gaudy silken colors: on the backs

> Of mules and asses I make asses ride,
> **Only for** sport to see the apish world
> Worship such beasts with sound idolatry.
> This Fortune does, **and** when all this is done,
> She sits and smiles to hear some curse her name,
> And some with adoration crown her fame."

The boundless beneficence of Dekkar's heart is especially embodied in the character of the opulent lord, **Jacomo** Gentili, in his play of The Wonder of a Kingdom. **When** Gentili's steward brings him the book in **which the** amount of his charities is recorded, **he exclaims** impatiently : —

> " Thou vain vainglorious fool, go burn that book;
> No herald needs to blazon charity's arms.
>
> .   .   .   .   .
>
> I launch not forth a ship, with drums and guns
> And trumpets, to proclaim my gallantry;
> He that will read the wasting of my gold
> Shall find it writ in ashes, which the wind
> Will scatter ere he spells it."
>
> .

He will have neither wife nor children. When, he says,

> " I shall have one hand in heaven,
> To write my happiness in leaves of stars,
> A wife would pluck me by the other down.
> This bark has thus long sailed about the world,
> My soul the pilot, and yet never listened
> **To such a** mermaid's song.
>
> .   .   .   .

> My heirs shall be poor children fed on alms;
> Soldiers that want limbs; scholars poor and scorned;
> And these **will** be a sure inheritance
> **Not** to decay; manors and towns will fall,
> Lordships and parks, pastures and woods, be sold;
> But this land still continues to the lord:
> No tricks of law can me beguile of this.
> But of the beggar's dish, I shall drink healths
> To last forever; whilst I live, my roof
> Shall cover naked wretches; when I die,
> 'T is dedicated to St. Charity."

We should not do justice to Dekkar's disposition, even after these quotations, did we omit that enumeration of positives and negatives which, in his **view,** make up the character of the happy man : —

> " He that in the sun is neither beam nor moat,
> He that 's not mad after a petticoat,
> He for whom poor men's curses dig no grave,
> He that is neither lord's nor lawyer's slave,
> He that makes This his sea and That his shore,
> He that in 's coffin is richer than before,
> He that counts Youth his sword and Age his staff,
> He whose right hand carves his own epitaph,
> He that upon his death-bed is a swan,
> And dead no crow, — he is a Happy Man."

As Dekkar wrote under the constant goad of necessity, he seems to have been indifferent to the require**ments** of art. That " wet-eyed wench, Care," was as absent from his ink, as from his soul. Even his best plays, Old Fortunatus, The Wonder of a Kingdom, and another whose title cannot be mentioned, are good in particular scenes and characters rather than good as wholes. Occasionally, as in the character of Signior Orlando Friscobaldo, he strikes off a fresh, original, and masterly creation, consistently sustained throughout, and charming us by its lovableness, as well as thrilling us by its power; but generally his sentiment and imagination break upon us in unexpected felicities, strangely better than what surrounds them. These have been culled by the affectionate admiration of Lamb, Hunt, and Hazlitt, and made familiar to all English readers. To prove how much finer, in its essence, his genius was than the genius of so eminent a dramatist as Massinger, we only need to compare Massinger's portions of the play of The Virgin Martyr with Dekkar's. The scene between Dorothea and Angelo, in which she recounts her first meeting with him as a "sweet-faced beggar-boy," and the scene in which Angelo brings to Theophilus the basket of fruits and flowers which Dorothea has plucked in Paradise, are inexpressibly beautiful in their exquisite subtlety of imagination and artless elevation of sentiment. It is difficult to understand how a writer capable of such refinements as these should have left no drama which is a part of the classical literature of his country.

One of these scenes — that between Dorothea, **the Virgin Martyr**, and Angelo, an angel who waits upon her in the disguise of a page — we cannot refrain from quoting, **familiar as** it must be to many readers: —

> " ***Dor.*** My book and taper.
>
> " ***Ang.*** Here, most holy mistress.
>
> " ***Dor.*** Thy voice sends forth such music, that **I never**
> **Was** ravished with a more **celestial** sound.
> Were every servant **in the world** like **thee**,
> So full of goodness, angels would **come down**
> To dwell with us: thy name is Angelo,
> And like that name thou art.   Get thee to **rest;**
> Thy youth with too much watching is oppressed.
>
> " *Ang.* **No, my dear lady; I** could weary stars,
> And force **the** wakeful moon to lose her eyes,
> By my late **watching,** but to wait on you.
> When at your prayers you kneel before the altar,
> Methinks I 'm singing with some quire in heaven,
> So blest I hold me in your company.
> Therefore, my most loved mistress, do not bid
> Your boy, so serviceable, to get hence,
> For then you break his heart.
>
> " *Dor.* Be nigh me still then.
> In golden letters down I 'll set that day
> Which gave thee to me.   Little did **I** hope
> To meet **such worlds of** comfort in thyself,
> This little **pretty body, when I,** coming
> Forth of the temple, heard **my beggar-boy,**
> My sweet-faced, godly beggar boy, crave an alms,
> Which with glad hand I gave, — with lucky hand!
> And when I took thee home, my most chaste bosom

Methought was filled with no hot wanton fire,
But with a holy flame, mounting since higher,
On wings of cherubim, than it did before.

"*Ang.*   Proud am I that my lady's modest eye
So likes so poor a servant.

"*Dor.*   I have offered
Handfuls of gold but to behold thy parents.
I would leave kingdoms, were I queen of some,
To dwell with thy good father. . . . . .

                         Show me thy parents;
Be not ashamed.

"*Ang.*   I am not: I did never
Know who my mother was; but by yon palace,
Filled with bright heavenly courtiers, I dare assure you,
And pawn these eyes upon it, and this hand,
My father is in heaven; and, pretty mistress,
If your illustrious hour-glass spend his sand,
No worse than yet it does, upon my life,
You and I both shall meet my father there,
And he shall bid you welcome.

"*Dor.*   O blessed day!
We all long to be there, but lose the way."

But the passage in all Dekkar's works which will be
most likely to immortalize his name is that often-quoted
one, taken from a play whose very name is unmention-
able to prudish ears : —

"Patience, my lord! why, 't is the soul of peace;
   Of all the virtues, 't is nearest kin to heaven;
   It makes men look like gods. — The best of men
   That e'er wore earth about him was a Sufferer,

> A soft, meek, patient, humble, tranquil spirit;
> The first true gentleman that ever breathed."

A more sombre genius than Dekkar, though a genius more than once associated with his own in composition, was John Webster, of whose biography nothing is certainly known, except that he was a member of the Merchant Tailors' Company. His works have been thrice republished within thirty years ; but the perusal of the whole does not add to the impression left on the mind by his two great tragedies. His comic talent was small; and for all the mirth in his comedies of Westward Hoe and Northward Hoe we are probably indebted to his associate, Dekkar. His play of Appius and Virginia is far from being an adequate rendering of one of the most beautiful and affecting fables that ever crept into history. The Devil's Law Case, a tragicomedy, has not sufficient power to atone for the want of probability in the plot and want of nature in the characters. The historical play of Sir Thomas Wyatt can only be fitly described by using the favorite word in which Ben Jonson was wont to condense his critical opinions, — " It is naught." But The White Devil and The Duchess of Malfy are tragedies which even so rich and varied a literature as the English could not lose without a sensible diminution of its treasures.

Webster was one of those writers whose genius consists in the expression of special moods, and who, outside of those moods, cannot force their creative faculties into vigorous action. His mind by instinctive sentiment was directed to the contemplation of the darker aspects of life. He brooded over crime and misery until his imagination was enveloped in their atmosphere, found a fearful joy in probing their sources and tracing their consequences, became strangely familiar with their physiognomy and psychology, and felt a shuddering sympathy with their " deep groans and terrible ghastly looks." There was hardly a remote corner of the soul, which hid a feeling capable of giving mental pain, into which this artist in agony had not curiously peered ; and his meditations on the mysterious disorder produced in the human consciousness by the rebound of thoughtless or criminal deeds might have found fit expression in the lines of a great poet of our own times : —

> " Action is momentary, —
> The motion of a muscle, this way or that.
> Suffering is long, obscure, and infinite."

With this proclivity of his imagination, Webster's power as a dramatist consists in confining the domain of his tragedy within definite limits, in excluding all variety of incident and character which could interfere with his main design of awaking terror and pity, and in the intensity with which he arrests, and the tenacity with which he holds the attention, as he drags the mind along the pathway which begins in misfortune or guilt, and ends in death. He is such a spendthrift of his stimulants, and accumulates horror on horror, **and crime on crime,** with such fatal facility, that he would render the mind callous to his terrors, were it not that what is acted is still less than what is suggested, and that the souls of his characters are greater than their sufferings or more terrible than their deeds. The crimes and the criminals belong to Italy as it was in the sixteenth century, when poisoning and assassination were almost in the fashion; the feelings with which they are regarded are English; and the result of the combination is to make the poisoners and assassins more fiendishly malignant in spirit than they actually were. Thus Ferdinand, in the Duchess of Malfy, is the conception formed by an honest, deep-thoughted Englishman of an Italian duke and politician, who had been educated in those maxims of policy which were generalized by Machiavelli. Webster makes him a devil, but a devil with a soul to be damned. The Duchess, his sister, is discovered to be secretly married to her steward; and in connection with his brother, the Cardinal, the Duke not only resolves on her death, but devises a series of **pre**liminary mental torments to madden and break down her proud spirit. The first is an exhibition of wax figures, representing her husband and children as they appeared in death. Then comes a dance of madmen, with dismal howls and songs and speeches. Then a tomb-maker whose talk is of the charnel-house, and who taunts her with her mortality. She interrupts his insulting homily with the exclamation, " **Am I not thy Duchess ?** " " Thou art," he scornfully replies, " some great woman sure, for riot begins to sit on thy forehead (clad in gray hairs) twenty years sooner than on a merry milkmaid's. **Thou sleepest worse than** if a mouse should be forced **to take up her** lodging in a cat's ear ; a little infant that breeds its teeth, should it lie with thee, would cry out, as if thou wert the more unquiet bedfellow." This mockery only brings from her firm spirit the proud assertion, " I am Duchess of Malfy still." Indeed, her mind becomes clearer and calmer as the tortures proceed. At first she had imprecated curses on her brothers, and cried,

> " Plagues that make lanes through largest families,
>   Consume them ! "

But now, when the executioners appear, when her dirge is sung, containing those tremendous lines,

> " Of what is 't fools make such vain keeping ?
>   Sin their conception, their birth weeping,
>   Their life a general mist of error,
>   Their death a hideous storm of terror," —

when all that malice could suggest for her torment has
been expended and the ruffians who have been sent to
murder her approach to do their office, her attitude is
that of quiet dignity, forgetful of her own sufferings,
solicitous for others.   Her attendant, Cariola, screams
out,

" Hence, villains, tyrants, murderers, alas!
 What will you do with my lady?   Call for help.
  " *Duchess.*   To whom, — to our next neighbors?
 They are mad folks.
  " *Bosola.*   Remove that noise.
  " *Duchess.*   Farewell, Cariola.
 In my last will I have not much to give:
 A many hungry guests have fed upon me;
 Thine will be a poor reversion.
  " **Cariola.**   I will die with **her.**
  " *Duchess.*   I pray thee, look thou giv'st my little boy
 Some syrup for his cold, and let the girl
 Say her prayers ere she sleep.   Now what you please:
 What death?
  " *Bosola.*   Strangling ; here are your executioners.

  " *Duchess.*   Pull, and pull strongly, for your able strength
 Must pull down heaven upon me:
 Yet stay, heaven-gates are not so highly arched
 As princes' palaces; they that enter there
 Must go upon their knees.   Come, violent death,
 Serve for mandragora to make me **sleep.**
 Go, tell my brothers; when I am laid out,
 They then may feed in quiet."

The strange, unearthly stupor which precedes the remorse of Ferdinand for her murder is true to nature, and especially his nature. Bosola, pointing to the dead body of the Duchess, says,

> " Fix your eye here.
>> " *Ferd.*   Constantly.
>> " *Bosola.*   Do you not weep?
> Other sins only speak; murther shrieks out:
> The element of water moistens the earth,
> But blood flies upwards and bedews the heavens.
>> " *Ferd.*   Cover her face; mine eyes dazzle:
> She died young.
>> " *Bosola.*   I think not so; her infelicity
> Seemed to have years too many.
>> " *Ferd.*   She and I were twins:
> And should I die this instant, I had lived
> Her time to a minute."

We have said that Webster's peculiarity is the tenacity of his hold on the mental and moral constitution of his characters. We know of their appetites and passions only by the effects of these on their souls. He has properly no sensuousness. Thus in The White Devil, his other great tragedy, the events proceed from the passion of Brachiano for Vittoria Corombona, — a passion so intense as to lead one to order the murder of his wife, and the other the murder of her husband. If either Fletcher or Ford had attempted the subject, the sensual and emotional motives to the crime would have

been represented with overpowering force, and expressed
in the most alluring images, so that wickedness would
have been almost resolved into weakness ; but Webster
lifts the wickedness at once from the region of the
senses into the region of the soul, exhibits its results in
spiritual depravity, and shows the satanic energy of purpose which may spring from the ruins of the moral will.
There is nothing lovable in Vittoria ; she seems, indeed,
almost without sensations ; and the affection between
her and Brachiano is simply the magnetic attraction
which one evil spirit has for another evil spirit.   Fran-
cisco, the brother of Brachiano's wife, says to him : —

> "**Thou hast** a wife, our sister; would I had given
>   Both her white hands to death, bound and locked fast
>   **In her last** winding-sheet, when I gave thee
>   But one."

This **is** the language of the intensest passion, but as
applied to the adulterous lover of Vittoria it seems little
more than the utterance of reasonable regret ; for devil
only can truly mate with devil, and Vittoria is Brachiano's real " affinity."

The moral confusion they produce by their deeds is
traced with more than Webster's usual steadiness of
nerve and clearness of vision.   The evil they inflict is
a cause of evil in others ; the passion which **leads to**
murder rouses the fiercer passion which aches for **ven-**

geance; and at last, when the avengers of crime have become morally as bad as the criminals, they are all involved in a common destruction. Vittoria is probably Webster's most powerful delineation. Bold, bad, proud, glittering in her baleful beauty, strong in that evil courage which shrinks from crime as little as from danger, she meets her murderers with the same self-reliant scorn with which she met her judges. "Kill her attendant first," exclaims one of them.

> "*Vittoria.*   You shall not kill her first; behold my breast:
> I will be waited on in death; my servant
> Shall never go before me.
>
>   "*Gasparo.*   Are you so brave?
>   "*Vittoria.*   Yes, I shall welcome death,
> As princes do some great ambassadors;
> I'll meet thy weapon half-way.
>   "*Lodovico.*   Strike, strike,
> With a joint motion.
>   "*Vittoria.*   'T was a manly blow;
> The next thou giv'st, murder some sucking infant,
> And then thou wilt be famous."

Webster tells us, in the Preface to The White Devil, that he does not "write with a goose-quill winged with two feathers"; and also hints that the play failed in representation through its being acted in winter in "an open and black theatre," and because it wanted "a full and understanding auditory." "Since that time," he sagely adds, "I have noted most of the

people that come to the playhouse resemble those ignorant asses **who,** visiting stationers' shops, their use is
not to inquire for good books, but new books." And
then comes the ever-recurring wail of the playwright,
Elizabethan as well as Georgian, respecting the taste
of audiences. "Should a man," he says, "present to
such an auditory the most sententious tragedy that ever
was written, observing all the critical laws, as height of
style and gravity of person, enrich it with the sententious chorus, and, as it were, enliven death in the passionate and weighty *Nuntius;* yet after all this divine
rapture, *O dura messorum ilia,* the breath that comes
from the uncapable multitude is able to poison it."

Of all the contemporaries of Shakespeare, Webster is
the most Shakespearian. His genius **was not only**
influenced by its contact with one side of Shakespeare's
many-sided mind, but the tragedies we have been considering abound in expressions and situations either
suggested by or directly copied from the tragedies of
him he took for his model. Yet he seems to have had
no conception of the superiority of Shakespeare to all
other dramatists; and in his Preface to The White
Devil, after speaking of the "full and heightened style
of Master Chapman, the labored and understanding
works of Master Jonson, the no less worthy composures
of the both worthily excellent Master Beaumont and

Master Fletcher," he adds his approval, " without wrong last to be named," of "the right happy and copious industry of Master Shakespeare, Master Dekkar, and Master Heywood." This is not half so felicitous a classification as would be made by a critic of our century, who should speak of the "right happy and copious industry" of Master Goethe, Master Dickens, and Master G. P. R. James.

Webster's reference, however, to "the full and heightened style of Master Chapman" is more appropriate ; for no writer of that age impresses us more by a certain rude heroic height of character than George Chapman. Born in 1559, and educated at the University of Oxford, he seems, on his first entrance into London life, to have acquired the patronage of the noble, and the friendship of all who valued genius and scholarship. He was among the few men whom Ben Jonson said he loved. His greatest performance, and it was a gigantic one, was his translation of Homer, which, in spite of obvious faults, excels all other translations in the power to rouse and lift and inflame the mind. Some eminent painter, we believe Barry, said that, when he went into the street after reading it, men seemed ten feet high. Pope averred that the translation of the Iliad might be supposed to have been written by Homer before he arrived at years of discretion ; and

Coleridge declares the version of the Odyssey to be as truly an original poem as the Faery Queen. Chapman himself evidently thought that he was the first translator who had been admitted into intimate relations with Homer's soul, and who had caught by direct contact the sacred fury of his inspiration. He says finely of those who had attempted the work in other languages : —

> " They failed to search his deep and treasurous heart.
>   The cause was, since they wanted the fit key
>   Of Nature, in their downright strength of art,
>   With Poesy to open Poesy."

Chapman was also a voluminous dramatist, and of his many comedies and tragedies some sixteen were printed. It is to be feared that the last twenty years of his long and honorable life were passed in a desperate struggle for the means of subsistence. But his ideas **of the** dignity of his art were so inwoven into his character that he probably met calamity bravely. Poesy he early professed to prefer above all worldly wisdom, being composed, in his own words, of the " sinews and souls of all learning, wisdom, and truth." " We have example sacred enough," he said, " that true Poesy's humility, poverty, and contempt are badges of divinity, not vanity. Bray then, and bark against it, ye wolf-faced worldlings, that nothing but riches, honors, and magistracy " can content. " I (for my part) shall ever esteem it much more manly and sacred, in this harmless and pious study, to sit until I sink into my grave, than shine in your vainglorious bubbles and impieties; all your poor policies, wisdoms, and their trappings, at no more valuing than a musty nut." These sentiments were probably fresh in his heart when, in 1634, friendless and poor, at the age of seventy-five, he died. Anthony Wood describes him as "a person of most reverend aspect, religious and temperate ; qualities," he spitefully adds, " rarely meeting in a poet."

Chapman was a man with great elements in his nature, which were so imperfectly harmonized that what he was found but a stuttering expression in what he wrote and did. There were gaps in his mind ; or, to use Victor Hugo's image, " his intellect was a book with some leaves torn out." His force, great as it was, was that of an Ajax, rather than that of an Achilles. Few dramatists of the time afford nobler passages of description and reflection. Few are wiser, deeper, manlier in their strain of thinking. But when we turn to the dramas from which these grand things have been detached, we find extravagance, confusion, huge thoughts lying in helpless heaps, sublimity in parts conducing to no general effect of sublimity, the movement lagging and unwieldy, and the plot urged on to the catastrophe by incoherent expedients. His imagination partook of **the** incompleteness of his intellect. Strong enough to clothe the ideas and emotions **of a common** poet, it was plainly inadequate to embody **the vast,** half-formed conceptions which gasped for expression in his soul in its moments **of** poetic exaltation. Often we feel his meaning, rather than apprehend it. The imagery has the indefiniteness of distant objects **seen** by moonlight. There are whole passages in his works in which he seems engaged in expressing **Chapman to** Chapman, like the deaf egotist who only placed his trumpet to his ear when he himself talked.

This criticism applies more particularly **to his** tragedies, and to his expression **of** great sentiments and passions. **His** comedies, though over-informed **with** thought, reveal him to us as a singularly sharp, **shrewd,** and somewhat cynical observer, sparkling with **worldly** wisdom, and not deficient in airiness any more than wit. Hazlitt, we believe, was the first to notice that Monsieur D'Olive, in the comedy of that name, is " the undoubted prototype of that light, flippant, gay, and infinitely delightful class of character, of the professed men **of wit and pleasure about** town, which we have in such perfection in Wycherley and Congreve, such as Sparkish, Witwould, Petulant, &c., both in the sentiments and the style of writing " ; and Tharsalio in **The** Widow's Tears, and Ludovico in May-Day, have **the hard** impudence and cynical distrust of virtue, the arrogant and glorying self-*un*righteousness, that distinguish another class of characters which the dramatists of the age of Charles and Anne were unwearied in providing with insolence and repartees. Occasionally we have a jest which Falstaff would not disown. Thus in May-Day, when Cuthbert, a barber, approaches Quintiliano, to get, if possible, "certain odd crowns" the latter owes him, Quintiliano says, "I think thou 'rt newly married?" "I am indeed, sir," is the reply. "I thought so ; keep on thy hat, man, 't will be the less perceived." Chapman, in his comedies generally, shows a kind of philosophical contempt for woman, as a frailer and flimsier, if fairer, creature than man, and he sustains his bad judgment with infinite ingenuity of wilful wit and penetration of ungracious analysis. In The Widow's Tears this unpoetic infidelity to the sex pervades the whole plot and sentiments, as well as gives edge to many an incisive sarcasm. "My sense," says Tharsalio, "tells me how short-lived widows' tears are, that their weeping is in truth but laughing under a mask, that they mourn in their gowns and laugh in their sleeves ; all of which I believe as a Delphian oracle, and am resolved to burn in that faith." "He," says Lodovico, in May-Day, — he "that holds religious and sacred thought of a woman, he that holds so reverent a respect to her that he will not touch her but with a kist hand and a timorous heart, he that adores her like his **god-dess**, let him be sure she will shun him like **her** slave. . . . . Whereas nature made " women " but half fools, we make 'em all fool : and this is our palpable flattery of them, where they had rather have plain dealing." **In** all Chapman's comic writing there is something **of Ben** Jonson's mental self-assertion and disdainful **glee** in his own superiority to the weakness he satirizes.

In passing from a comedy like May-Day to a tragedy like Bussy D'Ambois, we find some difficulty in recognizing the features of the same nature. Bussy D'Ambois represents **a** mind not so much in creation **as in** eruption, belching forth smoke, ashes, and stones, no less than **flame.** Pope speaks of it as full of fustian ; but **fustian** is rant in the words when there is no corresponding rant in the soul, whilst Chapman's tragedy, like Marlowe's Tamburlaine, indicates **a** greater swell **in the** thoughts and passions of his characters than in their expression. The poetry is to Shakespeare's what gold **ore** is to gold. Veins and lumps of the precious metal gleam **on** the eye from the duller substance in which it is imbedded. Here are specimens : —

> " *Man is a torch borne in the* **wind** *; a dream*
> *But of a shadow,* summed with all his substance;
> And as great seamen, using all their wealth

7 *

And skills in Neptune's deep invisible paths,
In tall ships richly built and ribbed with brass,
To put a girdle round about the world,
When they have done it (coming near their haven)
Are fain to give a warning piece, and call
A poor strayed fisherman, that never past
His country's sight, to waft and guide them in:
So when we wander furthest through the waves
Of glassy glory and the gulfs of state,
Topped with all titles, spreading all our reaches,
As if each private arm would sphere the earth,
We must to Virtue for her guide resort,
Or we shall shipwreck in our safest port."

"In a king
All places are contained.   His words and looks
Are like the flashes and the bolts of Jove;
His deeds inimitable, *like the sea*
That shuts still as it opes, and leaves no tracks,
Nor prints of precedent for mean men's acts."

"His great heart will not down: 't is like the sea,
That partly by his own internal heat,
Partly the stars' daily and nightly motion,
Their heat and light, and partly of the place
The divers frames, but chiefly by the moon
Bristled with surges, never will be won,
(No, not when th' hearts of all those powers are burst,)
To make retreat into his settled home,
Till he be crowned with his own quiet foam."

"Now, all ye peaceful regents of the night,
Silently gliding exhalations,

Languishing winds, and murmuring falls of waters,
Sadness of heart, and ominous secureness,
Enchantments, dead sleeps, all the friends of rest
That ever wrought upon the life of **man**
Extend your utmost strengths; and this charmed hour
Fix like the centre."

"There is One
That wakes above, whose eye no sleep can bind:
He sees through doors and darkness and our thoughts."

" O, the dangerous siege
Sin lays about us! and the tyranny
He exercises when he hath expugned:
Like to the horror of a winter's thunder,
Mixed with a gushing storm, that suffer nothing
To stir abroad on earth but their own rages,
Is sin, when it hath gathered head above us."

"Terror **of** darkness! O **thou king** of flames!
That with thy music-footed horse doth strike
The clear light out of crystal, on dark earth,
And hurl'st instinctive fire about the world,
Wake, wake, the drowsy and enchanted night,
That sleeps with dead eyes in this heavy riddle:
O thou great prince of shades, where never sun
Sticks his far-darted beams, whose eyes are made
To shine in darkness, and see ever best
Where men are blindest! open now the heart
Of thy abashed oracle, that for fear
Of some ill it includes would feign lie hid,
And rise thou with it in thy greater light."

It is hardly possible to read **Chapman's** serious verse without feeling that he had in him the elements of a great nature, and that he was a magnificent specimen of what is called " irregular genius." And one of his poems, the dedication of his translation of the Iliad to Prince Henry, is of so noble a strain, and from so high a mood, that, while borne along with its rapture, we are tempted to place him in the first rank of poets and of men. You can feel and hear the throbs of the grand old poet's heart in such lines as these : —

<blockquote>

" O, 't is wondrous much,
Though nothing prized, that the right virtuous touch
Of a well-written soul to virtue moves;
Nor have we souls to purpose, if their loves
Of fitting objects be not so inflamed.
How much were then this kingdom's main soul maimed,
To want this great inflamer of all powers
That move in human souls.

    .   .   .   .

Through all the pomp of kingdoms still he shines,
And graceth all his gracers.

    .   .   .   .

A prince's statue, or in marble carved,
Or steel, or gold, and shrined, to be preserved,
Aloft on pillars and pyramides,
Time into lowest ruins may depress;
But drawn with all his virtues in learned verse,
Fame shall resound them on oblivion's hearse,
Till graves gasp with their blasts, and dead men rise."

</blockquote>

WE have seen, in what has been already said of the intellectual habits of the Elizabethan dramatists, that it was a common practice for two, three, four, and sometimes five writers to co-operate in the production of one play. Thus Dekkar and Webster were partners in writing Northward Hoe! and Westward Hoe! Ben Jonson, Marston, and Chapman in writing Eastward Hoe! Drayton, Middleton, Dekkar, Webster, and Munday, in writing The Two Harpies. In the case of Webster and Dekkar, this union was evidently formed from a mutual belief that the sombre mind of the one was unsuited to the treatment of certain scenes and characters which were exactly in harmony with the sunny genius of the other; but the alliance was often brought about by the demand of theatre-managers for a new play at a short notice, in which case the dramatist who had the job hurriedly sketched the plan, and then applied to his brother playwrights to take shares in the enterprise, payable in daily or weekly instalments of mirth or passion. But there were two writers of the period, twins in genius, and bound together by more than brotherly affection, whose literary union was so much closer than the occasional combinations of other dramatists, that it is now difficult to dissociate, in the public mind, Francis Beaumont from John Fletcher, or even to change the order of their names, though it can easily be proved that the firm of Beaumont and Fletcher owes by far the greater portion of its capital to the teeming brain of the second partner.

The materials for their biographies are scanty. Beaumont was the son of a judge, was born about the year 1586, resided a short period at Oxford, but left without taking a degree, and, at the age of fifteen, was entered a member of the Inner Temple. Fletcher, the son of the " courtly and comely " Bishop Fletcher, was born in December, 1579, and was educated at Cambridge, but seems to have been designed for no profession. At what time and under what circumstances the poets met we have no record. The probability is, that, as both were esteemed by Ben Jonson, it was he who brought them together. It is more than probable that Fletcher, the elder of the two, had written for the theatres before his acquaintance with Beaumont began ; and that in The Woman-Hater and in Thierry and Theodoret he had proved his ability both as a comic and as a tragic dramatist before Beaumont had thought of dramatic composition. When they did meet, they found, in Aubrey's words, a "wonderful consimility of phansy" between them, which resulted in an exceeding "dearnesse of friendship"; and the old antiquary adds : "They lived together on the Banke side, not far from the playhouse, both bachelors, lay together," and "had the same cloths and cloak" between them. Their first joint composition was the tragi-comedy of Philaster, produced about the year 1608 ; and we may suppose that this community of goods as well as thoughts continued until 1613, when Beaumont was married, and that the friendship remained unbroken till it was broken in 1616 by Beaumont's death. Fletcher lived until August, 1625, at which time he was suddenly cut off by the plague, in his forty-sixth year.

In regard to the question as to Beaumont's share in the authorship of the fifty-two plays which go under the name of Beaumont and Fletcher, let us first quote the indignant doggerel which Sir Aston Cokaine addressed to the publisher of the first edition, in 1647 :—

> "Beaumont of those many writ in few:
> And Massinger in other few: the main
> Being sole issues of sweet Fletcher's brain.
> But how came I, you ask, so much to know?
> Fletcher's chief bosom-friend informed me so."

This gives no information touching the special plays which Beaumont assisted in producing. None of them were published as joint productions during his life, and only three during the nine or ten years that Fletcher survived him. Of the fifty-two dramas in the collection, fifty were written in the eighteen years which elapsed between 1607 and 1625. During the first years of their partnership neither seemed to be dependent on the stage for support; and it is almost certain that Beaumont's income continued to be adequate to his wants, and that his pen was never spurred into action by poverty. The result was that the earlier dramas were composed more slowly and carefully than the later. A year elapsed between the production of their first joint play, Philaster, in 1608, and the Maid's Tragedy, in 1609. In 1610 Fletcher alone brought out The Faithful Shepherdess. In 1611, A King and No King and the Knight of the Burning Pestle were acted. These five dramas — one exclusively by Fletcher, the others joint productions — are commonly ranked as their best works, and are considered to include all the capacities of their genius. If we suppose that after 1611 they wrote two plays a year, we have fifteen as the number produced up to the period of Beaumont's death, leaving thirty-five which were written by Fletcher alone in nine years. We do not think that

Beaumont's hand can be traced in more than fifteen **of** the plays, or that it is predominant in more than six.

With individual differences as to mind and temperament, these dramatists had some general characteristics in **common.** They agreed in **being** tainted with the fashionable slavishness and fashionable immorality of the court of James. They believed in the divine **right of** kings as piously as any bishop, and they violated **all** the decencies of life as recklessly as any courtier. The impurity of Beaumont, however, seems the result of elaborate thinking, that of Fletcher the running over of heedless animal spirits. They agreed also in certain leading dramatic conceptions and types of character; and they agreed, in regard to the morality **of their** plays, in subordinating their consciences to their audiences. But the mind of Beaumont was as slow, solid, and painstaking as his associate's was rapid, mercurial, and inventive. The tradition runs that his **chief** business was to correct the overflowings of Fletcher's fancy, **and** hold its volatile creativeness in check. Everybody of that age commended his judgment, and even Ben Jonson is said to have consulted him in regard to his plots. The plays in which he had a main hand exhibit a firmer hold upon character, a more orderly disposition of the incidents, and greater symmetry in the construction, than the others. His verse is also simpler, sweeter, more voluble, than Fletcher's, with few of the latter's double and triple endings and harsh pauses. Take, for example, the passage in which Philaster recounts his meeting with Bellario : —

> " Hunting the buck,
> I found him sitting by a fountain's side,
> Of which he borrowed some to quench his thirst,
> And paid the nymph again as much in tears.
> A garland lay him by, made by himself
> Of many several flowers bred in the vale,
> Stuck in that mystic order that the rareness
> Delighted me; but ever when he turned
> His tender eyes upon 'em he would weep,
> As if he meant to make 'em grow again."

Now contrast this with a characteristic passage from Fletcher : —

> " All shall be right again; and, as a pine,
> Rent from Oëta by a sweeping tempest,
> Jointed again, and made a mast, defies
> Those raging winds that split him; so will I
> Pieced to my never-failing strength and fortune,
> Steer through these swelling dangers, plough their prides up,
> And bear like thunder through their loudest tempests."

Beaumont also, though his general temperament was not so poetical as his partner's, had a vein of poetry in him, which was superior in quality and depth to Fletcher's, though sooner exhausted. Beaumont, we think it was, who conceived that beautiful type of womanhood of which Bellario in Philaster, Panthea in A King and No King, and Viola in The Coxcomb, are perhaps the most exquisite embodiments, and which also appears, somewhat dissolved in sentimentality, in Aspasia in The Maid's Tragedy. It is true that Shakespeare had already represented this type of character with even more force and purity in his Viola; but still Beaumont's mind appears to have penetrated to its ideal sources, and not to have copied from his greater contemporary. Beaumont could only repeat it under other names, after its first embodiment in Bellario; but it was too delicate and elusive for Fletcher even to repeat, and it never appears in the dramas he wrote after Beaumont's death. Fletcher has given us many examples of womanly virtue, devotion, and heroism; but he had a bad trick of disconnecting virtue from modesty, and the talk of his best and noblest women is often such as would scare womankind from any theatre of the present day. Beaumont alone could combine feminine innocence with feminine power, the most ethereal softness and sweetness with martyr-like heroism, knowledge of good with ignorance of evil, and invest the whole representation with a visionary charm, so that it affects us as Panthea did Arbaces:—

> " She is not fair
> Nor beautiful; these words express her not;
> They say her looks have something excellent,
> That wants a name."

Fletcher could not, we think, have written Bellario's account of her love for Philaster, as it runs in Beaumont's limpid verse : —

> " My father oft would speak
> Your worth and virtue; and as I did grow
> More and more apprehensive, I did thirst
> To see the man so praised.   But yet all this
> Was but a maiden-longing, to be lost
> As soon as found; till, sitting in my window,
> Printing my thoughts in lawn, I saw a god,
> I thought, (but it was you,) enter our gates;
> My blood flew out and back again, as fast
> As I had puffed it forth and sucked it in
> Like breath; then was I called away in haste
> To entertain you.   Never was a man,
> Heaved from a sheep-cote to a sceptre, raised
> So high in thoughts as I.   You left a kiss
> Upon these lips then, which I mean to keep
> From you forever; I did hear you talk,
> Far above singing.   After you were gone,
> I grew acquainted with my heart, and searched
> What stirred it so: alas, I found it love!"

With this superior fineness of perception, Beaumont also excelled his associate in solid humor.   The chief proof of this is to be found in his delineations, in

The Knight of the Burning Pestle, of the London citizen and his **wife.** These have a geniality, richness, and raciness, a closeness to nature and to fact, unexcelled by any contemporary pictures of Elizabethan **manners** and character, not excepting even Ben Jonson's. A more extravagant, but hardly less delicious, example of Beaumont's humor is his character of Bessus, **in A** King and No King; — a braggart whose cowardice is sustained **by** assurance so indomitable as to wear the aspect of courage; one who is too base to feel insult, who cannot be kicked out of his chirping self-esteem, but **presents as** cheerful a countenance to infamy as to honor.

After, however, awarding to **Beaumont all that he can** properly claim, he must still be placed below Fletcher, not merely in fertility, but in force and variety of genius. **Of** Fletcher, indeed, it is difficult to convey an **adequate** idea, without running into some of his own extravagance, and without quoting passages which would shock all modern notions of decency. He most assuredly was **not a** great man nor a great poet. He lacked seriousness, depth, purpose, principle, imaginative closeness of conception, imaginative condensation of expression. He saw everything at one remove from its soul and essence, and must be ranked with poets of the second class. But no other poet ever had such furious animal spirits, a keener sense of enjoyment, **a more perfect abandon-**

ment to whatever was uppermost in his mind at the moment. There was no conscience in his rakish and dissolute nature. Nothing in him — wit, humor, fancy, appetite, sentiment, passion, knowledge of life, knowledge of books, all his good and all his bad thoughts — met any impediment of taste or principle when rushing into expression. His eyes flash, his cheeks glow, as he writes; his air is hurried and eager; the blood that tingles and throbs in his veins flushes his words; and will and judgment, taken captive, follow with reluctant steps and half-averted faces the perilous lead of the passions they should direct. As there was no reserve in him, there was no reserved power. Rich as were the elements of his nature, they were never thoroughly organized in intellectual character; and as no presiding personality regulated the activity of his mind, he seems hardly to be morally responsible for the excesses into which he was impelled. Composition, indeed, sets his brain in a whirl. He sometimes writes as if inspired by a satyr; he sometimes writes as if inspired by a seraph; but neither satyr nor seraph had any hold on his individuality, and neither could put fetters on his caprice. There is the same gusto in his indecencies as in his refinements. Though an Englishman, he has no morality, except that morality which is connected with generous instincts, or which is awakened by the sense of beauty.

Though the son of a bishop, he had no religion, except that religion which consists in an alternate worship of Venus, Bacchus, and Mars. An incurable mental and moral levity is the characteristic of his writings, — a levity which has its source in an intoxication of the soul through an excess of feeling and sensation, and which is moral or immoral, sentimental or sensual, according to the impulse or temptation of the moment.

This giddiness of soul, in which decorum is ignored rather than denied, is most brilliantly and buoyantly exhibited in his comedies. In The Chances, The Spanish Curate, The Custom of the Country, Rule a Wife and have a Wife, The Wild-Goose Chase, and especially in Monsieur Thomas and The Little French Lawyer, we see the comic muse emancipated from all restraint, — loose, free-spoken, sportive, sparkling, indeed almost madly merry. It is not so much any quotable specimens of wit and humor as it is the all-animating spirit of frolic and mischief, which gives to these comedies their droll, equivocal power to please. In Fletcher's serious plays the same levity is displayed in pushing sentiment and passion altogether beyond the bounds of character; and the volatile fancy which, in his comedy, riots in fun, in his tragedy riots in blood. What lifts both into a poetic region is the tone of romantic heroism by which they are almost equally characterized. His coxcombs and profligates, as well as his conquerors and heroes, are all intrepid. They do not rate their lives at a pin's fee, — the first in comparison with the gratification of a passing desire or caprice; the second, in comparison with glory and honor. The peculiar life, indeed, of Fletcher's characters consists in their being careless of life. Wholly absorbed in the feeling or object of the instant, their action is ecstatic action, and flashes on us in a succession of poetic surprises. This is the great charm of Fletcher's plays; this gilds their grossness, and has kept them alive. You find it in his Monsieur Thomas as well as in his delineation of Cæsar. All the comic characters profess a sportive contempt for consequences, and startle us with unexpected audacities. Fear of disease, danger, or death never dissuades them from the rollicking action or expression of eccentricity and vice. Their concern is only for the free, wild, reckless whim of the moment. Thus, in the play of The Sea Voyage, Julietta, enraged at the jeers of Tibalt and the master of the ship, exclaims: —

"Why, slaves, 't is in our power to hang ye!"

"Very likely," retorts the jovial Master, —

"'T is in our powers then to be hanged, and scorn ye!"

This heroism of the blood, when it passes from an

instinct into some semblance of a principle, adopts the chivalrous guise of honor. Honor, in Fletcher's ethical code, is the only possible and admissible restraint on appetite and passion. Thus in the drama of The Captain, Julio, infatuated with the wicked Lelia, thinks of marrying her, and confesses to his friend Angelo that her bewitching and bewildering beauty has entirely mastered him. When she speaks, he says : —

> " Then music
> (Such as old Orpheus made, that gave a soul
> To aged mountains, and made rugged beasts
> Lay by their rages; and tall trees, that knew
> No sound but tempests, to bow down their branches,
> And hear, and wonder; and the sea, whose surges
> Shook their white heads in heaven, to be as midnight
> Still and attentive) steals into our souls
> So suddenly and strangely, that we are
> From that time no more ours, but what she pleases! "

Angelo admits the temptation, says he would be willing himself to sacrifice all his possessions, even his soul, to obtain her, but then adds : —

> " Yet methinks we should not dole away
>   That that is something more than ours, our honors;
>   I would not have thee marry her by no means."

Again : Curio, in Love's Cure, when threatened by his mistress with the loss of her affection if he fights with her brother, replies that he would willingly give his life, "rip every vein," to please her, yet still insists on his purpose.

> "Life is but a word, a shadow, a melting dream,
> Compared with essential and eternal honor."

In the plays of The Mad Lover, The Loyal Subject, Bonduca, and The False One, Fletcher attempts to portray this heroic element, not as a mere flash of courageous inspiration, but as a solid element of character. He strains his mind to the utmost, but the strain is too apparent. There is no calm, strong grasp of the theme. His heroes are generally too fond of vaunting themselves, too declamatory, too screechy, too much like embodied speeches. In his own words, they carry "a drum in their mouths"; and what they say of themselves would more properly and naturally come from others. Thus Memnon, in The Mad Lover, tells his prince, in apology for his roughness of behavior: —

> "I know no court but martial,
> No oily language but the shock of arms,
> No dalliance but with death, no lofty measures
> But weary and sad marches, cold and hunger,
> 'Larums at midnight Valor's self would shake at;
> Yet I ne'er shrunk. Balls of consuming wildfire,
> That licked men up like lightning, have I laughed at,
> And tossed 'em back again, like children's trifles.
> Upon the edges of my enemies' swords
> I have marched like whirlwinds, Fury at this hand waiting,

> Death at my right, Fortune my forlorn hope:
> When I **have** grappled with Destruction,
> And tugged with pale-faced **Ruin,** Night and Mischief
> **Frighted to see a** new day break in blood."

This is talk on stilts; **but it** is still resounding **talk, full of** ardor and the impatient consciousness **of personal** prowess. In the characterization **of Cæsar in The** False One, **the same feeling of** individual supremacy **is** combined with **a** haughtier self-possession, **as** befits a mightier and more imperial **soul.** We feel, through**out** this play, that there is power in the mere presence of Cæsar, and **that his words** derive their force from his character. **The very minds** and hearts **of** the Egyp**tians** crouch before him. He sways by disdaining them; **even his** clemency is allied to scorn. **"You have** found," he says, —

> " You have found me merciful in arguing with **ye;**
> Swords, hungers, fires, destruction of all natures,
> Demolishment of kingdoms, and whole ruins,
> Are wont to be my orators."

When they bring him the **head of** Pompey, whom they have slain for the purpose of propitiating him, his contempt for them breaks out in a noble tribute to his great enemy.

> "Egyptians, dare ye think your highest pyramids,
>   Built to out-dure the sun, as you suppose,

> Where your unworthy kings lie raked in ashes,
> **Are** monuments fit for him?   No, brood of Nilus,
> Nothing can cover his high fame but heaven,
> No pyramids set off his memories,
> But the eternal substance of his greatness;
> To which I leave him."

When he is besieged in the palace by the whole Egyptian army, he prepares, with his few followers, to cut his way to his ships. Septimius, a wretch who has been false to all parties, offers to show him safe means both of vengeance and escape. Cæsar's reply is one of the finest things in Fletcher.

> " **Cæsar scorns**
> To find his safety or revenge his wrongs
> So base a way, or owe the means of life
> To such a leprous traitor!   I have towered
> For victory like a falcon in the clouds,
> Not digged for 't like a mole.   Our swords and cause
> Make way for us: and that it may appear
> We took a noble course, and hate base treason,
> Some soldiers that would merit Cæsar's favor
> Hang him on yonder turret, and then follow
> The lane this sword makes for you."

But perhaps the play in which the heroic and martial spirit is most dominant is the tragedy of Bonduca; and the address of Suetonius, the Roman general, to his troops, as they prepare to close in battle with the Britons, is in Fletcher's noblest vein of manliness and imagination.

" And, gentlemen, to you now:
To bid you fight is needless; ye are Romans,
The name will fight itself.

.   .   .   .   .

Go on in full assurance: draw your swords
As daring and as confident as justice;
The gods of Rome fight for ye; loud Fame calls ye,
Pitched on the topless Apennine, and blows
To all the under-world, all nations, the seas,
And unfrequented deserts where the snow dwells;
Wakens the ruined monuments; and there,
Where nothing but eternal death and sleep is,
Informs again the dead bones with your virtues.
Go on, I say; valiant and wise rule heaven,
 And all the great aspects attend 'em.   Do but blow
Upon this enemy, who, but that we want foes,
Cannot deserve that name; and like a mist,
A lazy fog, before your burning valors
You 'll find him fly to nothing.   This is all.
We have swords, and are the sons of ancient Romans,
Heirs to their endless valors: fight and conquer!"

The maxim here laid down, that " Valiant and wise
rule heaven," is much better, or worse, than Napoleon's,
that " Providence is always on the side of the heaviest
battalions."

It might be supposed that the extreme susceptibility of
Fletcher — the openness of his nature to all impressions,
ludicrous, romantic, heroic, or indecent — would have
made him a great delineator of the varieties of life and
character.   But the truth is, it made him versatile with-

out making him universal. He wrote a greater number of plays than Shakespeare, and he has between five
and six hundred names of characters; but two or three
plays of Shakespeare cover a wider extent of human
life than all of Fletcher's. To compare them is like
comparing a planet with a comet, — a comet whose
nucleus is only a few hundred miles in diameter, though
its nebulous appendage flames millions of leagues behind. Fletcher's susceptibility to the surfaces of things
was almost unlimited; his vital sympathy and inward
vision were confined to a few kinds of character and a
few aspects of life. His variety is not variety of character, but variety of incident and circumstance. He
contrives rather than creates; and his contrivances,
ingenious and exhilarating as they are, cannot hide his
constant repetition of a few types of human nature.
These types he conceived by a process essentially different from Shakespeare's. Shakespeare individualized
classes; Fletcher generalized individuals. One of
Shakespeare's characters includes a whole body of persons; one of Fletcher's is simply an idealized individual, and that often an exceptional individual. This
individual, repeated in play after play, never covers so
large a portion of humanity as Shakespeare's individualized class, which he disdains to repeat. But, more than
this, the very faculties of Fletcher, — his wit, humor,

understanding, **fancy,** imagination, — though we **call** them by the **same** words **we** use in naming Shakespeare's, differ from Shakespeare's both in **kind and** degree. Shakespeare was **a great** and comprehensive man, whose faculties all partook **of his general** greatness. The man Fletcher was so much **smaller and** narrower, and the materials on which his faculties worked so much more limited, that we are fooled by words if, following the example of his contemporaries, we place any **one of** his qualities or faculties above **or on a level with** Shakespeare's.

Keeping, then, in view the fact that the **man is the** measure of **the poet, let** us glance for a **moment at** Fletcher's poetic faculty as distinguished from his **dramatic.**

As a poet he is best judged, perhaps, **by his pastoral** tragi-comedy of **The** Faithful **Shepherdess, the most** elaborate and one of the **earliest of his works. It** failed on the stage, being, in his own phrase, "hissed to **ashes";** but **the** merits which the many-headed mon-**ster of the pit could** not discern **so** enchanted Milton that **they were** vividly in his memory when **he** wrote Comus. The melody, the romantic sweetness of **fan-**cy, the luxuriant and luxurious descriptions of nature, **and the true** lyric inspiration, **of large** portions of this **drama, are** not more striking **than** the deliberate desecration of its beauty by the introduction of impure sentiments and images. The hoof-prints of unclean beasts are visible all over Fletcher's pastoral paradise; and they are there by design. Why they are there is a question which can be answered only by pointing out the primal defect of Fletcher's mind, which was an incapacity to conceive or represent goodness and innocence except as the ideal opposites of evil and depravity. He took depravity as the positive fact of life, and then framed from fancy a kind of goodness out of its negation. The result is, that, in the case of The Faithful Shepherdess, Chloe and the Sullen Shepherd, the depraved characters of the play, are the most natural and lifelike, while there is a sickliness and unreality in the very virtue of Amoret. It is not, therefore, as some critics suppose, the mere admission of vicious characters into the play that gives it its taint. Milton, whose conceptions both of good and evil were positive, and who represented them in their right spiritual relations, entirely avoided this error in Comus, while he availed himself of much in The Faithful Shepherdess that is excellent. In Comus it is virtue which seems most real and permanent, and the vice and wickedness represented in it do not mar the general impression of moral beauty left by the whole poem. But Fletcher, having no positive imaginative conception of the good, and feeling for

depravity neither mental nor moral disgust, reverses
this order. His vice is robust and prominent ; his virtue is vague, characterless, and fantastic ; and though his
play has a formal moral, it has an essential impurity.

But, if the general effect of the pastoral is not beautiful, none can deny its beauty in parts, especially in the
lyrical portions. What Milton condescended to copy
everybody must be delighted to applaud. But not
merely in The Faithful Shepherdess is this lyric genius
displayed. Scattered all over his plays are exquisite
songs and short poems, representing almost every variety of the poet's mood, and each perfect of its kind.
As an example of the softness, sweetness, and melody
of these we will quote the hymn to Venus from The
Mad Lover : —

> " O divinest star of heaven,
>   Thou, in power above the seven;
>   Thou, sweet kindler of desires,
>   Till they grow to mutual fires;
>   Thou, O gentle queen, that art
>   Curer of each wounded heart;
>   Thou, the fuel and the flame;
>   Thou, in heaven, here, the same;
>   Thou, the wooer and the wooed;
>   Thou, the hunger and the food;
>   Thou, the prayer and the prayed;
>   Thou, what is or shall be said;
>   Thou, still young and golden tresséd,
>   Make me by thy answer blesséd ! "

8 *

Fletcher died in 1625, and the dramatist who suc ceeded him in popular esteem was a less fiery and ebullient spirit, PHILIP MASSINGER. Massinger, the son of a gentleman in the service of the Earl of Pembroke, was born in 1584, was educated at Oxford, left the University without taking a degree, and about the year 1606 went to London to seek his fortune as a dramatist. Here he worked obscurely for some sixteen years ; the only thing we know about him being this, that in 1614, in connection with Field and Daborne, he was a suppliant to old Manager Henslowe for five pounds to relieve him and them from the most pinching pecuniary distress. In 1622 The Virgin Martyr, a play written in connection with Dekkar, was published, and from this period to his death, in 1640, his most celebrated dramas were produced. He wrote thirty-seven plays, twenty of which have perished. Eleven of them, in manuscript, were in the possession of a Mr. Warburton, whose cook, desirous of saving what she considered better paper, used them in the kindling of fires and the basting of turkeys, and would doubtless have treated the manuscript of the Faery Queene and the Novum Organum in the same way had Providence seen fit to commit them to her master's custody.

Massinger's life seems to have been one long struggle with want. The price for a play in his time ranged

from ten to twenty pounds ; if published, the copyright
brought from six to ten pounds more ; and the dedication
fee was **forty** shillings. The income of a successful dramatist, **who** wrote two or three plays a **year, was** about
fifty pounds, equivalent to some twelve hundred dollars
at the present time. But it is doubtful if even Fletcher
could count on so large an income as this, as some of
his plays failed in representation, great master of theatrical effect as he undoubtedly was. Massinger was
always poor, and, by his own admission in one of his
dedications, depended at times on the casual charity of
patrons. When poverty was not present, it seems to
have been always in prospect. He had a morbid vision
of approaching calamities, as —

> " Creeping billows
> **Not got to shore yet."**

It is difficult to determine how **far his** popular principles
in politics interfered with his success **at the** theatre.
Fletcher's slavish political doctrines **were** perfectly
suited **to** the court of James **and** Charles. We are,
says one of his characters, —

> **" We are but subjects, Maximus.** Obedience
> To what is done, and grief for what is ill done,
> **Is all we** can call ours."

Massinger, on the contrary, **was as strong a Liberal**

as Hampden or Pym. The political and social abuses
of his time found in him an uncompromising satirist.
Oppression in every form, whether of the poor by the
rich, or the subject by the king, provoked his amiable
nature into unwonted passion. In his plays he frequently violates the keeping of character in order to in-
trude his own manly political sentiments and ideas.
There are allusions in his dramas which, if they were
taken by the audience, must have raised a storm of mingled applause and hisses. Though more liberty seems
to have been allowed to playwrights than to members
of Parliament, Massinger sometimes found it difficult to
get his plays licensed. In 1631 the Master of the
Revels refused to license one of his pieces, on the
ground that it contained "dangerous matter"; and
the dramatist had to pay the fee, while he lost all the
results of his labor. In 1638, in the height of the dispute about ship-money, he wrote a drama, now lost,
called The King and the Subject. On looking it over,
the Master of the Revels was startled at coming upon
the following passage : —

> "Moneys? we 'll raise supplies which way we please,
> And force you to subscribe to blanks, in which
> We 'll mulct you as we shall think fit. The Cæsars
> In Rome were wise, acknowledging no laws
> But what their swords did ratify; the wives
> And daughters of the senators bowing to
> Their wills as deities."

The play was shown to King Charles, and he, marking the obnoxious passage, wrote with his own hand: "This is **too insolent,** and to be changed." It is, however, to be mentioned to his honor, that he allowed the **piece to be** acted after the **daring lines had** been expunged.

Massinger's spirit, though sufficiently independent and self-respectful, was as modest **as** Addison's. He chid his friends when they placed him as a dramatist by the side of Beaumont and Fletcher. All the commendatory poems prefixed to his plays evince affection for the man as well as admiration for the genius. But there is **a** strange absence of distinct memorials of his career; and his death and burial were in harmony with the loneliness of his life. We are told that, on the 16th of March, 1640, he went to bed, seemingly in good health, and was found dead in the morning. In the parish register of the Church of St. Saviour's, under the date of March 20, we **read :** " Buried, Philip Massinger, a stranger." No stone indicates where in the churchyard he was laid. " His sepulchre," says Hartley Coleridge, " was like his life, obscure ; like the nightingale he sung darkling, — it is to be feared like the nightingale of the fable, with his breast against a thorn."

Massinger possessed a large though not especially poetic **mind, and a** temperament equable rather than energetic. He lacked strong passions, vivid conceptions, creative imagination. In reading him we feel that the exulting, vigorous life of the drama of the age has begun to decay. But though he has been excelled by obscurer writers in special qualities of genius, he still attaches us by the harmony of his powers, and the uniformity of his excellence. The plot, style, and characters of one of his dramas all conduce to a common interest. His plays, indeed, are novels in dialogue. They rarely thrill, startle, or kindle us, but, as Lamb says, "are read with composure and placid delight." The Bondman, The Picture, The Bashful Lover, The Renegado, A Very Woman, The Emperor of the East, interest us specially as stories. The Duke of Milan, The Unnatural Combat, and The Fatal Dowry are his nearest approaches to the representation of passion, as distinguished from its description. The leading characters in The City Madam and A New Way to pay Old Debts are delineated with more than common power, for they are embodiments of the author's hatred as well as of his genius. Massinger's life was such as to make him look with little favor on the creditor portion of the British people ; and when creditors were also oppressors, he was roused to a pitch of indignation which inspired his conceptions of Luke and Sir Giles Overreach.

Massinger's style, though it does not evince a single

great quality of the poet, has always charmed English
readers by its dignity, flexibility, elegance, clearness,
and ease. His metre and rhythm Coleridge pronounces
incomparably good. Still his verse, with all its merits,
is smooth rather than melodious; the thoughts are not
born in music, but mechanically set to a tune; and even
its majestic flow is frequently purchased at the expense
of dramatic closeness to character and passion.

Though there is nothing in Massinger's plays, as
there is in Fletcher's, indicating profligacy of mind and
morals, they are even coarser in scenes; for as Massinger had none of Fletcher's wit and humor, he made his
low and inferior characters, whether men or women,
little better than beasts. As even his serious personages
use words and allusions which are now banished from
all respectable books, we must suppose that decorum, as
we understand it, was almost unknown in the time of
James and Charles. Thus The Guardian, one of the
most mellifluous in diction and licentious in incident of
all Massinger's works, was acted at the court of Charles
I., and acted, too, by order of the king, on *Sunday*,
January 12, 1633. This coarseness is a deplorable blot
on Massinger's plays; but that it is to be referred to the
manners of his time, and not to his own immorality,
is proved by the fact that his vital sympathies were
for virtue and justice, and that his genius never dis-

played itself in his representations of coarse depravity.
As a man he seems to have had not merely elevated
sentiments, but strong religious **feelings.** If his **unim-**
passioned spirit ever rose to fervor, **the** fervor was
moral ; his best things are ethically, as **well** as poetically
the best ; and in reading him we often **find** passages
like the following, which leap up from the **prosaic level**
of his diction as by an impulse of ecstasy : —

> " When good men pursue
> The path marked out by virtue, the blest saints
> With joy look on it, and seraphic angels
> Clap their celestial wings in heavenly plaudits."

> " Honor is
> Virtue's allowed ascent ; honor, that clasps
> All perfect justice in her arms, that craves
> No more respect than what she gives, that does
> Nothing but what she 'll suffer."

> " As you have
> A soul moulded from heaven, and do desire
> To have it made a star there, make the means
> Of your ascent to that celestial height
> Virtue winged with brave action : they draw near
> The nature and the essence of the gods
> Who imitate their goodness."

> " By these blessed feet
> That pace the paths of equity, and tread boldly
> On the stiff neck of tyrannous oppression,

> "By these tears by which I bathe them, I conjure you
> With pity to look on me."

We now come to a very different dramatist, JOHN
FORD, whose genius and personal appearance are
shrewdly indicated in a rugged couplet from a contemporary satire : —

> "Deep in a dump, John Ford by himself sat,
> With folded arms and melancholy hat."

In that somewhat dainty mental loneliness, and under
that melancholy hat, the mind of the poet was absorbed
in the intensest meditation of the ideal possibilities of
grief and guilt, and the strange aberrations of the passions. Massinger has little sway over the heart; but
Ford was not merely the poet of the heart, but of the
broken heart, — the heart bending under burdens, or
torn by emotions, almost too great for mortality to bear.
In reading his tragedies, as in reading Webster's, we are
fretfully conscious of being shut up in the sultry atmosphere of one morbid mind, deprived of all companionship with healthy nature and genial human life, and
forced into a shuddering or sickly sympathy with the
extremes of crime and suffering. But the power of
Webster lies in terror; the power of Ford, in tenderness. Out of his peculiar walk, Ford is the feeblest of
finical fine writers. His attempts at liveliness and

humor excite, not laughter, but rather a dismal feeling
of pitying contempt. His great gift is displayed in
the tragedy of The Broken Heart, and in two or
three thrilling scenes of the tragedy of Love's Sacrifice. In The Broken Heart, the noblest of his works,
our sympathies are on the whole rightly directed ; and
the death of Calantha, after enduring the most soul-
crushing calamities, concealed from others under a show
of mirth, is exquisitely pathetic : —

> " O my lords,
> I but deceived your eyes with antick gesture,
> When one news straight came huddling on another,
> Of death, and death, and death, still I danced forward;
> But it struck home, and here, and in an instant.
>
> .   .   .   .   .
>
> They are the silent griefs which cut the heartstrings;
> Let me die smiling."

Of another of Ford's tragedies, which can hardly
be named here, Campbell justly remarks : " Better that
poetry should cease to exist than have to do with such
subjects." But it is characteristic of Ford, that his
power and tenderness are seldom so great as in their
worst perversions. Without any austerity of soul, dis-
eased in his sympathies, a sentimentalist rather than a
man of sentiment, he brooded over guilt until all sense
of its wickedness was lost in a morbid pity for its afflic-

tions, and the tears **he** compels us to shed are rarely the tears of honest and manly feeling.

Ford **died, or** disappeared, **about** the year 1640, **and** with him died the last original dramatist of the Elizabethan age ; for Shirley, though **his** plays **fill six** thick **volumes, was** but a faint echo of Fletcher. Thus, **in a** short period of fifty years, from 1590 to 1640, **we** have the names of thirteen dramatists, varying in **power and variety of power** and perversion of power, **but each** individual **in** his genius, and **one** the greatest **genius of** the world, — the names of Marlowe, Shakespeare, Ben Jonson, **Heywood,** Middleton, Marston, Dekkar, **Web-**ster, Chapman, Beaumont, Fletcher, Massinger, **and** Ford. **Though** little **is known of their lives, it is** through **them we learn** the life **of** their **time, — the** manners, **customs,** character, **ideas, habits,** sentiments, and passions, the form and the spirit, **of** the Elizabethan age. And they are all intensely and audaciously human. Taking them in the mass, they have much to offend our artistic and shock **our** moral sense ; but still the **dra-matic** literature **of the** world would be searched in vain for another instance **of** so broad and bold a representa-**tion** of the varieties **of** human nature, — one in which **the** conventional restraints both on depravity and excel-**lence are so** resolutely set aside, — **one in which the many-charactered** soul of man **is so vividly** depicted, in its weakness and in its strength, in its mirth and in its passion, in the appetites which sink it below the beasts that perish, in the aspirations which lift it to regions of existence of which the visible heavens are but the veil.

IN the last chapter we closed our remarks on the Dramatic Literature of the Age of Elizabeth. In the present we propose to treat of Spenser, with some introductory observations on the miscellaneous poets who preceded him. And it is necessary to bear in mind that, in the age of which we treat, as in all ages, the versifiers far exceeded the seers, and the poetasters the poets. It has been common to exercise a charity towards the early English poets which we refuse to extend to those of later times; but mediocrity has identical characteristics in all periods, and there was no charm in the circumstances of the Elizabethan age to convert a rhymer into a genius. Indeed, leaving out the dramatists, the poetry produced in the reigns of Elizabeth and James can hardly compare in originality, richness, and variety, with the English poetry of the nineteenth century. Spenser is a great name; but he is the only undramatic poet of his time who could be placed above, or on a level with, Wordsworth, Byron, Shelley, Coleridge, or Tennyson. There is a list, somewhere, of two hundred names of poets who belonged to the Eliza-

bethan age, — mostly mere nebulous appearances, which
it requires a telescope of the greatest power to resolve
into individual stars. Few of them can be made to
shine with as steady a lustre as the ordinary versemen
who contribute to our magazines. Take England's
Helicon and the Paradise of Dainty Devices, — two
collections of the miscellaneous poetry written during
the last forty or fifty years of the sixteenth century,
— and, if we except a few pieces by Raleigh, Sidney,
Marlowe, Greene, Lodge, Breton, Watson, Nash, and
Hunnis, these collections have little to dazzle us into
admiration or afflict us with a sense of inferiority.
Reading them is a task, in which an occasional elegance
of thought, or quaintness of fancy, or sweetness of sentiment does not compensate for the languor induced
by tiresome repetitions of moral commonplaces, varied
by repetitions, as tiresome, of amatory commonplaces.
In the great body of the poetry of the time there is
more that is bad than tolerable, more that is tolerable
than readable, and more that is readable than excellent.

One person, however, stands out from this mob of
versifiers the most noticeable elevation in English poetry from Chaucer to Spenser, namely, Thomas Sackville, afterwards Lord Buckhurst, and, still later, Earl
of Dorset. Born in 1536, and educated at both universities, his poetic genius was but one phase of his general

ability. In 1561 his tragedy of Gorboduc was acted with great **applause** before the Queen. Previously to this, in 1559, at the age of twenty-three, he had joined two dreary poetasters — Baldwyne and Ferrers — in the **production** of a work called The Mirrour **for** Magistrates, the design of which was to exhibit, in **a series of** metrical narratives and soliloquies, the calamities of men prominent in the history of England. **The work passed to a** third edition in 1571, and received such constant additions from other writers, in the fourth, fifth, and sixth editions, that its bulk finally became enormous. Its poetical value is altogether in the comparatively meagre contributions of Sackville, consisting **of** the Induction, and the complaint **of** the Duke of **Buck**ingham. The Induction, especially, **is a** masterpiece of meditative imagination, working under the impulse of sternly serious sentiment. **Misery and sorrow seem** the dark inspirers of Sackville's Muse; **and** his allegoric pictures of Revenge, Remorse, Old Age, Dread, **Care,** Sleep, Famine, Strife, **War,** and Death exhibit **such a** combination of reflective and analytic with imaginative power, **of** melody of verse with compact, massive strength and certainty of verbal expression, that our wonder is awakened that a man with such **a** conscious mastery **of** the resources of thought and language should have written **so** little. If **political** ambition —

the ambition that puts thoughts into facts instead of
putting them into words — was the cause of his with-
drawal from the Muse, — if Burleigh tempted him from
Dante, — it must be admitted that his choice, in a worldly
sense, was justified by the event, for he became an eminent statesman, and in 1598 was made Lord High
Treasurer of England.   He held that great office at the
time of his death, in 1608.   But it is probable that
Sackville ceased to cultivate poetry because he failed
to reap its internal rewards.   His genius had no joy in
it, and its exercise probably gave him little poetic
delight.   With great force of imagination, his was still
a somewhat dogged force.   He could discern clearly,
and shape truly, but no sudden ecstasy of emotion gave
a "precious seeing" to his eye or unexpected felicity
to his hand.   There is something bleak in his noblest
verse.   The poet, we must ever remember, is paid, not
by external praise, or fortune, or fame, but by the deep
bliss of those inward moods from which his creations
spring.   The pleasure they give to others is as nothing
compared with the rapture they give to him.

But Sackville was to be succeeded by a man who,
though he did not exhibit at so early an age equal
power of shaping imagination, had that perception of
the loveliness of things, and that joy in the perception,
which make continuous poetic creation a necessity of

existence. In the meagre memorials of the external career of this man, Edmund Spenser, there is little that stands in intelligible connection with the wondrous inner life embodied in the enchantments of The Faery Queene. He was born in London in 1552, and was the son of parents who, though in humble circumstances, were of gentle birth. We first hear of him, at the age of seventeen, as a sizar, or charity student, in Pembroke Hall, Cambridge. While there he made acquaintance and formed a lasting friendship with Gabriel Harvey, — a man of large acquirements, irritable temper, and pedantic taste, who rendered himself the object of the sarcastic invectives of the wits of the time, and to be associated with whom was to run the risk of sharing the ridicule he provoked. One of the most beautiful traits of Spenser's character was his constancy to his friends; to their persons when alive, to their memory when dead. It is difficult to discover what intellectual benefits Spenser derived from Harvey's companionship, though we know what the world has gained by his refusal to follow his advice. It was Harvey who tried to persuade Spenser into writing hexameter verse, and dissuade him from writing the Faery Queene. After seven years' residence at the university, Spenser took his degree, and went to reside with some friends of his family in the North of Eng-

land.   Here he fell in love with a beautiful girl, whose
real name he has concealed under the anagrammatic
one of Rosalind, and who, after having tempted and
balked the curiosity of English critics, has, by an American writer,* who has raised guessing into a science,
been satisfactorily proved to be Rose Daniel, a sister
of the poet Daniel.   It is mortifying to record that she
rejected the great exalter of her sex, — the creator of
some of the most exquisite embodiments of female excellence, — the man who had the high honor of saying
of women,

> " For demigods they be, and first did spring
>   From heaven, though graft in frailness feminine,"

— she rejected him, we say, for a ridiculous and irascible
pedant, John Florio, and one so prominent in his folly
that Shakespeare condescended to lampoon him in
Love's Labor Lost.

But the graces of soul and person which had no effect
on the heart of Rosalind were not lost on the mind of
Sir Philip Sidney.   Introduced to Spenser, — it is supposed by Gabriel Harvey, — Sidney recognized his
genius, and warmly recommended him to his uncle, the
Earl of Leicester, who, in 1579, took him into his service.   In December of that year he published his

---

* In the Atlantic Monthly for November, 1858.

Shepherd's Calendar, **a series** of twelve pastorals, —
one for every **month.** In these, avoiding the affectation
of refinement, **he** falls into the opposite affectation of
rusticity ; and, by a profusion of obsolete and uncouth
expressions, hinders the free movement **of his** fancy.
It may be absurd for shepherds to talk in the style of
courtiers, as they **do in** many pastoral poets ; but **it is**
also absurd to give them the sentiments and ideas **of**
priests and philosophers. Campbell, who **is** a sceptic
in regard to all English pastorals, is especially severe **on**
the Shepherd's Calendar. Spenser's shepherds, **he**
says, " are parsons **in** disguise, who converse about
heathen divinities and points of Christian theology.
Palinode defends the luxuries **of** the Catholic **clergy,**
and Piers extols the purity of Archbishop **Grindal, con-**
cluding with the story of a fox who came to the house
of a goat in the character of a pedler, and obtained ad-
mittance by pretending **to be a sheep.** This may be
burlesquing Æsop, but certainly **it is** not imitating
Theocritus." These eclogues are, however, important,
considered in reference to **their** position in the history of
English poetry, and **to** their connection with the history
of the poet's **heart.** No descriptions of external nature
since Chaucer's had equalled those in the Shepherd's
Calendar **in** the combination of various excellences,
though the excellences were still second-rate, exhibiting

the beautiful genius of the author struggling with the pedantries and affectations of his time, and the pedantries and affectations which overlaid his own mind. Even in his prime, it was difficult for him to grasp a thing in itself, after the manner of the greatest poets, and flash its form and spirit upon the mind in a few vivid words, vital with suggestive meaning. In the Shepherd's Calendar this defect is especially prominent, his imagination playing round objects, illustrating and adorning them, rather than penetrating at once to their essence. Even in those portions where, as Colin Clout, he celebrates the beauty and bewails the coldness of Rosalind, we have a conventional discourse about love, rather than the direct utterance of the passion.

Spenser's ambition was to obtain some office which, by placing him above want, would enable him to follow his true vocation of poet, and he seems to have looked to Leicester as a magnificent patron through whom his wish could be realized. The great design of the Faery Queene had already dawned upon his mind; he

> " By that vision splendid
> Was on his way attended ";

and he ached for leisure and competence to enable him to embody his gorgeous and noble dreams. All that Leicester did for him was to get him appointed secretary to Lord Grey of **Wilton,** who, in 1580, went over to Ireland as lord deputy. Here he passed the largest **remaining** portion of his life ; and, though moaning **over** the **hard** fortune which banished him from England, he appears to have exhibited sufficient talent for affairs, and **to** have performed services of sufficient note, **to deserve** the attention of **the** government. In 1586 he received **a grant** of three thousand and twenty-eight **acres of land, — a** portion **of the** confiscated estates of the **Earl of** Desmond. **The** manor and the castle of Kilcolman, situated amidst the most beautiful scenery, constituted a portion of this **grant.** In 1589 the restless and chivalrous Raleigh, transiently out **of favor** with the haughty coquette who ruled England, came over **to Ireland for** the purpose of looking **after his own immense estates in that** country, wrung, like **Spenser's, from the native pro-**prietors. He visited **the lone** poet at Kilcolman ; **and** to him,

> " Amongst the coolly shade
> **Of** the green alders by the Mullaes shore,"

Spenser **read** the first three **books of The Faery** Queene. Campbell finely **says:** " **When we conceive** Spenser reciting **his** compositions **to** Raleigh in a scene so beautifully appropriate, the mind casts pleasing retrospect over that influence which the enterprise **of the dis-coverer** of Virginia and the genius of the author of the

Faery Queene have respectively produced in the fortune and language of England. The fancy might easily be pardoned for a momentary superstition, that the genius of their country hovered, unseen, over their meeting, casting her first look of regard on the poet that was destined to inspire her future Milton, and the other on her maritime hero, who paved the way for colonizing distant regions of the earth, where the language of England was to be spoken, and the poetry of Spenser to be admired."

Raleigh, his imagination kindled by the enchantments of Spenser's verse, and feeling that he had discovered in an Irish wilderness the greatest of living poets, prevailed on the too-happy author to accompany him to England. Spenser was graciously received by Elizabeth, and was smitten with a courtier's hopes in receiving a poet's welcome.

In the early part of 1590 the first three books of The Faery Queene were published. Who that has read it can ever forget the thrill that went through him as he completed the first stanza?

> " Lo, I the man whose Muse whilom did mask,
>   As Time her taught, in lowly shepherd's weeds,
>   Am now enforced, — a far unfitter task, —
>   For trumpets stern to change my oaten reeds;
>   And sing of knights' and ladies' gentle deeds,
>   Whose praises, having slept in silence long,

> Me, all too mean, the sacred muse areeds,
>> To blazon broad amongst her learned throng:
> Fierce wars and faithful loves shall moralize my song."

' **The admiration,"** says Hallam, "of this great poem **was** unanimous and enthusiastic. **No** academy had been trained to carp at his genius with minute cavilling; no recent popularity, no traditional fame, interfered with the immediate recognition of his supremacy. The Faery Queene became at once the delight of every accomplished gentleman, the model of every poet, the solace of every scholar."

But if the aspirations of the poet were thus gratified, those of the courtier and politician were cruelly disappointed. Burleigh, the Lord Treasurer, to whom Spenser was merely a successful maker of **ballads, and one** pushed forward by the faction which was constantly intriguing for his lordship's overthrow, contrived to intercept, delay, or divert the favor which the queen was willing to bestow on her melodious flatterer. The **irritated** bard, **in** a few memorable couplets, **has** recorded, for the warning of all office-seekers and supplicants for the patronage of the great, his wretched experience during the year and a half he danced attendance on the court. Rage is a great condenser; and the most diffuse of poets became the most concentrated when wrath brooded over the memory of wrong.

> " To fret thy soul with crosses and with cares;
> To eat thy heart through comfortless despairs;
> To fawn, to crouch, to wait, to ride, to run,
> To spend, to give, to want, to be undone," —

this was the harsh experience of the laurelled minstrel, fresh from the glories of fairy-land. But it is only charitable to allow for the different points of view from which different minds survey the poet. To Burleigh, Spenser was a rhyming suitor, clamorous for the queen's favor, and meditating designs on her treasury. To a Mr. Beeston, according to Aubrey, " he was a little man, who wore short hair, little band, and little cuffs." Did not the sullen Burleigh have a more profound appreciation of Spenser than the great world of commonplace gossips, represented by friend Beeston? At last, in February, 1591, Spenser succeeded in obtaining a pension of fifty pounds, and returned, but half satisfied, to Ireland. In a graceful poem, called Colin Clout 's Come Home Again, full of gratitude to Raleigh and adulation of Elizabeth, he described the glories and the vanities he had witnessed at the English Court.

A deeper passion than that which inspired the amorous plaints of the Shepherd's Calendar, and one destined to a happier end, he now recorded in a series of exquisitely thoughtful and tender sonnets, under the general name of Amoretti; and he celebrated its long

deferred consummation in a rapturous Epithalamion.
We have no means of judging of Elizabeth, the Irish
maiden who prompted these wonderful poems, except
from her transfigured image as seen reflected in Spenser's verse, — verse which has made her perfect and has
made her immortal. The Epithalamion is the grandest
and purest marriage-song in literature. Even Hallam,
the least enthusiastic of critics, and one who too often
writes as if judgment consisted, not in the inclusion, but
exclusion of sympathy, cannot speak of this poem without an unwonted touch of ecstasy in the words which
convey his magisterial decision. And John Wilson grows
wild in its praise. "Joy," he says, — "Joy, Love,
Desire, Passion, Gratitude, Religion, rejoice, in presence of Heaven, to take possession of Affection, Beauty,
and Innocence. Faith and Hope are bridesmaids, and
holiest incense is burning on the altar." But the raptures of critics can convey no adequate idea of the
deep, thoughtful, satisfying delight that breathes through
the Epithalamion, and harmonizes its occasional starts
of ecstasy into unity with its pervading spirit of tranquil bliss. How simple and tender, and yet how intensely imaginative, is this exquisite picture of the
bride !

"Behold, whiles she before the altar stands,
    Hearing the holy priest that to her speaks

9 *

> And blesseth her with his two happy hands,
> How the red roses flush up in her cheeks,
> And the pure snow with goodly vermeil stain
> Like crimson dyed in grain:
> That even the angels, which continually
> About the sacred altar do remain,
> Forget their service and about her fly,
> Oft peeping in her face, that seems more fair
> The more they on it stare.
> But her sad eyes, still fastened on the ground,
> Are governed with goodly modesty,
> That suffers not one look to glance awry,
> Which may let in a little thought unsound.
> Why blush ye, Love, to give to me your hand,
> The pledge of all our band?
> Sing, ye sweet angels, Allelujah sing,
> That all the woods may answer, and your echoes ring!"

Nothing can be more delicately poetic than the line in which the hands of the priest, lifted over the head of the bride in the act of benediction, receive a reflected joy from the beauty they bless:—

> "And blesseth her with his two *happy* hands."

At the time of his marriage, in 1594, Spenser had completed three more books of The Faery Queene, and in 1595 he visited England for the purpose of publishing them. They appeared in 1596. During this visit he presented to the queen his View of the State of Ireland,—a prose tract, displaying the sagacity of an

English statesman, but a spirit towards the poor native Irish as ruthless as Cromwell's. He felt, in respect to the population of the country in which he was forced to make his home, as a Puritan New-Englander might have felt in regard to the wild Indians who were skulking round his rude cabin, peering for a chance at the scalps of his children. Returning to Ireland, with the queen's recommendation for the office of Sheriff of Cork, his worldly fortunes seemed now to be assured. But in 1598 the Insurrection of Munster broke out. Spenser, who appears, not unnaturally, to have been especially hated by the Irish, lost everything. His house was assailed, pillaged, and burned; and in the **hurry of his** departure from **his** burning dwelling, **it is said that his** youngest child **was** left to **perish** in **the flames. He** succeeded, with the remaining portion of **his family, in** escaping to London, where, in a common inn, overcome by his misfortunes, and broken in heart and brain, on **the** 16th of January, 1599, he died. The saddest thing **of** all remains to be recorded. Soon after his death — such is the curt statement — "his widow married one Roger Seckerstone." Did Edmund Spenser, then, after all, appear to his wife Elizabeth as he appeared to Mr. Beeston, — simply as "**a** little man, who wore **short** hair, little band, and little cuffs"? One would suppose that the memory of so much genius and glory

and calamity would have been better than the presence
of "one Roger Seckerstone"! Among the thousands
of millions of men born on the planet, it was her fortune to be the companion of Edmund Spenser, and
"soon after his death she married one Roger Seckerstone"! It required two years of assiduous courtship,
illustrated by sonnets which have made her name immortal, before the adoring poet could hymn, in a trans-
port of gratitude, her acceptance of his hand; but fortunate Mr. Seckerstone did not have to wait! She saw
her husband laid in Westminster Abbey, mourned by
all that was noble in rank or high in genius, and then,
as in the case of another too-celebrated marriage,

> " The funeral baked meats
> Did coldly furnish forth the marriage tables! "

The work to which Spenser devoted the largest portion of his meditative life was The Faery Queene ; and
in this poem the whole nature and scope of his genius
may be discerned. Its object, as he tells us, " was to
fashion a gentleman or noble person in virtuous and
gentle discipline " ; and, as doctrine embodied in persons
is more efficient than doctrine embodied in maxims, he
proposed to do this by means of a historical fiction, in
which duty should be infused into the mind by the process of delight, and Virtue, reunited to the Beauty from

which she **had unwisely** been severed, should be presented as **an object to** be passionately loved as well as reverently obeyed. He chose for his subject the history **of Arthur,** the fabulous hero and **king of** England, as familiar to readers of romance then **as the** heroes of Scott's novels are to the readers **of our time; and he** purposed " to portray in him, before he was king, **the** image of a brave knight, perfected in the twelve private **moral virtues."** This plan was to be comprised in twelve books; and then he proposed, in case his plan succeeded, " to frame the other part of politic virtues in his **person,** after he came to be king." As only one half of **the first** portion of this **vast** design was completed, as this half makes one **of the longest poems in** the world, **and as** all but the poet's resolute admirers profess their incapacity to **read** without weariness more than the first three **books, it must** be admitted that Spenser's conception of the abstract capabilities of human patience was truly heroic, and that his confidence **in his** own longevity was founded on a reminiscence of Methuselah rather than on a study of vital statistics.

But the poem was also intended by the author to be " one long-continued allegory **or** dark conceit." The story and the characters are symbolic as well as representative. The pictures that please the eye, the melody that charms the ear, the beauty that would seem " its

own excuse for being," cover a latent meaning, not perceptible to the senses they delight, but to be interpreted
by the mind. Philosophical ideas, ethical truths, historical events, compliments to contemporaries, satire on
contemporaries, are veiled and sometimes hidden in
these beautiful forms and heroic incidents. Much of
this covert sense is easily detected; but to explain all
would require a commentator who could not only think
from Spenser's mind, but recall from oblivion all the
gossip of Elizabeth's court. The general intention of
the allegorical design is given by the poet himself, in
his letter to Raleigh. He supposes Prince Arthur, after
his long education by Timon, " to have seen in a dream
or vision the Faery Queene, with whose excellent
beauty ravished, he, awaking, resolved to seek her out ";
and, armed by the magician Merlin, Arthur went to
seek her in fairy-land. Spenser is careful to inform us
that by the Faery Queene he means Glory in his general intention, but in his particular, " the excellent and
glorious person of our sovereign the queen, and her
kingdom in fairy-land." And considering that she bears
two persons, " the one of a most royal queen or empress, the other of a virtuous and beautiful lady, the
latter part in some places I do express in Belphœbe."
Arthur he intends to be the embodiment of the virtue
of Magnificence, or Magnanimity, as this contains all

the other virtues, and **is** the perfection of them all ; **but**
of the twelve separate virtues he takes twelve different
knights for the patrons, making the adventures of each
the subject of a whole book, though the magnificent
Arthur appears in all, exercising **with ease** the special
virtue, whether it be temperance, or holiness, or chas-
tity, or courtesy, **or** justice, which is included in the
rounded perfection **of his** moral being. The explana-
tion of the causes of these several adventures was, in
the poem, **to be** reserved to the twelfth book, of which
the rude Irish kerns unwittingly deprived us, in depriv-
ing us of the brain in which alone it had existence ; but
we know that the poet's plan was, in that book, to represent the Faery Queene as keeping her annual feast
twelve days, " upon which the occasions of the twelve
separate adventures happened, which, being undertaken
by twelve separate knights," were in the twelve books
of the poem to be severally described. Spenser defends
his course in thus putting what might be deemed the
beginning **at** the end, by discriminating between the
poet historical **and the** historiographer. A historiographer, he says, "discourseth of affairs orderly, as **they**
were done, accounting **as** well the times as the actions :
but a poet thrusteth into the middest, ever where it
most concerneth him, and there recoursing to things fore-
past, and divining of things to come, maketh a pleasing
analysis of all."

In judging of the plan of the Faery Queene, we
must remember that it is a fragment. Spenser only
completed six books, of twelve cantos each, and a portion of another. The tradition that three unpublished
books were destroyed by the fire which consumed his
dwelling has, by the latest and ablest editor of his
works, Professor F. J. Child, been rejected as un-
founded and untenable. But, though the poem was never
completed, we know the poet's design; and, much as
this design has been censured, it seems to us that the
radical defect was not in what Spenser proposed to do,
but in the way he did it, — not in the plan of the poem,
but in the limitations of the poet. He conceived the
separate details — the individual objects, persons, and
incidents — imaginatively; but he conceived the whole
plan logically. He could give, and did give, elaborate
reasons for the conduct of his story, — better reasons,
perhaps, than Homer, or Shakespeare, or Cervantes,
or Goethe could have given to justify the designs of his
works; but do you suppose that he could have given
reasons for Una, or Florimel, or Amoret? The truth is,
that his design was too large and complicated for his imagination to grasp as a whole. The parts, each organically conceived, are not organically related. The result
is a series of organisms connected by a logical bond,
— an endless procession of beautiful forms, but no such

vital combination of them as would convey unity of impression. The cumbrousness and confusion and diffusion which critics **have** recognized in the poem are to be referred to the fact that the processes of the understanding, coldly contemplating the general plan, are in hopeless antagonism to the processes of the imagination, rapturously beholding and bodying forth the separate facts. The moment the poet abandons himself to his genius he forgets, and makes us forget, the purpose he had in view at the start ; and he and we are only recalled from the delicious dream in order that he may moralize, and that we may yawn. A dozen lines might be selected from any canto which are of more value than his statement of the idea of the whole **poem.** In truth, the combining, co-ordinating, centralizing, fusing imagination of the highest order of genius, — an imagination competent to seize and hold such a complex design as our poet contemplated, and to flash in brief and burning words details over which his description lovingly lingers, — this was a power denied **to Spenser.** He has auroral lights in profusion, but no lightning. **It is not** that he lacks power. The Cave of Despair, the description of Mammon and of Jealousy, the Binding of Furor, not to mention other examples, **are** full of power ; but it is not condensed into that di-**rect** executive efficiency which, in the same instant, **irradiates, smites, and is gone.** He has not so much of

N

this power as Byron, though he greatly exceeds him in fulness of matter and depth and elevation of thought.

The poem has another defect which also answers to a limitation of Spenser's character. His disposition was soft and yielding ; and, to honor a friend or propitiate a patron, he did not hesitate to make his verse a vehicle of flattery as well as of truth. If by Prince Arthur he intended any real person, it was probably Sir Philip Sidney ; but in the sixth book he allows himself to associate the name of Arthur with the ignominious campaign of Leicester in the Netherlands, — Leicester who represented the seven deadly sins rather than the twelve moral virtues. Sir Arthegall, again, stands for Lord Grey of Wilton, the Irish lord deputy, whom Spenser served as secretary ; but Grey was the exponent of ruthlessness rather than of justice. The flattery of Queen Elizabeth is so gross, that the wonder is that she did not behead him for irony instead of pensioning him for panegyric. The queen's hair was red, or, as some still chivalrously insist, auburn ; and Spenser, like the other poets of the day, is too loyal to permit the ideal head of beauty to wear any locks but those which are golden. In the first book, the Red-Cross Knight, who is the personification of Holiness, after being married to Una, who is the personification of Truth or True Religion, leaves her at the end of the twelfth canto to go to the court of Gloriana, the Faery Queene. Now if Gloriana means Glory, Holiness very improperly leaves True Religion to seek it; if Gloriana means Queen Elizabeth, it is probable that Holiness never arrived at his destination.

We have thus a poet ungifted with the smiting directness of power, the soaring and darting imagination, of the very highest order of minds; a man sensitive, tender, grateful, dependent; reverential to the unseen realities of the spiritual world, deferential to the crowned and coroneted celebrities of the world of fact; but we still have not yet touched the peculiarities of his special genius. If we pass into the inner world of the poet's spirit, where he really lived and brooded, we forget criticism in the loving wonder and admiration evoked by the sight of that "paradise of devices," both "dainty" and divine. We are in communion with a nature in which the most delicate, the most voluptuous, sense of beauty is in exquisite harmony with the austerest recognition of the paramount obligations of goodness and rectitude. The beauty of material objects never obscures to him the transcendent beauty of holiness. In his Bowers of Bliss and his Houses of Pride he surprises even voluptuaries by the luxuriousness of his descriptions, and dazzles even the arrogant by the towering bravery of his style; but his Bowers of Bliss repose on caverns of bale, and the glories of his House of Pride are built over human carcasses.

This great mind ripened late; for it was cumulative before it was creative, and inventiveness brooded over memory. With great subtlety and strength of reason, disciplined, exalted, and connected with imagination by deep study of the philosophy of Plato, his intellect, under the guidance of fixed spiritual ideas, roamed over the field of history and fiction, selecting from every quarter fit nutriment to feed and increase its energies. The mythology of Greece and Rome, the creeds and martyrologies of Christendom, the romance and superstitions of the Middle Ages, the ideals and facts of chivalry, the literatures of every civilized nation, were all received into his hospitable intelligence, and more or less assimilated with its substance. Gradually his imagination, working on these multifarious materials, gave them form and life. Divinities, fairies, magicians, goblins, embodied passions, became real objects to his inward vision. He had

> "*Sight* of Proteus coming from the sea,"

and *heard*

> "Old Triton blow his wreathèd horn."

He began to believe, with more than the usual faith of the poet, in the beautiful or terrible or fantastic shapes with which his fancy was peopled. As they had been modified, re-created, associated with his own sympathies and antipathies, — *Spenserized*, — in the imaginative process they had gone through, he felt spiritually at home **in their** company. Even when they were falsified by actual facts, he knew they were still the appropriate images of essential truths, having a **validity** independent of experience. And it was this wondrous and various troop of ideal shapes, palpable to his **own eye** and domesticated in his own heart, that he sent forth, in an endless succession of pictures, through **the** magical **pages of the** Faery Queene.

It was the necessary condition **of a** poem, thus sociably blending Christian and Pagan beliefs, Platonic ideas, and barbaric superstitions, that its action should **occur** in what Coleridge happily calls " mental space." Truth **of** scenery, truth of climate, **truth** of locality, **truth of** costume, could have **no** binding authority **in** the everywhere and nowhere of Fairy-Land. Spenser's life was too inward to allow his observation of external nature to be close and exact. **He** had not, of course, the pert pretension of the artist who said that nature put him out, or **of the** French abstractionist who, when told that his theory did not agree with facts, blandly replied, " So much **the** worse for the facts "; but his fault, if fault **it was,** arose **from a** predominance **of his** reflective and imaginative powers over **his**

powers of observation, — from his instinctive habit of subordinating, in Bacon's phrase, " the shows of things to the desires of the mind " ; and, as the scene of his poem is mental and not material space, his lack of local truth is hardly a real defect. It is objected, for example, that, in his enumeration of the trees in one of his forests, he associates trees which in nature do not coexist; but his forest is in Fairy-Land. Again, the following stanza, — one of the most beautiful in the poem, describing the melody which arose from the Bower of Bliss, — has been repeatedly criticised : —

> " The joyous birds, shrouded in cheerful shade,
>   Their notes unto the voice attempered sweet;
>   The angelical, soft, trembling voices made
>   To th' instruments divine respondence meet;
>   The silver-sounding instruments did meet
>   With the base murmur of the water's fall;
>   The water's fall, with difference discreet,
>   Now soft, now loud, unto the wind did call;
> The gentle warbling wind low answeréd to all."

It is objected that the result of such a combination of sounds, voices, and instruments would be discord, and not melody. We may be sure it made music to Spenser's soul, though he admits that it was not the music of earth.

> " Right hard it was for wight who did it hear
>   To read what manner music that mote be;

> For all that pleasing is to living ear
>   Was there consorted in one harmony;
> Birds, voices, instruments, winds, waters, all agree."

Again, Hallam says that the image conjured **up by** the description of Una riding

> " Upon a lowly ass more white than snow,
>   But she much whiter,"

is a hideous image **; but it is** evident he does **not follow** the thought of the poet, who, rapidly passing from snow as a material fact to snow as an emblem of innocence, intends to **say** that the white purity **of** Una's soul, shining in her face and transfiguring its expression, cannot be expressed by **the** purest **material** symbol. **The** image of **a** woman's face ghastly white passed before Hallam's eye ; we may be sure that no such uncomely image was in Spenser's mind. The real meaning is **so** obvious, that its perversion by so distinguished a critic **proves** that acuteness has **no irreconcilable** feud with imaginative insensibility, and can be spiritually dull when **it** prides itself most **on** being intellectually keen.

To this inwardness — this ideal and idealizing **quality** of Spenser's soul — we must add its melodiousness. His best thoughts were born in music. The spirit of **poetry** is not only felt in his sentiments and made visible in his imagery, but it steals out in the recurring chimes of his complicated stanza. Accordingly, Spenser, rather than Shakespeare and Milton, — who, as Coleridge has remarked, had "deeper and more inwoven harmonies," — is commonly adduced in support of the accredited dogma, that verse is as much an essential constituent of poetry as passion and imagination. But it seems to us that poetry is not necessarily opposed to prose, but to what is prosaic. It doubtless finds in the verse of the greatest poets its happiest and most vital expression ; but sometimes verse is a clog, and its management a mechanical exercise. Much of Spenser's, especially in the last three books of The Faery Queene, is mere ingenuity in rhythm and rhyme ; and even in the first three books we continually light on passages which are essentially prosaic. Take, for example, the following stanza, descriptive of Immodest Mirth, and it will readily be seen that only the first four lines are poetic : —

> " And therein sat a lady fresh and fair,
>   Making sweet solace to herself alone:
>   Sometimes she sang as loud as lark in air,
>   Sometimes she laughed, that nigh her breath was gone;
>   Yet was there not with her else any one,
>   That to her might move cause of merriment;
>   Matter of mirth enough, though there were none,
>   She could devise, and thousand ways invent
> To feed her foolish humor and vain jolliment."

In Shakespeare's line,

"How sweet the moonlight sleeps upon this bank!"

the poetry is in the single epithet **" sleeps "**; substitute "lies," and though the rhythm would be as perfect, the poetry would be gone. The soul of poetry, indeed, is impassioned imagination, using words, but not necessarily verse, in **its** expression. Bacon wrote verse, **and** execrable verse it **is**; but was not Bacon a poet? **Is not** Milton a poet in his prose? Are not the prose translations of the Psalms **of** David poetic? The poetic faculty, which is vital, cannot be made to depend on a form which, even in undisputed poets, is so apt **to** be mechanical. Even should we admit that verse **is the** body of which poetry is the soul, cannot **a soul manifest** itself in a body which does not in **all** respects correspond to it? Cannot the essential spirit of poetry transfigure the rudest, unrhythmic expression, as the soul of Socrates glorified his homely face? **It** is not, of course, mere imagination which makes **a** poet; for Aristotle **and** Newton were men of great imagination, scientifically directed to the discovery **of** new truth, not to the creation of new beauty. But imagination directed by poetic sentiment and passion to poetic ends **does** make **the** poet. And **that** these conditions **are** often fulfilled **in** prose, and a purely poetic impression

10

produced, cannot be denied without resisting the evi.
dence of ordinary experience.

And, though there is a delicious charm in Spenser's
sweetest verse, the finest and rarest elements of his
genius were independent of music. That celestial light
which occasionally touches his page with an ineffable
beauty, and which gave to him in his own time the
name of "the heavenly Spenser," is a more wonderful
emanation from his mind than its subtlest melodies.
We especially feel this in his ideal delineations of
woman, in which he has only been exceeded by Shakespeare.   He has been called the poet's poet ; he should
also be called the woman's poet, for the feminine element in his genius is its loftiest, deepest, most angelic
element.   The tenderness, the ethereal softness and
grace, the moral purity, the sentiment untainted by
sentimentality, which characterize his impersonations of
feminine excellence, show, too, that the poet's brain had
been fed from his heart, and that reverence for woman
was the instinct of his sensibility before it was con-
firmed by the insight of his imagination.

The inwardness of Spenser's genius, the constant
reference of his creative faculty to internal ideals rather
than to objective facts, has given his poem a special
character of remoteness. It is often objected to his
female characters that they are not sufficiently individ-

ualized, and are too far **removed** from ordinary life to awaken human sympathy. It is to be hoped **that the** latter **part of this** charge is not true; for a person who **can** have no sympathy with Una, and Belphœbe, and Florimel, and Amoret, can have no sympathy with the woman in women. But it must be conceded, that though Shakespeare, like Spenser, draws his women from ideal regions of existence, he has succeeded better in naturalizing them on the planet. The creations of both are characterized by remoteness; but Shakespeare's are *direct* perceptions of objects ideally *remote*, and strike us both by their naturalness and their distance from common nature; Spenser really sees the objects as distant, and sees them through a visionary **medium.** The strong-winged Shakespeare penetrates to **the region of** spiritual **facts which** he embodies; **Spenser surveys** them wonderingly from below. Shakespeare goes up; Spenser looks up; and our **poet** therefore lacks the great dramatist's "*familiar* grasp **of** things divine."

It remains to be said, that though Spenser's outward life was vexed with discontent, and fretted by his resentment of the indifference with which he supposed his claims were treated **by** the great and powerful, his poetry breathes the very soul of contentment and cheer. This cheer **has** no connection with mirth, either **in the** form of wit or humor, but springs from **his** perception

of an ideal of life, which has become a reality to his
heart and imagination. The Faery Queene proves that
the perception of the Beautiful can make the heart
more abidingly glad than the perception of the ludicrous. In the soul of this seer and singer, who shaped
the first vague dreams and unquiet aspirations of the
youth into beautiful forms to solace the man, there is a
serene depth of tender joy, ay, "a sober certainty of
waking bliss"; and, as he has not locked up in his own
breast this precious delight, but sent it in vital currents
through the marvels and moralities of The Faery
Queene to refresh the world, let no defects which criticism can discern hinder the reader from participating
in the deep satisfaction of that happy spirit and the
visionary glories of that celestialized imagination.

IN the present chapter we propose to speak of a **few** of Spenser's contemporaries and successors, **who** were rated as poets in their **own** generation, how- ever neglected they may be in ours. **We shall select** those who have some pretensions to originality **of** character as well as mind; and, though **we** shall not mention all who claim the attention of students **of** literary history, we fear we shall gain the gratitude **of** the reader for those omitted, rather than **for those** included, in the survey. Sins **of** omission are some- times exalted **by** circumstances into a high rank among the negative virtues.

Among the minor poets of this era were two imita- **tors of** Spenser,—Phineas and Giles Fletcher. **They were** cousins of Fletcher the dramatist, but with none of his wild blood **in** their veins, and none of his flashing creativeness in their souls, to give evidence of the rela- tionship. The Purple Island, a poem in twelve cantos, by Phineas, is a long allegorical description of **the body** and soul of man, perverse in design, melodious **in ver-** sification, occasionally felicitous in the personification of abstract qualities, but on the whole to be considered as an exercise of boundless ingenuity to produce insufferable tediousness. Not in the dissecting-room itself is anatomy less poetical than in the harmonious stanzas of The Purple Island. Giles, the brother of Phineas, was the more potent spirit of the two, but his power is often directed by a taste even more elaborately bad. His poem of Christ's Victory and Triumph, in parts almost sublime, in parts almost puerile, is a proof that imaginative fertility may exist in a mind with little imaginative grasp. Campbell, however, considers him a connecting link between Spenser and Milton.

Samuel Daniel, another poet of this period, was the son of a music-master, and was born in 1562. Fuller says of him, that " he carried, in his Christian and surname, two holy prophets, his monitors, so to qualify his raptures that he abhorred all profaneness." Amiable in character, gentle in disposition, and with a genius meditative rather than energetic, he appears to have possessed that combination of qualities which makes men personally pleasing if it does not make them permanently famous. He was patronized both by Elizabeth and James, was the friend of Shakespeare and Camden, and was highly esteemed by the most accomplished women of his time. A most voluminous writer in prose and verse, he was distinguished in both for the purity, simplicity, **and elegance of his** diction. Browne calls him "the well-languaged Daniel." But if he **avoided** the pedantry **and** quaintness which were too apt to viti-**ate the style of** the period, **and wrote** what might be called modern English, it has still been found **that mod-**ern Englishmen cannot be **coaxed** into reading what is so lucidly written. **His** longest work, a versified His-tory of the Civil **Wars,** dispassionate as a chronicle and unimpassioned as a poem, is now only read by those **critics** in whom the sense of duty is victorious over the disposition to doze. The best expressions of his pen-sive, tender, and thoughtful nature are his epistles and his sonnets. Among the epistles, that to the Countess **of** Cumberland is the best. It is a model for all **adula-**tory addresses to women; indeed, a masterpiece **of** subtile compliment; for it assumes in its object a sym-pathy with whatever is noblest in sentiment, and an understanding of whatever is most elevated in thought. **The** sonnets, first published in 1592, in his thirtieth year, record the strength and the disappointment of a youthful passion. The lady, whom he addresses under the name of Delia, refused him, it is said, for a wealth-ier lover, and the pang of this baffled affection made him wretched for years, and sent him

> "Haunting untrodden paths to wail apart."

Echo, — **he** tells us, while **he** was aiming **to overcome** the indifference of the maiden, —

> " Echo, daughter of the air,
>   Babbling guest of rocks and rills,
>   Knows the name of my fierce fair,
>   And sounds the accents of my ills."

Throughout the sonnets, the matchless perfection of this Delia is ever connected with her disdain of the poet who celebrates it : —

> " Fair is my love, and cruel as she 's fair;
>   Her brow shades frowns, although her eyes are sunny;
> Her smiles are lightning, though her pride despair;
>   And her disdains are gall, her favors honey.
> A modest maid, decked with a blush of honor,
>   Who treads along green paths of youth and love,
> The wonder of all eyes that gaze upon her,
>   Sacred on earth, designed a saint above."

This picture of the " modest maid, decked with a blush of honor," is exquisite ; but it is still a picture, and not a living presence. Shakespeare, touching the same beautiful object with his life-imparting imagination, suffuses at once the sense and soul with a feeling of the vital reality, when he describes the French princess as a " maiden rosed over with the virgin crimson of modesty."

The richest and most elaborately fanciful of these sonnets is that in which the poet calls upon his mistress to give back her perfections to the objects from which she derived them : —

" Restore thy tresses to the golden ore;
  Yield Cytherea's son those arcs of love;
Bequeath the heavens the stars that I adore;
  And to the orient do thy pearls remove.
Yield thy hand's pride unto the ivory white;
  To Arabian odors give thy breathing sweet;
Restore thy blush unto Aurora bright;
  To Thetis give the honor of thy feet.
Let Venus have thy graces, her resigned;
  And thy sweet voice give back unto the spheres;
But yet restore thy fierce and cruel mind
  To Hyrcan tigers and to ruthless bears;
Yield to the marble thy hard heart again;
  So shalt thou cease to plague and I to pain."

There is a fate in love. This man, who could not conquer the insensibility of one country girl, was the honored friend of the noblest and most celebrated woman of his age. Eventually, at the age of forty, he was married to a sister of John Florio, to whom his own sister, the Rosalind who jilted Spenser, is supposed to have been previously united. He died in retirement, in 1619, in his fifty-eighth year.

A more powerful and a more prolific poet than Daniel was Michael Drayton, who rhymed steadily for some forty years, and produced nearly a hundred thousand lines. The son of a butcher, and born about the year 1563, he early exhibited an innocent desire to be a poet, and his first request to his tutor at college was to make him one.　Like Daniel, he enjoyed the friendship and patronage of the noble favorers of learning and genius. His character seems to have been irreproachable.　Meres, in his Wit's Treasury, says of him, that among all sorts of people "he is held as a man of virtuous disposition, honest conversation, and well-governed carriage, which is almost miraculous among good wits in these declining and corrupt times, when there is nothing but roguery in villanous man, and when cheating and craftiness is counted the cleanest wit and soundest wisdom."　But the market-value, both of his poetry and virtue, was small, and he seems to have been always on bad terms with the booksellers.　His poems, we believe, were the first which arrived at second editions by the simple process of merely reprinting, with additions, the title-pages of the first, — a fact which is ominous of his bad success with the public.　The defect of his mind was not the lack of materials, but the lack of taste to select, and imagination to fuse, his materials.　His poem of The Barons' Wars is a metrical chronicle; his Poly-Olbion is an enormous piece of metrical topography, extending to thirty thousand twelve-syllabled lines.　In neither poem does he view his subject from an eminence, but doggedly follows the course of events and the succession of objects.　As a description of England, the Poly-Olbion is in general so accurate that it is quoted as authority by such antiquaries as Hearne and Wood and Nicholson. Campbell has felicitously touched its fatal defect in saying that Drayton "chained his poetry to the map." The only modern critic who seems to have followed all its wearisome details with loving enthusiasm is Charles Lamb, who speaks of Drayton as that "panegyrist of my native earth who has gone over her soil with the fidelity of a herald and the painful love of a son; who has not left a rivulet (so narrow that it may be stepped over) without honorable mention; and has animated hills and streams with life and passion above the dreams of old mythology." But, in spite of this warm commendation, the essential difficulty with the Poly-Olbion is, that, with all its merits, it is unreadable. The poetic feeling, the grace, the freshness, the pure, bright, and vigorous diction, which characterize it, appear to more advantage in the poet's minor pieces, where his subjects are less unwieldy, and the vivacity of his fancy makes us forget his lack of high imagination. His fairy poem of Nymphidia, for instance, is one of the most deliciously fanciful creations in the language; and many of his smaller pieces have the point and sparkle of Carew's and Suckling's. In his longer poems, too, we frequently light upon passages as perfect of their kind as this description of Queen Isabella's hand: —

> " She laid her fingers on his manly cheek,
>   The God's pure sceptres and the darts of love,
>   That with their touch might make a tiger meek,
>   Or might great Atlas from his seat remove,
>   So white, so soft, so delicate, so sleek,
>   As she had worn a lily for a glove."

A more popular poet than Daniel, or Drayton, or the Fletchers, was William Warner, an attorney of the Court of Common Pleas, who was born about the year 1558, and who died in 1609. His Albion's England, a poem of some ten thousand verses, was published in 1586, ran through six editions in sixteen years, and died out of the memory of mankind with the last, in 1612. After having conscientiously waded through immense masses of uninteresting rhyme, as we have been compelled to do in the preparation of these notices, we confess, with a not unmalicious exultation, that we know Warner's poem only by description and extracts. Albion is an ancient name for Great Britain; and Albion's England is a metrical history — " not barren," in the author's own words, " of inventive intermixtures " — of the southern portion of the island, beginning at the deluge, and ending with the reign of James I. As James might have said, " After me the deluge," Warner's poem may be considered as ending in some such catastrophe as that with which it begins. The merit of Warner is that of a story-teller, and he reached classes

of readers to whom Spenser was hardly known by
name. The work is a strange mixture of comic and
tragic fact and fable, exceedingly gross in parts,
with little power of imagination or grace of language,
but possessing the great popular excellence of describing persons and incidents in the fewest and simplest words. The best story is that of Argentile and
Curan, and it is told as briefly as though it were
intended for transmission by telegraph at the cost of
a dollar a word. Warner has some occasional touches
of nature and pathos which almost rival the old ballads
for directness and intensity of feeling. The most remarkable of these, condensed in two of his long four-
teen-syllabled lines, is worth all the rest of his poems.
It occurs in his description of Queen Eleanor striking
the Fair Rosamond.

> " With that she dashed her on the lips, so dyéd double red:
> Hard was the heart that gave the blow, soft were those lips that
> bled."

It is a rapid transition from Warner, the poet of
the populace, to Donne, the poet of the metaphysicians,
but the range of the Elizabethan literature is full
of contrasts. In the words of the satirist, Donne is a
poet

> " Whose muse on dromedary trots,
> Wreathes iron pokers into true-love-knots;

> Rhyme's sturdy cripple, fancy's maze and clew,
> Wit's forge and fire-blast, meaning's press and screw.
>
> .   .   .   .   .
>
> See lewdness with theology combined, —
> A cynic and a sycophantic mind,
> A fancy shared party per pale between
> Death's-heads and skeletons and Aretine! —
> Not his peculiar defect and crime,
> But the true current mintage of the time.
> Such were the established signs and tokens given
> To mark a loyal churchman, sound and even,
> Free from papistic and fanatic leaven."

John Donne, the heterogeneous qualities of whose intellect and character are thus maliciously sketched, was one of the strangest of versifiers, sermonizers, and men. He was the son of a wealthy London merchant, and was born in 1573. One of those youthful prodigies who have an appetite for learning as other boys have for cakes and plums, he was, at the age of eleven, sufficiently advanced in his studies to enter the University of Oxford, where he remained three years. He was then transferred to Cambridge. His classical and mathematical education being thus completed, he, at the age of seventeen, was admitted into Lincoln's Inn to study the law. His relations being Roman Catholics, he abandoned the law at the age of nineteen, in order to make an elaborate examination of the points in dispute between the Romanists and the Reformers. Having in a **year's** time exhausted this controversy, he spent several years in travelling in Italy and Spain. On his return to England he became chief secretary of Lord Chancellor Ellesmere, — and held the office five years. **It was** probably during **the period** between his twentieth and thirtieth years that most of his secular poetry was **written,** and that his nature **took** its decided eccentric **twist. An** insatiable **intellectual** curiosity seems, up to this time, to have been his leading characteristic; and as this led him **to** all kinds of literature for mental nutriment, his faculties, in their formation, were inlaid with the oddest varieties of opinions and crotchets. With vast learning, with a subtile and penetrating intellect, with a fancy singularly fruitful and ingenious, he still contrived to disconnect, more **or less,** his learning from what was worth learning, his intellect from what was reasonable, his fancy from what was beautiful. His poems, or rather his metrical problems, **are** obscure in thought, rugged in versification, and full **of** conceits which are intended to surprise rather than to please; but they still exhibit a power of intellect, both analytical and analogical, competent at once to separate the minutest and connect the remotest ideas. This power, while it might not have given his poems grace, sweetness, freshness, and melody, would still, if properly directed, have made them valuable for their thoughts;

but in the case of Donne it is perverted to the production of what is *bizarre* or unnatural, and his muse is thus as hostile to use as to beauty. The intention is, not to idealize what is true, but to display the writer's skill and wit in giving a show of reason to what is false. The effect of this on the moral character of Donne was pernicious. A subtile intellectual scepticism, which weakened will, divorced thought from action and literature from life, and made existence a puzzle and a dream, resulted from this perversion of his intellect. He found that he could wittily justify what was vicious as well as what was unnatural ; and his amatory poems, accordingly, are characterized by a cold, hard, labored, intellectualized sensuality, worse than the worst impurity of his contemporaries, because it has no excuse of passion for its violations of decency.

But now happened an event which proved how little the talents and accomplishments of this voluptuary of intellectual conceits were competent to serve him in a grapple with the realities of life. Lady Ellesmere had a niece, the daughter of Sir George Moore, with whom Donne fell in love ; and as, according to Izaak Walton, his behavior, when it would entice, had " a strange kind of elegant, irresistible art," he induced her to consent to a private marriage, without the knowledge of her father. Izaak accounts for this on the perhaps tenable ground, "that love is a flattering mischief, that hath denied aged and wise men a foresight of those evils that too often prove **to** be children of that blind father; a passion that carries us to commit errors with as much ease as whirlwinds move feathers, and be-**gets** in us an unwearied industry to the attainment of what we desire." But Sir George Moore, the father of the lady, an arrogant, avaricious, and passionate **brute,** was so enraged at the match, that he did not rest until he had induced Lord Ellesmere to dismiss Donne from his service, and until **he** had placed his son-in-law in prison. Although Sir George, compelled to submit to what was inevitable, became at last reconciled to Donne, he refused to contribute anything towards his daughter's maintenance. As Donne's **own** fortune had been by this time all expended in travel, books, and other intellectual dissipations, and as he had been deprived of his office, he was now stripped of everything but his power **of** framing conceits ; and accordingly, in a dismal letter to his wife, recounting his miseries, he has nothing but this quibble to support her under affliction: "John Donne, **Ann** Donne, Undone." A charitable kinsman of the Ellesmeres, however, Sir Francis Wolly, seeing the helplessness of this man of brain, took him and his wife into his own house. Here they resided until the death of their benefactor, Donne occupying his time in studying the civil and canon laws, and probably also in composing his Thesis on Self-Homicide, — a work in which his ingenuity is thought to have devised some excuses for suicide, but the reading of which, according to Hallam, would induce no man to kill himself unless he were threatened with another volume.

During his residence with Sir Francis Wolly, Donne, whose acquirements in theology were immense, was offered a benefice by Dr. Morton, then Dean of Gloucester; but he declined to enter the Church, from a feeling of spiritual unfitness. It is probable that his habits of intellectual self-indulgence, while they really weakened his conscience, made it morbidly acute. He would not adopt the profession of law or divinity for a subsistence, though he was willing to depend for subsistence on the charity of others. Izaak Walton praises his humility; but Donne's humility was only another name for indisposition to practical labor, — a humility which makes self-depreciation an excuse for moral laziness, and shrinks as nervously from duty as from pride. Both law and divinity, therefore, he continued to make the luxuries of his existence.

In good time this selfish intellectuality resulted in that worst of intellectual diseases, mental disgust. After the death of his patron, his father-in-law allowed him eighty pounds a year to support his family. Sickness

and affliction and comparative poverty came to wake
him from his **dream** and reveal him **to** himself. In some
affecting **letters,** which have been preserved, **he** moans
over his moral inefficiency, and **confesses to an** "over-
earnest desire for the next life," to **escape from the per-**
plexities of this. " I grow older," **he** says, " and not
better ; my strength diminisheth, **and** my load grows
heavier ; **and yet I would** fain be or **do** something ; but
that I cannot tell **what, is no wonder in** this time **of** my
sadness ; for to choose is **to do ;** but **to** be no part of any
body is as to be nothing : and so **I** am, and shall so
judge myself, unless I could be so incorporated into a
part of the world as by business to contribute some sus-
tenation to the whole. This I made **account ; I began**
early, when I undertook the **study of our laws ; but was**
diverted by leaving that, **and embracing** the **worst**
voluptuousness, **an** hydroptic immoderate desire **of hu-**
man learning and languages. . . . . . **Now I** am become
so little, or such a nothing, that I am not a subject good
enough for one of my own letters. . . . . . I am rather a
sickness **or** disease **of** the world than any part of it, and
therefore neither **love it** nor life." And he closes with
the words, " Your poor friend and God's poor patient,
John Donne."

And this was the mental state **to** which Donne was
reduced by thirty years of incessant study, — of study

that sought only the gratification of intellectual caprice
and of intellectual curiosity, — of study without a practical object. From this wretched mood of self-disgust
and disgust with existence, this fret of thought at the
impotence of will, we may date Donne's gradual eman-
cipation from his besetting sins ; for life, at such a point
of spiritual experience, is only possible under the form
of a new life. His theological studies and meditations
were now probably directed more to the building-up of
character, and less to the pandering to his gluttonous
intellectuality. His recovery was a work of years ; and
it is doubtful if he would ever have chosen a profession,
if King James, delighted with his views regarding the
questions of supremacy and allegiance, and amazed at
his opulence in what was then called learning, had not
insisted on his entering the Church. After much hesi-
tation and long preparation, Donne yielded to the royal
command. He was successively made Chaplain in Ordinary, Lecturer at Lincoln's Inn, and Dean of St.
Paul's, was soon recognized as one of the ablest and
most eloquent preachers of his time, and impressed those
who sat under his ministrations, not merely with admiration for his genius, but with reverence for his holy life
and almost ascetic self-denial. The profession he had
adopted with so much self-distrust he came to love with
such fervor that his expressed wish was, to die in the

pulpit, or in consequence of **his** labors therein. **This** last wish **was** granted in 1631, in his fifty-eighth **year;** "and that body," says Walton with quaint pathos, "which once was **a** temple of **the** Holy Ghost" now became "but a small quantity of Christian dust."

Donne's published sermons **are in form nearly as** grotesque as his **poems,** though **they** are characterized **by** profounder qualities of heart and mind. **It was his** misfortune to know thoroughly the works of fourteen hundred writers, most of them necessarily worthless; · and he could not help displaying his erudition in his discourses. **Of** what is now called taste he was **ab-** solutely destitute. His sermons are a curious mosaic of quaintness, quotation, wisdom, puerility, subtilty, and ecstasy. The pedant and the seer possess him **by turns,** and in reading no other divine are our transitions from yawning to rapture so swift and unexpected. He has passages of transcendent merit, passages which evince a spiritual vision so piercing, and a feeling **of** divine things so intense, that for the time we seem to be com- muning with a religious genius of the most exalted and exalting order; but soon he involves us in a maze of quotations and references, and our minds are hustled by what Hallam calls "the rabble of bad authors" that this saint and sage **has** always at his skirts, even when **he** ascends to the highest heaven of contemplation.

Doubtless what displeases this age added to his reputation in his own. Donne was more pedantic than his clerical contemporaries only because he had more of that thought-suffocating learning which all of them regarded with irrational respect. One of the signs of Bacon's superiority to his age was the cool audacity with which he assailed sophists, simpletons, bigots, and liars, even though they wrote in Latin and Greek.

A poet as intellectual as Donne, but whose intelligence was united to more manliness and efficiency, was Sir John Davies. He was born in 1570, and was educated for the law. The first we hear of him, after he had been called to the bar, was his expulsion from the Society of the Middle Temple, for quarrelling with one Richard Martin and giving him a sound beating. This was in 1598. The next recorded fact of his biography was the publication, a year afterwards, of his poem on the Immortality of the Soul. A man who thus combined so much pugilistic with so much philosophic power could not be long kept down in a country so full of fight and thought as England. He was soon restored to his profession, won the esteem both of Elizabeth and James, held high offices in Ireland, and in 1626 was appointed Chief Justice of England, but died of apoplexy before he was sworn in.

The two works on which his fame as a poet rests are

on the widely different themes of Dancing, and the Immortality of **the** Soul. The first is in the form of **a** dialogue between Penelope and one of her wooers, and most melodiously expresses "the antiquity and excellence of dancing." Only in the Elizabethan age could such a great effort of intellect, learning, and fancy have arisen from the trifling incident of asking a lady to dance. It was left unfinished ; and, indeed, as it is the object of the wooer to prove to Penelope that dancing is the law of nature and life, the poem could only be brought to an end by the exhaustion of the writer's ingenuity in devising subtile analogies for the wooer and answers as subtile from Penelope, who aids

> " The music of her tongue
> With the sweet speech of her alluring eyes."

To think logically from his premises was the necessity of Davies's mind. In the poem on Dancing the premises are fanciful ; in the poem on the Immortality of the Soul the premises are real ; but the reasoning in both is equally exact. It is usual among critics, even such critics as Hallam and Campbell, to decide that the imaginative power of the poem on the Immortality of the Soul consists in the illustration of the arguments rather than in the perception of the premises. But the truth would seem to be that the author exhibits his imagination **more** in his insight than in his imagery.

The poetic excellence of the work comes from the power of clear, steady beholding of spiritual facts with the spiritual eye, — of beholding them so clearly that the task of stating, illustrating, and reasoning from them is performed with masterly ease. In truth, the great writers of the time *believed* in the soul's immortality, because they were conscious of having souls ; the height of their thinking was due to the fact that the soul was always in the premises; and thought, with them, included imaginative vision as well as dialectic skill. From a lower order of minds than Shakespeare, Hooker, and Bacon, than Chapman, Sidney, and Davies, proceed the theories of materialism, for no thinking *from* the soul can deny the soul's *existence*. It is curious to observe the advantage which Davies holds over his materialistic opponents, through the circumstance that, while his logical understanding is as well furnished as theirs, it reposes on central ideas and deep experiences which they either want or ignore. No adequate idea of the general gravity and grandeur of his thinking can be conveyed by short extracts ; yet, opening the poem at the fourth section, devoted to the demonstration that the soul is a spirit, we will quote a few of his resounding quatrains in illustration of his manner : —

> " For she all natures under heaven doth pass,
>   Being like those spirits which God's face do see,

Or like /itusolf, whose image once she was,
    Though now, alas! she scarce his shadow be.

Were she a body, how could she remain
    Within the body which is less than she?
Or how could she the world's great shape **contain,**
    And in our narrow breasts containéd be?

" All bodies are confined within some place,
    But she **all** place within herself confines;
All bodies have their measure and their space;
    But who can draw the soul's dimensive lines? "

The next poet we shall mention was a link of con
nection between the age of Elizabeth and Cromwell;
a contemporary equally of Shakespeare and Milton;
a man whose first work was published ten years **before**
Shakespeare had produced his greatest tragedies, **and**
who, later in life, defended Episcopacy against Milton.
We refer of course to Joseph **Hall.** He was born in
1574, was educated at Cambridge, and in 1597, at the
age of twenty-three, published his satires. Originally
intended for **the** Church, he was now presented with a
living by Sir Robert Drury, who was also a munificent
patron of Donne. He rose gradually to preferment,
was made Bishop of Exeter in 1627, and translated to
the see of Norwich in 1641. In 1643 he was deprived
of his place and revenue by the Parliamentary Com-
mittee **of** Sequestration, and died in 1656, in his eighty-

second year. As a churchman, he was in favor of moderate measures, and he had the rare good fortune to oppose Archbishop Laud, and to suffer under Oliver Cromwell.

As a satirist, if we reject the claim of Gascoigne to precedence, he was the earliest that English literature can boast. In his own words,

> "I first adventure: follow me who list,
> And be the second English satirist."

He had two qualifications for his chosen task, — penetrating observation and unshrinking courage. The follies and vices, the manners, prejudices, delusions, and crimes of his time, form the materials of his satires; and these he lashes, or laughs at, according as the subject-matter provokes his indignation or his contempt. "Sith," he says in his Preface, " faults loathe nothing more than the light, and men love nothing more than their faults," it follows that, " what with the nature of the faults and the faults of the persons," it is impossible "that so violent an appeachment should be quietly brooked." But to those who are offended he vouchsafes but this curt and cutting defence of his plain-speaking: " Art thou guilty? Complain not, thou art not wronged. Art thou guiltless? Complain not, thou art not touched." These satires, however, striking as they are for their compactness of language and vigor of characterization, convey but an inadequate idea of the depth, devoutness, and largeness **of** soul displayed in Hall's theological writings. His Meditations, especially, **have** been read by thousands who never heard **of** him **as a tart** and caustic wit. But the one characteristic **of** sententiousness marks equally the sarcasm of the youthful satirist and the raptures of the aged saint.

The next writer we shall consider, Sir Henry Wotton, possessed one of the most accomplished and enlightened minds of the age, though, unhappily for us, he has left **few** records of it in literature. He was born in 1568, educated at Oxford, and, leaving the university in his twenty-second year, **passed** nine years in travelling **in** Germany **and Italy. On his** return his conversation showed such wit and information that it was said **to be** " **one of** the delights of mankind." **He entered the** service of the Earl **of** Essex, and, on the discovery **of the** Earl's treason, prudently escaped to the Continent. While in Italy he rendered **a** great service to **the** Scottish King; and James, on his accession to the English throne, knighted him, and sent him as ambassador to Venice. He remained abroad over twenty years. On his return he was made provost of Eton College. He died in 1639, in his seventy-first year.

Wotton is one of the few Englishmen who have suc-

ceeded in divesting themselves of English prejudices
without at the same time divesting themselves of English virtues. He was a man of the world of the kind
described by Bacon, — a man " whose heart was not
cut off from other men's lands, **but a** continent that
joined to them."   One of the ablest and most sagacious
diplomatists that England ever sent abroad to match
Italian craft with Saxon sense, he was at the same time
chivalrous, loyal, and true. Though the author of the
satirical definition of an ambassador, as " an honest
man sent to lie abroad for the commonwealth," his own
course **was the** opposite of falsehood. Indeed, he laid
this down as an infallible aphorism to guide an English
ambassador, that he should always tell the truth : first,
because he will secure himself if called to account; second, because he will never be believed, and he will thus
" put his adversaries, who will ever hunt counter, at a
loss." **One of** his many accomplishments was the art
of saying pointed things in pithy language. At Rome,
a priest asked him, " Where was your religion be-
fore Luther ? " To which Wotton answered, " My
religion was to **be** found then where yours is not to
be found now, — in the written Word of God." **He**
then put to the priest this question: " Do you be-
lieve all those many thousands **of** poor Christians
were damned, that were excommunicated because the

Pope and the Duke of Venice could not agree about their temporal power, — even those poor Christians that knew not why they quarrelled? Speak your conscience." The priest's reply was, " Monsieur, excuse me." Wotton's own Protestantism, however, did not consist, like that of too many others **of his** time and of ours, in hating Romanists. He was once asked whether a papist may be saved. His answer was: " You may be saved without knowing that. Look to yourself." The spirit of this reply is of the inmost essence of toleration.

Cowley, in his elegy on Wotton, has touched wittily on those felicities of his nature and culture which made him so admired by his contemporaries : —

> " What shall we say ? since silent now is he,
>   Who when he spoke, all things would silent be;
>   Who had so many languages in store,
>   That only fame shall speak of him in more;
>   Whom England now no more returned must see:
>   He 's gone to heaven on his fourth embassy.
>   .   .   .   .
>   So well he understood the most and best
>   Of tongues — that Babel sent into the west, —
>   Spoke them so truly, that he had, you 'd swear,
>   Not only lived but been born everywhere.
>   .   .   .   .
>   Nor ought the language of that man be less,
>   Who in his breast had all things to express."

As a poet Sir Henry Wotton is universally known by one exquisite little poem, The Character of a Happy Life, which is in all hymn-books. The general drift of his poetry is, to expose the hollowness of all the objects to which as a statesman and courtier the greater portion of his own life was devoted. His verses are texts for discourses, uniting economy of words with fulness of thought and sentiment. His celebrated epitaph on a married couple is condensed to the point of converting feeling into wit.

> " He first deceased.   She, for a little, tried
> To do without him, liked it not, and died."

In one of his hymns he has this startling image : —

> " No hallowed oils, no gums I need,
> No new-born drams of purging fire;
> One rosy drop from David's seed
> Was worlds of seas to quench their ire."

Excellent, however, of its kind as Wotton's poetry is, it is not equal to that living poem, his life. He was one of those men who are not so much makers of poems as subjects for poems.

The last poet of whom we shall speak, George Herbert, was one in whom the quaintness of the time found its most fantastic embodiment. He began life as a courtier; and on the disappointment of his hopes, or on his conviction of the vanity of **his** ambitions, he suddenly changed his whole course **of** thought and life, became a clergyman, **and is** known **to** posterity only as "holy George Herbert." His poetry is the *bizarre* expression **of a** deeply religious and intensely thoughtful nature, sincere at heart, but strange, far-fetched, **and** serenely crotchety in utterance. Nothing can be more frigid **than** the conceits in which he clothes the great majority **of his pious** ejaculations and heavenly ecstasies. Yet every reader feels that his fancy, quaint as it often is, **is** a part of the organism of his character; and that his quaintness, his uncouth metaphors and comparisons, his squalid phraseology, his holy charades and pious riddles, **his** inspirations crystallized into ingenuities, **and his** general disposition to **represent the divine through the** exterior guise of **the** odd, are vitally connected with that essential beauty and sweetness of soul which give his poems their wild flavor and fragrance. Amateurs in sanctity, and men of fine religious taste, will tell you that genuine emotion can never find an outlet in such **an** elaborately fantastic form; **and** the proposition, according, as it does, with the rules of Blair and Kames and Whately, commands your immediate assent; but still you feel that genuine emotion is there, and, if you watch sharply, **you** will find that Taste, entering holy **George Herbert's "Temple,"** after **a** preliminary sniff

of imbecile contempt, somehow slinks away abashed
after the first verse at the " Church-porch : "

> " Thou whose sweet youth and early hopes enhance
>   Thy rate and price, and mark thee for a treasure,
>   Hearken unto a verser, who may chance
>   Rhyme thee to good, and make a bait of pleasure:
>   A verse may find him whom a sermon flies,
>   And turn delight into a sacrifice."

And that fine gentleman, Taste, having relieved us
of his sweetly-scented presence, redolent with the "balm
of a thousand flowers," — let us, in closing, quote one
of the profoundest utterances of the Elizabethan age,
George Herbert's lines on Man : —

> " Man is all symmetrie,
>   Full of proportions, one limbe to another,
>   And all to all the world besides:
>   Each part may call the farthest, brother;
>   For head with foot hath private amitie,
>   And both with moon and tides.

> " Nothing hath got so farre
>   But man hath caught and kept it, as his prey.
>   His eyes dismount the highest starre:
>   He is in little all the sphere.
>   Herbs gladly cure our flesh, because that they
>   Finde their acquaintance there.

.   .   .   .

" The starres have us to bed;
Night draws the curtain, which the sun withdraws:
  Musick **and** light attend our head.
  All things unto our *flesh* are kinde
In their *descent* and *being;* to our minde
  In their *ascent* and *cause.*

  .   .   •   •

" More servants wait on Man
Than he 'll take notice of; in every path
  He treads down that which doth befriend him
  When sickness makes him pale and wan.
O mightie love!   Man is one world, and hath
  Another to attend him.

" Since then, my God, thou hast
So brave a Palace built; O dwell in it,
  That it may dwell with thee at last!
  Till then afford us **so much wit,**
That as the world serves us we may serve thee,
  And both thy servants be."

11 *

THE characteristic of a good prose style is, that, while it mirrors or embodies the mind that uses it, it also gives pleasure in itself. The quality which decides on its fulfilment of these conditions is commonly called taste.

Though taste is properly under law, and should, if pressed, give reasons for its decisions, many of its most authoritative judgments come directly from its instinct or insight, without regard to rules. Indeed, a fine feeling of the beauty, melody, fitness, and vitality of words is often wanting in men who are dexterous in the application of the principles of style; and some of the most philosophic treatises on æsthetics betray a lack of that deep internal sense which directly perceives the objects and qualities whose validity it is the office of the understanding laboriously to demonstrate.

But whether we judge of style by our perceptions or by principles, we all feel that there is a distinction between persons who write books and writers whose books belong to literature. There is something in the mere wording of a description of **a** triviality of dress or manner, by Addison or Steele, which gives greater mental delight than the description of a campaign or a revolution **by Alison.** The principle that style is thus a vital element in the expression of thought and emotion, that it **not** only measures the quality and quantity of the mind it conveys, but has a charm in itself, makes the task of an historian of literature less difficult than it **at first** appears. **Among the** prose-writers of the age of Elizabeth we do not, accordingly, include all who wrote in prose, but those **in** whom prose composition was laboring to fulfil the conditions of art. In many cases this endeavor resulted in the substitution of artifice for **art;** and the bond which connects the invisible thought with the visible **word, and** through which the word is **sur**charged with the life of the thought, being thus severed, **the** effect was to produce a factitious dignity, sweetness, and elegance by mental sleight **of hand and** tricks of modulation and antithesis.

In one of the earliest prose-writers of the reign of Elizabeth, John Lyly, we perceive how easily the **de**mand in the cultivated classes for what is fine in diction may degenerate into admiration of what is superfine, **how** elegant imbecility may pass itself off for elegance, and how hypocrisy and grimace may become a fashion in that high society which constitutes itself the arbiter of taste. Lyly, a scholar of some beauty, and more ingenuity, of fancy, was especially fitted to corrupt a language whose rude masculine vigor was beginning to be softened into harmony and elegance; for he was one of those effeminate spirits whose felicity it is to be born affected, and who can violate general nature without doing injustice to their own. The court of Elizabeth, full of highly educated men and women, was greatly pleased with the fopperies of diction and sentiment, the dainty verbal confectionery, of his so-called classic plays, and seems to have been entirely carried away by his prose romance of Euphues and his England, first published in 1579. In this persons of fashion might congratulate themselves that they could find a language which was not spoken by the vulgar. The nation, Sir Henry Blunt tells us, was in debt to him for a new English which he taught it; "all our ladies were his scholars"; and that beauty in court was disregarded "who could not parley Euphuism, that is to say, who was unable to converse in that pure and reformed English." Those who have studied the jargon of Holofernes in Shakespeare's Love's Labor's Lost, of Fastidious Brisk in Ben Jonson's Every Man out of his Humour, and, later still, of Sir Piercie Shafton, in Scott's novel of The Monastery, can form some idea of this "pure and reformed English," the peculiarities

of which have been happily characterized to consist in
"pedantic and far-fetched allusion, elaborate indirect-
ness, **a** cloying smoothness and monotony of diction,"
and great fertility in " alliteration and punning."   Even
when Lyly seems really sweet, elegant, and eloquent,
he evinces a natural suspicion of the graces of nature,
and contrives to divorce his rhetoric from all sincerity
of utterance.   There is something pretty and puerile
even in his expression of heroism; and to say a good
thing in a way it ought not to be said was to realize his
highest idea **of** art.   His attitude towards what was
natural had a touch of that condescending commisera-
tion which Colman's perfumed, embroidered, and **man-
nered** coxcomb extended to the blooming country **girl**
he stooped **to** admire : " Ah, my dear ! Nature **is very**
well, for she made you ; but then Nature could not
have made me ! "

This infection of the superfine in composition was felt
even by writers for the multitude ; and in the romances
of Greene and Lodge we have euphuism as an affectation of an affectation.   Even their habits of vulgar
dissipation could not altogether keep them loyal to the
comparative purity of the vulgar language.   The fashion
subtly affected even the style of Sidney, conscious as he
was of its more obvious fooleries ; and to this day every
man who has anything of the coxcomb in his brain, who

desires a dress for his thought more splendid than his thought, slides unconsciously into euphuism.

The name of Sir Philip Sidney stands in the English imagination for more than his writings, more than his actions, more than his character, — for more, we had almost said, than the qualities of his soul. The English race, compound of Saxon and Norman, has been fertile in great generals, great statesmen, great poets, great heroes, saints, and martyrs, but it has not been fertile in great gentlemen ; and Mr. Bull, plethoric with power but scant in courtesy, recognizes, with mingled feelings of surprise and delight, his great ornamental production in Sidney. He does not read the Sonnets or the Arcadia of his cherished darling ; he long left to an accomplished American lady the grateful task of writing an adequate biography of the phenomenon ; but he gazes with a certain pathetic wonder on the one renowned gentleman of his illustrious house, speculates curiously how he came into the family, and would perhaps rather part with Shakespeare and Milton, with Bacon and Locke, with Burleigh and Somers, with Marlborough and Wellington, with Latimer and Ridley, than with this chivalrous youth, whose "high-erected thoughts" were "seated in a heart of courtesy." It is not for superior moral or mental qualities that he especially prizes his favorite, for he has had children who have exceeded Sidney in both; but he feels that in Sidney **alone has** equal genius and goodness been expressed in *behavior*.

Sidney was born on the 29th of November, 1554. His father was Sir Henry Sidney, a statesman of ability and integrity. His mother was Mary, sister of Robert Dudley, afterwards Earl of Leicester. No pains were spared in the harmonious development of **his** powers, physical, mental, and moral; and his instructors were fortunate in a pupil blessed, not only with the love of knowledge, but with the love of that virtue which he considered the proper end of knowledge. He was intended for public life; and, leaving the university at the age of seventeen, he was shortly after sent abroad **to** study the languages, observe the manners, and mingle in the society of the Continent. He went nowhere without winning the hearts of those with whom he associated. Scholars, philosophers, artists, and men of letters, all were charmed with the ingenuous and high-spirited English youth, who visited foreign countries, not like the majority of his young countrymen, to partake of their dissipations and become initiated in their vices, but to fill and enlarge his understanding, and ennoble his soul. Hubert Languet, a scholar of whom **it is** recorded "that he lived as the best of men should **die,"** was especially captivated by Philip, became through

life his adviser and friend, and said, "That day on which
I first beheld him with my eyes shone propitious to
me!"

After about three years' absence Sidney returned to
England variously accomplished almost beyond any man
of his years; brave, honorable, and just; ambitious of
political, of military, of literary distinction, and having
powerful connections, competent, it might be supposed,
to aid him in any public career on which his energies
should be concentrated. But his very perfections seem
to have stood in the way of his advancement. Such a
combination of the scholar, the poet, and the knight-
errant, one so full of learning, of lofty imagination, of
chivalrous sentiment, was too precious as a courtier to
be employed as a man of affairs; and Elizabeth admired, petted, praised, but hesitated to employ him.
So fine an ornament of the nation could not be spared
for its defence. Even his uncle Leicester, all-powerful
as he seemed, failed in his attempts to aid the kinsman
who was perhaps the only man that could rouse in his
dark and scheming soul the feeling of affection. Sidney, who did not lack the knowledge — we had almost
said the conceit — of his own merits, and whose temper
was naturally impetuous, was far from being contented
with the lot which was to make him the "mirror of
courtesy," the observed and loved of all beholders, the

Beau Brummel of the Age of Elizabeth, but which was to shut him out from the nobler ambitions of his manly and ardent nature, and prevent his taking that part which, both **as a** Protestant and as a patriot, he ached to perform in the stirring contests and enterprises of the time. Still, he submitted and waited; and the result is, that the incidents of the career of this man, born a hero and educated a statesman, were ludicrously disproportioned to his own expectations and to his fame. In **1576** he was sent on an ornamental embassy to the Emperor of Germany. Soon after his return he successfully vindicated his father, who was Governor of Ireland, from some aspersions which had excited the anger of Elizabeth, and threatened his father's secretary, whom he suspected of opening his own letters to Sir Henry, that he would **thrust** his dagger into him if the treachery was repeated; "and trust to it," he adds, "I speak it in earnest." **He** wrote a bold letter to the Queen, against her projected matrimonial alliance with the little French duke, on whose villanous person, and still more villanous soul, this "imperial votaress," so long walking the earth

"In maiden meditation, fancy-free,"

had pretended to fix her "virgin" affections. He was shortly after, while playing at tennis, called a puppy by

the Earl of Oxford ; and it is a curious illustration of
the aristocratic temper of the times, that our Philip,
who saw no reasons to prevent him from thrusting his
dagger, without heeding the usual forms of the duel,
into the suspected heart of his father's secretary, could
not force this haughty and insolent Earl to accept his
challenge ; and the Queen put an end to the quarrel by
informing him that there was a great difference in degree between earls and private gentlemen, and that
princes were bound to support the nobility, and to insist
on their being treated with proper respect.

Wearied with court life, he now retired to Wilton,
the seat of his famous sister, the Countess of Pembroke, and there embodied in his Arcadia the thoughts,
sentiments, and aspirations he could not realize in
practice. Campbell has said that Sidney's life " was
poetry expressed in action "; but up to this time it had
been poetry expressed in character, and denied an outlet in action. It now found an outlet in literature.
From day to day he wrote under the eye of his beloved
sister, with no thought of publication, page after page of
this goodly folio. The form of the Arcadia, it must be
confessed, is somewhat fantastic, and the story tedious ;
but the work is still so sound at the core, so pure, strong,
and vital in the soul that animates it, and so much inward freshness and beauty are revealed the moment we

pierce its outward crust of affectation, that no changes in
the fashions of literature have ever been able to dislodge
it from its eminence of place. There we may still learn
the sweet lore of friendship and love ; there we may
still feed the heart's hunger, equally for scenes of pastoral innocence and heroic daring. **A ray of**

" The light that never was on sea or land "

gleams here and there over its descriptions, and **pro-**
claims the poet. The style of the book, in its good elements, was the best prose style which had, as yet, appeared in English literature, — vigorous, harmonious,
figurative, and condensed. In the characterizations of
feminine **beauty and** excellence Spenser **and Shake-**
speare are anticipated, if not sometimes rivalled. But
all these merits are apt to be lost on the modern reader,
owing to the fact that, though Sidney's thoughts were
noble and his feelings genuine, his fancy was artificial,
and incessantly labored to lift his rhetoric on stilts. It
will not trust Nature in her " homely russet brown," but
bedizens her in court trappings, belaces and embroiders
her, is sceptical of everything in sentiment and passion
which is easily great, and sometimes so elaborates all life
out of expression, that language is converted from the
temple of thought into its stately mausoleum. It cannot,
we fear, be doubted that **Sidney's court life had made**

him a little affected and conceited on the surface of his fine nature, if not in its substance. The Arcadia is **rich** in imagery, but in the same sentence we often find images that glitter like dew-drops, followed by images that glitter like icicles; and there is every evidence that to his taste the icicles were finer than the dew-drops.

It may not here be out of place to say, that, though we commonly think of Sidney as beautiful in face no less than in behavior, he was not in fact a comely gentleman. **Ben** Jonson told Drummond that he " was no pleasant man in countenance, his face being spoiled with pimples, **of high blood,** and long."

In 1581 we find Sidney in Parliament. Shortly after, he wrote his Defence of Poesy, in which, assuming that the object of knowledge is right action, he attempted **to** prove the superiority of poetry to all other branches of knowledge, on the ground that, while the other branches merely coldly pointed the way to virtue, poetry enticed, animated, inspired the soul to pursue it. Fine as this defence of poetry is, the best defence of poetry is to write that which **is** good. In 1583 he was married to the daughter of Sir Francis Walsingham. As his whole heart and imagination were at this time absorbed by the Stella of his sonnets, the beautiful Penelope Devereux, **sister of the** Earl of Essex, and **as** his passion does not **appear to** have abated after her marriage with Lord

Rich, Sidney must be considered to have failed in love as in ambition, marrying the woman he respected, and losing the woman he adored. And it is curious that the woman he did marry, soon after his death, married the Earl of Essex, brother of the woman he **so** much desired to marry.

In 1585 the Queen, having decided to **assist the** United Provinces, in their war against Philip of Spain, with an English army, under the command of Leicester, gratified Sidney's long thirst for honorable action by appointing him Governor of Flushing. In this post, and as general of cavalry, he did all that valor and sagacity could do to repair the blunders and mischiefs **which** resulted from the cowardice, arrogance, knavery, **and** military impotence of Leicester. On the **22d of Sep**-tember, 1586, in a desperate engagement **near** Zutphen, he was dangerously wounded in attempting to **rescue a** friend hemmed in by the enemy; and as he **was** carried bleeding from the field, he performed the crowning act of his life. The cup **of** water, which his lips ached to touch, but which he passed to the dying soldier with the words, "Thy necessity is greater than mine,"—this beautiful Deed, worth a thousand Defences **of** Poetry, will consecrate his memory in the hearts of millions who will never read **the** Arcadia.

Sidney lingered many days in great agony. The

prospect of his death stirred Leicester with unwonted emotion. "This young man," he writes, "he was my greatest comfort, next her Majesty, of all the world: and if I could buy his life with all I have, to my shirt, I would give it." The account of his death, by his chaplain, is inexpressibly affecting. When the good man, to use his own words, "proved to him out of the Scriptures, that, though his understanding and senses should fail, yet that faith which he had now could not fail, he did, with a cheerful and smiling countenance, put forth his hand, and slapped me softly on the cheeks. Not long after, he lifted up his eyes and hands, uttering these words, 'I would not change my joy for the empire of the world.' . . . . Having made a comparison of God's grace now in him, his former virtues seemed to be nothing; for he wholly condemned his former life. 'All things in it,' he said, 'have been vain, vain, vain.'"

His sufferings were brought to a close on the 17th of October, 1586. Among the throng of testimonials to his excellence, called forth by his death, only two were worthy of the occasion. The first was the simple remark of Lord Buckhurst, that "he hath had as great love in this life, and as many tears for his death, as ever any had." The second is a stanza from an anonymous poem, usually printed with the elaborate, but cold and pedantic, eulogy of Spenser, whose tears for his friend and patron seemed to freeze in their passage into words. The stanza has been often quoted, but rarely in connection with the person it celebrates.

> " A sweet, attractive kind of grace,
>   A full assurance given by looks,
>   Continual comfort in a face,
>   The lineaments of Gospel Books."

In passing from Sidney to Raleigh, we pass to a less beautiful and engaging, but far more potent and comprehensive spirit. We despair of doing justice to the various efficiency of this most splendid of adventurers, all of whose talents were abilities, and all of whose abilities were accomplishments; whose vigorous and elastic **nature** could adapt itself to **all occasions** and all **pursuits**; and who, as soldier, sailor, courtier, colonizer, statesman, historian, and poet, seemed specially gifted to do the thing which absorbed him **at** the moment. Born **in** 1552, and the son of a Devonshire gentleman of ancient family, straitened income, and numerous children, fortune denied him wealth, only to lavish on him all the powers by which wealth is acquired. In his case, one of the most happily constituted of human intellects was lodged in a physical frame of perfect soundness and strength, so that **at** all periods of his life, in the phrase of the spiteful and sickly Cecil, he could " toil terribly."

Action, adventure, was the necessity of his being. Imaginative and thoughtful as he was, the vision of imagination, the suggestion of thought, went equally to enlighten and energize his will. Whatever appeared possible to his brain he ached to make actual with his hand. Though distinguished at the university, he left it at the first opportunity for active life presented to him, and at the age of seventeen joined the band of gentlemen volunteers who went to France to fight on the Protestant side in the civil war by which that kingdom was convulsed. In this rough work he passed five years. Shortly after his return in 1580, an Irish rebellion broke out; and Raleigh, as captain of a company of English troops, engaged in the ruthless business of putting it down. A dispute having occurred between him and the Lord Deputy, Grey, it was referred to the Council Board in England. Raleigh, determined, if possible, to escape from the squalid, cruel, and disgusting drudgery of an Irish war, exerted every resource of his pliant genius to ingratiate himself with Elizabeth, and urged his own views with such consummate art that he got, says the chronicler, " the Queen's ear in a trice." His graces of person took her fancy, as much as his ready intelligence, his plausible elocution, and his available union of the large conceptions of the statesman with the intrepidity of the soldier, impressed her discerning mind. The tradition that he first attracted her regard by casting his rich cloak into a puddle to save the royal feet from contaminating mud, though characteristic, is probably one of those stories which are too good to be true. His promotion was as rapid as Sidney's was slow; for he had a mind which, on all occasions, darted at once to the best thing to be done; and, not content with deserving to be advanced, he outwitted all who intrigued against his advancement. He was knighted, made Captain of the Guard, Seneschal of the County of Cornwall, Lord Warden of the Stannaries, and received a large grant of land in Ireland, in less than three years after his victorious appearance at the Council Board. Though now enabled to gratify those **luxurious** tastes which poverty had heretofore **mortified, and** though so susceptible to all that can charm the senses through the imagination that his friend Spenser described him as a man

"In whose high thoughts Pleasure had built her bower,"

still pleasure, though intensely enjoyed, had no allurements to weaken the insatiable activity of his spirit or moderate the audacity of his ambition. Patriot as well as courtier, and statesman as well as adventurer, with **an** intelligence so flexible that **it** could grasp great designs as easily **as** it could manage petty intrigues, and

12

impelled by an impatient feeling that he was the ablest man of the nation, in virtue of individualizing most thoroughly the spirit and aspirations of the people and the time, he now engaged in those great maritime enterprises which are inseparably associated with his name, — to found a colonial empire for England, and to break down the power and humble the pride of Spain. In 1585 he obtained a patent from the Queen " to appropriate, plant, and govern any territorial possessions he might acquire in the unoccupied portions of North America." The result was the first settlement of Virginia, which failed from the misconduct of the colonists and the hostility of the Indians. He then engaged extensively in those privateering — those somewhat buccaneering — expeditions against the commerce and colonies of Spain which can be justified on no general principles, but which the instinct of the English people, hating Spaniards, hating Popery, and conscious that real war existed under formal peace, both stimulated and sanctioned. Spain, to Raleigh, was a nation to be detested and warred against by every honest Englishman for " her bloody and injurious designs, purposed and practised against Christian princes, over all of whom she seeks unlawful and ungodly rule and empiry."

In the height of Raleigh's favor with the Queen the

discovery of his intrigue and subsequent private marriage with one **of her** maids **of** honor brought **down** on his head the full storm of the royal virago's wrath. He was deprived of all the offices which gave him admission to her august presence, and imprisoned with his wife in the Tower. Any other man would have been hopelessly ruined; but, by counterfeiting the most romantic despair at the Queen's displeasure, and by representing his whole misery to proceed from being deprived of the sight of her red hair and painted face, he was, in two or three weeks, released from imprisonment. When free, he performed such important parliamentary services that he partially regained her favor, and he managed so well as to induce her to grant him the manor of Sherborne. As this was church property, and **as Raleigh** was accused by his enemies of **being an atheist,** the grant occasioned great scandal. His disgrace and imprisonment had filled his rivals with hope. They naturally thought that his offence, which mortified the coquette's vanity as well as the sovereign's pride, was of such a nature that even Raleigh's management could not gloss it over; but now they trembled with apprehensions of his complete restoration to favor. One of them writes: "It is feared of all honest men, that Sir Walter Raleigh shall presently come to court; and yet it is well withstood. God grant him some further resistance, and that place he better deserveth if he had his right."

Raleigh, unsuccessful in regaining the affection and esteem of his royal mistress, now thought to dazzle her imagination with a shining enterprise. He believed, with millions of others, in the fable of El Dorado, and conceived the place to lie somewhere in Guiana, in the region between the Orinoco and the Amazon. His imagination was fired with the thought of penetrating to the capital city, where the houses were roofed with gold, where the common sand glistened, and the very rocks shone, with the precious deposit. Should he succeed, the consequences would be immense wealth and fame for himself, and immense addition to the power and glory of England ; and as he purposed to induce the native chiefs to swear allegiance to the Queen, and eventually to establish an English colony in the country, he flattered himself, in Mr. Napier's words, "that he would be able, by the acquisition of Guiana, vastly to extend the sphere of English industry and commerce, to render London the mart of the choicest productions of the New World, and to annex to the Crown a region which, besides its great colonial recommendations, would enable it to command the chief possessions of its greatest enemy, and from which his principal resources were derived." Possessed by these kindling ideas, and with the personal magnetism to make them infectious, Raleigh does not seem to have found any difficulty in obtaining money and men to carry them out; and in February, 1595, with a fleet of five ships, he set out for the land of gold. The enterprise was, of course, unsuccessful, for no El Dorado existed; but on his return, at the close of the summer, he published his account of "The Discovery of the Large, Rich, and Beautiful Empire of Guiana," in which the failure of the expedition is recorded in connection with a profession of undisturbed faith in the reality of its object, and some astounding stories are told, concerning which it is now difficult to decide whether Raleigh unconsciously exaggerated or deliberately lied. It was his professed intention to renew the search at once; but, the Queen having by this time nearly forgiven his offence, his ambition was stimulated by objects nearer home, and the quest of El Dorado was postponed to a more convenient season.

In 1596 he won great fame for his intrepidity and skill as Rear Admiral of the fleet which took Cadiz; and in 1597 he further distinguished himself by the capture of Fayal. Restored to his office of Captain of the Guard, he was again seen by envious rivals in personal attendance on the Queen. Between the court factions of Essex and Cecil he first tried to mediate;

but, being hated by Essex, he joined Cecil for the purpose of crushing the enemy of both. The intention of Cecil was, to use Raleigh to depress Essex, and then to betray his own instrument. Essex fell ; but, as long as Elizabeth lived, Raleigh was safe. Cecil, however, took care to poison in advance the mind of her successor with suspicions of Raleigh ; and, on James's accession to the throne, Raleigh discovered that he was distrusted, and would probably be disgraced. Such a man was not likely to give up his offices and abdicate his power without a struggle ; and, as he could hope for no favor, he tried the desperate expedient of making himself powerful by making himself feared. In our time he would have " gone into opposition " : in the time of James the First " His Majesty's Opposition " did not exist ; and he became connected with a mysterious plot to raise Arabella Stuart to the English throne, — trusting, as we cannot but think, in his own sagacity to avoid the appearance and evidence of treason, and to use the folly of the real conspirators as a means of forcing his claims on the attention of James. In this game, however, Cecil proved himself a more astute and unscrupulous politician than his late accomplice. The plot was discovered ; Raleigh was tried on a charge of treason ; the jury, being managed by the government, found him guilty, and he was sentenced to death. The sentence, however, was so palpably against the law and the evidence **that it** was not executed. By the exceeding grace of the good King, Raleigh was only plundered of his estate, sent to the Tower, and confined there for thirteen years.

The restless activity of his mind now found a vent in experimental science and in literature; and, taking a theme as large as the scope of his own mind, he set himself resolutely to work to write the History of the World. Meanwhile he spared no arts of influence, bribery, and flattery to get his liberty; and at last, in **March,** 1615, was released, without being pardoned, on his tempting the cupidity of James with circumstantial **details of** the mineral wealth **of Guiana,** and by offering to conduct an expedition there to open **a** gold-mine. With a fleet of thirteen ships he set **sail,** arrived on the coast in November, and sent a large party up the Orinoco, who, after having attacked and burnt the Spanish town of St. Thomas, — an engagement in which Raleigh's eldest son lost his life, — returned to their sick and mortified commander with the intelligence that they had failed to discover the mine. The accounts of what afterwards occurred in this ill-fated expedition are so confused and contradictory that it is difficult to obtain a clear idea of the facts. It is sufficient to say that Raleigh returned to England, laboring under

imputations of falsehood, treachery, and contemplated
treason and piracy, and that he there found the Spanish
ambassador clamoring in the court of James for his life.
His ruin was resolved upon ; and, as he never had been
pardoned, it was thought more convenient to execute
him on the old sentence than to run the risk of a new
trial for his alleged offences since. In other words, it
was resolved to use the technicalities of law to violate
its essence, and to employ certain legal refinements as
instruments of murder. On the 29th of October, 1618,
he was accordingly beheaded. His behavior on the
scaffold was what might have been expected from the
dauntless spirit which, in its experience of nearly the
whole circle of human emotions, had never felt the sensation of fear. After vindicating his conduct in a manly
and dignified speech to the spectators, he desired the
headsman to show him the axe, which not being done
at once, he said, " I pray thee, let me see it. Dost thou
think that I am afraid of it ? " After he had taken it
in his hand, he felt curiously along the edge, and then
smilingly remarked to the sheriff, " This is a sharp
medicine, but it is a physician for all diseases." After
he had laid his head on the block, he was requested to
turn it on the other side. " So the heart be right," he
replied, " it is no matter which way the head lieth."
After his forgiving the headsman, and praying a few

moments, the signal was made, which not being immediately followed by **the** stroke, Raleigh said to the exe-
cutioner: "Why dost thou not strike? Strike, man!"
Two strokes of the axe, under which his frame did not
shrink or move, severed his head from **his** body. The
immense effusion of blood, in a man of sixty-six, amazed
everybody that saw it. "**Who** would have thought,"
King James might have said, with another distinguished
ornament of the royal house of Scotland, "that the old
man had so much blood in him!" Yes, blood enough
in his veins, and thought enough in his head, and hero-
ism enough in his soul, to have served England for
twenty years more, had folly and baseness not otherwise willed it!

The superabundant physical and mental vitality **of**
this extraordinary man is seen almost equally in his actions and his writings. A courtier, riding abroad **with**
the Queen in his suit of silver armor, or in attendance
at her court, dressed, as the antiquary tells us, in "a
white satin doublet all embroidered with white pearls,
and a mighty rich chain of great pearls about his neck,"
he was still not imprisoned by these magnificent vanities,
but could abandon them joyfully to encounter pestilen-
tial climates and lead desperate maritime enterprises.
As an orator he was not only powerful in the Commons,
but persuasive with individuals. Nobody could resist

his tongue. The Queen, we are told, " was much taken
with his elocution, loved to hear his reasons, and took
him for a kind of oracle." To his counsel, more than
to any other man's, England was indebted for the destruction of the Spanish Armada.   He spoke and wrote
wisely and vigorously on policy and government, on
naval architecture and naval tactics.   Among his public
services we may rank his claim to be considered the in-
troducer into Europe of tobacco and the potato.   In
political economy, he anticipated the modern doctrine of
free trade and freedom of industry ; he first stated also
the theory regarding population which is associated
with the name of Malthus ; and, though himself a gold-
seeker, he saw clearly that gold had no peculiar pre-
ciousness beyond any other commodity, and that it was
the value of what a nation derived from its colonies,
and not the kind of value, which made colonies important.   In intellectual philosophy Dugald Stewart admits
that he anticipated his own leading doctrine in respect
to " the fundamental laws of human belief."   His curious and practical intellect, stung by all secrets, showed
also an aptitude for the experimental investigation of
natural phenomena.

And he was likewise a poet. It was one of his inten-
tions to write an English epic ; but his busy life only
allowed him leisure for some miscellaneous pieces.

Among these, his sonnet on his friend Spenser's Faery
Queene would alone be sufficient to demonstrate the
depth **of his** sentiment and the strength of **his imagination.**

> " Methought I saw the grave where Laura lay,
> Within that Temple where the vestal flame
> Was wont to burn; and, passing by that way
> To see that buried dust of living fame,
> Whose tomb fair Love and fairer Virtue kept,
> All suddenly I saw the Faery Queen:
> **At** whose approach the soul of Petrarch wept,
> And from thenceforth those Graces were not seen
> (For they this Queen attended), in whose stead
> Oblivion laid him down on Laura's hearse;
> Hereat the hardest stones were seen to bleed,
> And groans of buried ghosts the heavens did perse:
> Where Homer's spright did tremble all for grief,
> And cursed the access of that celestial thief."

But his great literary work was his History of the
World, written during his imprisonment in the Tower.
As might be supposed, his restless, insatiable, capacious,
and audacious mind could not be content with the modern practice, even as followed by philosophical historians, of narrating events and elucidating laws. He
began with the Creator and the creation, pressing into
his service all the theology, the philosophy, and the
metaphysics of his time, and boldly grappling with the
most insoluble problems, even that of the Divine Es-

sence. Nearly half of the immense folio is devoted
to sacred history; and though the remaining portions,
devoted to the Assyrians, the Persians, the Greeks, and
the Romans, are commonly considered the most readable, inasmuch as they exhibit Raleigh, the statesman and
warrior, sociably treating of statesmen and warriors, —
Raleigh, who had lived history, penetrating into the life
of historical events, — we must confess to having been
more attracted by the earlier portions, which show us
Raleigh the scholar, philosopher, and divine, in his attempts to probe the deepest secrets of existence, his brain
crowded with all the foolish and all the wise sayings of
Pagan philosophers and Christian fathers and schoolmen,
and throwing his own judgments, with a quaint simplicity and a quaint audacity, into the general mass of theological and philosophical guessing he has accumulated.
The style of the history is excellent, — clear, sweet,
flexible, straightforward and business-like, discussing the
question of the locality of Paradise as Raleigh would
have discussed the question of an expedition against
Spain at the council-table of Elizabeth. There is an
apocryphal story that he completed another volume of
the History of the World, but, on learning that his publisher had lost money by the first, burnt the manuscript,
not willing that so good a man should suffer any further
harm through him. But the story must be false; for

such tenderness to a publisher is equally against human nature and author-nature.

The **defect** of Raleigh's character, even when his ends were patriotic and noble, was unscrupulousness, — a flashing impatience with all moral obstacles obtruded **in** the path of his designs. He had a too confident belief in the resources of his wit and courage, in the infallibility of his insight, foresight, and power of combination, in the unflagging vigor by which he had so often **made** his will march abreast of his swiftest thought; and in carrying out his projects he sometimes risked his conscience with almost the same joyous recklessness with which he risked his **life.** The noblest passage in his History of the World, that in which he condenses in the bold and striking image of a majestic tree the power of Rome, has some application to his own splendid rise and terrible fall. "We have left Rome," he says, "flourishing in the middle of the field, having rooted up or cut down all that kept it from the eyes and admiration of the world. But, after some continuance, it shall begin to lose the beauty it had; the storms of ambition shall beat her great boughs and branches **one** against another; her leaves shall fall off, her limbs wither, and a rabble of barbarous nations enter the field and cut her down."

BACON.

I.

NEXT to Shakespeare, the greatest name of the Elizabethan age is that of Bacon. His life has been written by his chaplain, Dr. Rawley, by Basil Montagu, by Lord Campbell, and by Macaulay; yet none of these biographies reconciles the external facts of the man's life with the internal facts of the man's nature.

Macaulay's vivid sketch of Bacon's career is the most acute, the most merciless, and for popular effect the most efficient, of all; but it deals simply with external events, evinces in their interpretation no deep and detecting glance into character, and urges the evidence for the baseness of Bacon with the acrimonious zeal of a prosecuting attorney, eager for a verdict, rather than weighs it with the candor of a judge deciding on the nature of a great benefactor of the race, who in his will had solemnly left his memory to " men's charitable speeches." When he comes to treat of Bacon as a philosopher, he passes to the opposite extreme of panegyric. The impression left by the whole representation is not the impression of a man, but of a monstrous huddling together **of** two men, — one infamous, the other glorious, — which he calls by the name of Bacon.

The question therefore arises, Is it possible to harmonize, in one individuality, Bacon the courtier, Bacon the lawyer, Bacon the statesman, Bacon the judge, with Bacon the thinker, philosopher, and philanthropist? The antithesis commonly instituted **between these is** rather a play of epigram than an exercise of characterization. The "meanest of mankind" could not have written The Advancement of Learning; yet everybody feels that some connection there must be between the meditative life which produced The Advancement **of** Learning, and the practical life devoted to the advancement of Bacon. Who, then, *was* the man who **is so** execrated for selling justice, and so exalted for writing the Novum Organum?

This question can never be intelligently answered, unless we establish some points of connection between the spirit which animates his works and the external events which constituted what is called his life. As a general principle, it is well for us to obtain some conception of a great man from his writings, before we give much heed to the recorded incidents of his career; for these incidents, as historically narrated, are likely to be false, are sure to be one-sided, and almost always need

to be interpreted in order to convey real knowledge to
the mind. It is ever for the interest or the malice of
some contemporary, that every famous politician, who
by necessity passes into history, should pass into it
stained in character; and it is fortunate that, in the case
of Bacon, we are not confined to the outside records of
his career, but possess means of information which conduct us into the heart of his nature. Indeed, Bacon
the man is most clearly seen and intimately known in
Bacon the thinker. Bacon thinking, Bacon observing,
Bacon inventing, — these were as much *acts* of Bacon
as Bacon intriguing for power and place. "I account,"
he has said, "my ordinary course of study and meditation more painful than most parts of action are." But
his works do not merely contain his thoughts and observations; they are all informed with the inmost life of
his mind and the real quality of his nature; and, if he
was base, servile, treacherous, and venal, it will not require any great expenditure of sagacity to detect the
taint of servility, baseness, treachery, and venality in
his writings. For what was Bacon's intellect but Bacon's nature in its intellectual expression? Everybody
remembers the noble commencement of the Novum Organum: "*Francis of Verulam thought thus.*" Ay! it is
not merely the understanding of Francis of Verulam,
but Francis himself that thinks; and we may be sure

that the thought will give us the spirit and average
moral quality **of** the man ; for it is not faculties, but
persons using faculties, persons behind faculties and
within faculties, that invent, combine, discover, create ;
and in the whole history of the human intellect, in the
department of literature, there has been no exercise of
live creative faculty without an escape of **character.**
The new thoughts, the novel combinations, the fresh
images, are all enveloped in an atmosphere, or borne on
a stream, which conveys into the recipient mind the fine
essence of individual life and individual disposition.   It
is more difficult to detect this in comprehensive individualities like Bacon **and** Shakespeare than in narrow
individualities like Ben Jonson and Marlowe ; **but still,**
if we sharply scrutinize the impression which Bacon
and Shakespeare have left on our minds, we shall find
that they have not merely enlarged our reason with new
truth, and charmed our imagination with new beauty,
but that they have stamped on our consciousness the
image of their natures, and touched the finest sensi-
bilities of our souls with the subtile but potent influence
of their characters.

   Now if we discern and feel *this* image and *this* life
of Bacon, derived from his works, **we** shall find that his
individuality — capacious, flexible, fertile, far-reaching
as it was — was still deficient in heat, and that this de-

ficiency was in the very centre of his nature and sources of his moral being. Leaving out of view the lack of stamina in his bodily constitution, and his consequent want of those rude, rough energies and that peculiar Teutonic pluck which seem the birthright of every Englishman of robust health, we find in the works as in the life of the man no evidence of strong appetites or fierce passions or kindling sentiments. Neither in his blood nor in his soul can we discover any of the coarse or any of the fine impulses which impart intensity to character. He is without the vices of passion, — voluptuousness, hatred, envy, malice, revenge ; but he is also without the virtues of passion, — deep love, warm gratitude, capacity of unwithholding self-committal to a great sentiment or a great cause. This defect of intensity is the source of that weakness in the actions of his life which his satirists have stigmatized as baseness.; and, viewing it altogether apart from the vast intellectual nature modifying and modified by it, they have tied the faculties of an angel to the soul of a sneak. While narrating the events of his career, and making epigrams out of his frailties, they have lost all vision of that noble brow, on which, it might be said, " Shame is ashamed to sit." Shame may be there, but it is shame shamefaced, — aghast at its position, not glorying in it !

With this view of the intellectual character of Bacon, let us pass to the events of his life. He was born in London on the 22d of January, 1561, and was the youngest son of Sir Nicholas **Bacon, Keeper** of the Great Seal. His mother, sister to the wife of Lord Treasurer Burleigh, possessed uncommon accomplishments even in that age of learned women. " Such being his parents," quaintly says Dr. Rawley, " you may easily imagine what the issue was likely to be ; having had whatsoever nature or breeding could put into him." Sir Nicholas was a capable, sagacious, long-headed, cold-blooded, and **not** especially scrupulous man of the world, who, like all the eminent statesmen of Elizabeth's reign, acted for the public interest without prejudicing his own. Lady Bacon had, **among other** works, translated from the Italian some sermons on Predestination and Election, written by Ochinus, a divine **of** that Socinian sect which Orthodox religionists, who hated each other, could still unite in stigmatizing as preeminently wicked ; and, if we may judge from this circumstance, she must have had a daring and discursive as well as learned spirit. The mind of the son, if it derived its weight, moderation, and strong practical bent from the father, derived no less its intellectual self-reliance and audacity from the mother ; and, as Francis was **the** favorite child, we may presume that the parents

saw in him their different qualities exquisitely combined.
As a boy, he was weak in health, indifferent to the
sports of youth, of great quickness, curiosity, and flexibility of intellect, and with a sweet sobriety in his de-
portment which made the Queen call him "the young
Lord Keeper."   He was a courtier, too, at an age when
most boys care as little for queens as they do for
nursery-maids.   Being asked by Elizabeth how old he
was, he replied that he was "two years younger than
her Majesty's happy reign," with which answer, says the
honest chronicler, "the Queen was much taken."   Receiving his early education under his mother's eye, and
freely mixing with the wise and great people who visited
his father's house, he was uncommonly mature in mind
when, at the age of thirteen, he was sent to the University of Cambridge.   With his swiftness and facility of
acquisition, it was but natural that he should easily
master his studies ; but he did more, he subjected them
to his own tests of value and utility, and despised them.
Before he had been two years at college, this smooth,
decorous stripling, who bowed so low to Dr. Whitgift,
and was outwardly so respectful to the solemn trumpery
about him, but was still inwardly unawed by the authority of traditions and accredited forms, coolly removed the mask from the body of learning, to find, as
he thought, nothing but ignorance and emptiness within.

The intellectual dictator of forty generations, Aristotle himself, was called up before the judgment-seat of this young brain, the pretensions of his philosophy silently sifted, and then dismissed and disowned, — not, he condescended to say, "for the worthlessness **of the** author, to whom he would ever ascribe all high attributes," but for the barrenness of the method, "the unfruitfulness of the way." By profound and self-reliant meditation, he had already caught bright glimpses of a new path for the human intellect to pursue, leading to a more fertile and fruitful domain, — its process experience, not dogmatism; its results discoveries, not disputations; its object "the glory of God and the relief of man's estate." . This aspiring idea was the constant companion of **his** mind through all the vicissitudes of his career, — never forgotten in poverty, in business, in glory, in humiliation, — the last word on his lip, and alive in the last beat of his heart ; and it is this which lends to his large reason and rich imagination that sweet and pervasive beneficence, which is felt to be the culminating charm of his matchless compositions, and which refuses to allow his character to be deprived of benignity, even after its pliancy to circumstances may have deprived it of **its** title to respect.

Before he was sixteen, he left the university, without taking a degree ; **and** his father, who evidently intended

him for public life, sent him to France, in the train of the
English ambassador, in order that he might learn the
arts of statecraft. Here he resided for about two years
and a half, enjoying rare opportunities for observing men
and affairs, and of mingling in the society of statesmen,
philosophers, and men of letters, who were pleased
equally by the originality of his mind and the amenity
of his manners. He purposed to stay some years
abroad, and was studying assiduously at Poitiers, when,
in February, 1579, an accident occurred which ruined
his hopes of an early entrance upon a brilliant career,
converted him from a scholar into an adventurer, and, in
his own phrase, made it incumbent on him "to think
how to live, instead of living only to think." A barber
it was who thus decided the fate of a philosopher. His
father, while undergoing the process of shaving, happened to fall asleep ; and, so deep was the reverence of
the barber for the Lord Keeper of the Great Seal, that
he did not presume to shake into consciousness so august
a personage, but stood gazing at him in wondering admiration. Unfortunately a draft of air from an open win-
dow was blowing all the while on "the second prop of
the kingdom," and murdering him by inches. Sir Nicholas awoke shivering ; and, on being informed by the
barber that respect for his dignity was the cause
of his not having been roused, he quietly said, "Your

politeness has cost me my life." In two days after he died. A considerable sum of money, which he had laid **by in order to purchase** a landed estate for Francis, was left unappropriated to that purpose; **and** Francis, on his return from France, found that he had to share with four others the amount which his father had intended for him alone. Thus left comparatively poor, he solicited his uncle, the Lord Treasurer, for some political office, and, had his abilities been less splendid, he would doubtless have succeeded in his suit; but Burleigh's penetrating eye recognized in him talents in comparison with which the talents of his own favorite son, Robert Cecil, were dwarfed; **and,** as his heart was set **on** Cecil's succeeding to **his** own great offices, **he is suspected** to have systematically "suppressed" the nephew in order that the nephew should not have the opportunity of making himself a powerful rival of the son.

Bacon, therefore, had no other resource but the profession of the law; and for six years, between 1580 and 1586, he bent his powerful mind to its study. He then again applied to Burleigh, hoping, through the latter's influence, to be "called within bars," and to be able at once to practise. **He** was testily denied. Two years afterwards, however, he was made "counsel learned extraordinary" to the Queen. This was an office of honor rather **than** profit; but, **as it** gave him access to

Elizabeth, it might have led to his political advancement, had not his good cousin Cecil, ever at her **ear,**
represented him as a speculative man, "indulging in
philosophic reveries, and calculated **more** to perplex
than promote public business." **Probably** he obtained
this idea from a letter written by Bacon to Burleigh, in
1591, in which — wearied with waiting on fortune,
troubled with poverty, and haunted by the rebuking **vis-**
ion of his grand philosophical scheme — he solicits him
for some employment adequate for his support, and which
will, at the same time, leave him **leisure to** become a
"pioneer in the deep mines of truth." " Not being
born," he says, " under Sol, that loveth **honor,** nor under
Jupiter, that loveth business, but **being wholly carried**
away by the contemplative planet," he proceeds **to fol-**
low **up** this modest disclaimer of being influenced by the
ambitions which engrossed the Cecils, with the proud,
the imperial declaration, that **he has** " vast contemplative
ends, though moderate civil ends," and " has taken all
knowledge for his province." This appeal had no effect;
and as the reversion he held of the registrarship of the
Star Chamber, worth £ 1,600 a year, did not fall in
until twenty years afterwards, he was still fretted with
poverty, and had to give **to law** and politics the precious
hours to which **philosophy would have** asserted an exclusive claim.

But politics, and law as connected with politics, were, in Bacon's time, occupations by which Bacon could succeed only at the expense of discrediting himself with posterity. Whatever may have been his motives for desiring power, — and they were doubtless neither wholly selfish nor wholly noble, — power could be obtained only by submitting to the conditions by which power was then hampered. In submitting to these conditions, Bacon the politician may be said to have agreed with Bacon the philosopher; as the same objectivity of mind which, as a philosopher, led him to seek the law of phenomena in nature, and not in the intelligence, led him as a politician to seek the law of political action in **circumstances**, and not in conscience. " Nature **is commanded** by obeying her," **is** his great **philosophical** maxim. Events are commanded by obeying **them, was** probably his guiding maxim of civil prudence. In each case the principle was derived from without, and not from within; and he doubtless thought that, as in the one **case it** led to power over nature, so in the other it would lead to power over states. As his political life must be considered **an** immense mistake; as the result of his theory in civil affairs was, to make him the servant, and not the master, **of** his intended instruments; as he was constantly inferior in power to persons inferior to him in **mind; as** he had to do the bidding of masters who would

not profit by his advice; and as his wisdom was no
match, in the real tug of affairs, for men who acted either
from good or from bad impulses and instincts, — it is
well to trace his failure to its source. The fault was
partly in Bacon, partly in his times, and partly inherent
in politics. He thought he possessed the genius of
action, because, in addition to his universality of mind
and universality of acquirement, he was the deepest observer of men, had the broadest comprehension of
affairs, and could give the wisest counsel, of any statesman of his time. He was practically sagacious beyond
even the Cecils; for if they could, better than he, see
an inch before the nose, he could see the continuation
of that inch along a line of a thousand miles. Still his
was not specially the genius of action, but the genius
which tells how to act wisely. In the genius of action,
the mind is passionately concentrated in the will; in the
genius which tells how to act wisely, the force of the
will is somewhat expended in enlarging the area over
which the mind sends its glance. In the genius of action, there is commonly more or less effrontery, wilful-
ness, cunning, narrowing of the mind to the mere business of the moment, with little foresight of consequences;
in the genius which tells how to act wisely there is true
practical wisdom. Unhappily, principles are, in politics,
so complicated with passions, and power is so often the

prize of insolent demerit, that the two have rarely been combined in one statesman ; and history exhibits scores of sterile and stunted intellects, pushed by rough force into ruling positions, for one instance of comprehensive intelligence impelled by audacious will.

As a politician, Bacon had a difficult game **to play.** Entering the House of Commons in 1593, he at once showed himself the ablest speaker and debater of his time. It is said that Lord Eldon, the stanchest of Tories, declared in his old age, that, if he could recommence his political career, he would begin " in the sedition line "; and Bacon at first tried the expedient of attacking a government measure, in order to force his abilities on the notice of Burleigh, and perhaps obtain by fear what he could not obtain by favor. But the reign **of the** haughty and almost absolute Elizabeth **was** not the period for such tactics, and he narrowly escaped arrest and punishment. He then recurred to a design, formed three years before, of opposing the Lord Treasurer by means of a rival ; for at the court and in the councils of the Queen there were two factions, — one devoted to Burleigh, the counsellor of Elizabeth, the other to the Earl of Essex, her lover. These factions were divided by no principle ; the question was not, *how* should the government be carried on, but *by whom* should the government be carried on ; and the object of each was to

engross the favor of Elizabeth, in order to engross the
power and patronage of office. Bacon, judging that
Essex, who held the Queen's affections, would be successful over Burleigh, who only held her judgment, had
already attached himself to the fortunes of Essex. It
may be added that, as his grand philosophical scheme
for the interpretation of nature depended on the patronage of government for its complete success, he saw that,
if Essex triumphed, he might be able to gratify his
philosophic as well as political ambition ; for the Earl,
with every fault that can coexist with valor, generosity,
and frankness, — fierce, proud, wilful, licentious, and
headstrong, — had still a soul sensitive to literary as to
military glory, while Burleigh was indifferent to both.
It may be doubted if Bacon was capable of intense, all-
sacrificing friendship for anybody, especially for a man
like Essex. It is probable that what his sagacity detected as the rule which governed the political friend-
ships of Cæsar may to some extent apply to his own.
" Cæsar," he says, "made choice of such friends as a man
might easily see that he chose them rather to be instruments to his ends than for any good-will to them." But
it is still certain that for ten years he was the wisest
counsellor of Essex, by his admirable management kept
the Earl's haughty and headlong spirit under some control of wisdom, and never allowed him to take a false

step without honestly pointing out its folly. He was the
Philippe de Commines to this Charles the Rash.

Essex, on his part, urged the claims of **Bacon with
the** same impetuosity with which he threw himself into
everything he undertook. But he constantly failed. In
1594 he tried to get Bacon appointed Attorney-General,
and he failed. He then tried to get **Bacon** appointed
Solicitor-General, **and** failed, — failed not because the
Queen was hostile to Bacon, but because she desired to
show that she was not enslaved **by** Essex. He then
urged Bacon's suit to Lady Hatton, whom Bacon desired to marry, not for her temper, which was that of an
eccentric termagant, but for her fortune ; and here, for-
tunately for Bacon, he again failed. He then **gave**
Bacon a landed estate, which Bacon sold **for £ 1,800 ;**
and soon afterwards Bacon was in such pecuniary distress as to be arrested and sent to a sponging-house, for
a debt of £ 500. Such were the obligations of Bacon
to Essex. What were the obligations of Essex to
Bacon ? Ten years of faithful service, ten years of the
" time and talents " of the best head for large affairs in
Europe. At last the Queen and Essex quarrelled.
Bacon, himself serenely superior to passion, but adroit
in calming the passions of others, exerted infinite skill
and address to reconcile them ; but the temper of each
was too haughty to yield. The occasion of the final

and deadly feud between them looks ludicrous as the decisive event in the life of a hero. Essex held a monopoly of sweet wines; that is, the Queen had granted to him, for a certain period, the exclusive privilege of plundering all her subjects who drank sweet wines. He asked for a renewal of his patent, and was refused. Taking this refusal as a proof that his enemies were triumphant at court, he then organized a formidable conspiracy against the government, and, for a purely personal object, without the pretence of any public aim, attempted to seize the Queen's person, overturn her government, and convulse the kingdom with civil war. He was arrested, tried, and executed. Bacon, as Queen's counsel, appeared against him on his trial, and, by the Queen's command, wrote a narrative of the facts which justified the government in its course. For this most of his biographers represent him as guilty of the foulest treachery, ingratitude, and baseness. Let us see how it probably appeared to Bacon. The association of politicians of which Essex was the head, and to which Bacon belonged, was an association to obtain power and office by legal means; treason and insurrection were not in the " platform "; and the rule of honor which applies to such a body is plain. It is treacherous for any of the followers to betray the leader, but it is also treacherous for the leader to betray any of the followers. Nobody pretends that Bacon betrayed Essex, but it is very evident that Essex betrayed Bacon; for Bacon, the confidant, as he supposed, of the most secret thoughts and designs of Essex, liable to be compromised by his acts, and already lying under the suspicion and displeasure of Elizabeth on account of his strenuous advocacy of the Earl's claims to her continued favor, suddenly discovers that Essex had given way to passions as selfish as they were furious; that he had committed high-treason, and recklessly risked the fortunes of his political friends, as well as personal confederates, on the hazard of an enterprise as wicked as it was mad. Henry Wotton, who was private secretary to Essex, but not engaged in the conspiracy, still thought it prudent to escape to the Continent, and not trust to the chances of a trial; and Bacon was more in the confidence of Essex than Wotton. If Essex had no conscience in extricating himself from his difficulties by treason, why blame Bacon for extricating himself from complicity with Essex by censuring his treason? To the indignation that Bacon must have felt in finding himself duped and betrayed by the man whose interests he had identified with his own must be added his indignation at the treason itself; for the politician had not so completely absorbed the patriot but that he may have felt genuine horror at the idea of compassing personal ends by civil war. In the case of Essex, the crime was really aggravated by the ingratitude which Bacon's critics charge on himself. Bacon, it seems, was a mean-spirited wretch, because he did not see the friend who had given him £1,800 in the public enemy. But is it to be supposed that a friend will be more constant than a lover? And Essex, the lover of the Queen, made war upon her, — upon her who, frugal as she was in dispensing honors and money, had lavished both on him. She had given him in all what would now be equivalent to £300,000 ; and then, on her refusal to allow him to continue cheating those of her subjects who drank sweet wines, the exasperated hero attempted to overthrow her government. But Essex acted from his passions, — and passions, it seems, atone for more sins than even charity can cover. History itself has here sided against reason; and the fame of Bacon, the intellectual bene-factor of the world, will probably, through all time, be sacrificed to that of this hot-blooded, arrogant, self-willed, and greedy noble. Intellect is often selfish ; but nothing is more frightfully selfish, after all, than passion.

It would be well if the character of Bacon were justly open to no severer charge than that founded on his connection with Essex. But " worse remains be-hind." In 1603 Elizabeth died, and James, King of Scotland, succeeded to the English throne. Bacon at

once detected in him the characteristic defect of all the
Stuarts. " Methought," he wrote to a friend, "his
Majesty rather asked counsel of the time past than of
the time to come." Yet he paid assiduous court to
James, and especially won his favor by advocating in
Parliament the union of England and Scotland. By a
combination of hard work and soft compliances he gradually obtained the commanding positions, though not
the commanding influence, of his political ambition. In
1609 he was made Solicitor-General; in 1613, Attorney-General; in 1616, Privy Councillor; in 1617, Lord
Keeper; in 1618, Lord Chancellor and Baron Verulam; in 1621, Viscount St. Albans. These eighteen
years of his life exhibit an almost unparalleled **activity**
and fertility of mind in law, politics, literature, **and phi-**
losophy; but in the reign of James I. no man could
rise to the positions which Bacon reached without compromises with conscience and compromises with intelligence which it is doubtless provoking that Bacon did not
scorn. Even if we could pardon these compromises on
the principle that events must be obeyed in order to be
commanded, it is still plain that his obedience did not
lead to real command. He unquestionably expected
that his position would enable him to draw the government into his philosophical scheme of waging a
systematic war on Nature, with an army of investi-

13 *

gators, to force her to deliver up her secrets ; but the
Solomon who was then king of England preferred to
spend his money on quite different objects ; and Bacon's
compliances, therefore, gave him as little real power
over Nature as real power in the direction of affairs.

As it is our purpose not to excuse, but to explain,
Bacon's conduct, — to identify the Bacon who during
this period wrote The Advancement of Learning, The
Wisdom of the Ancients, and the Novum Organum,
with the Bacon who within the same period was connected with the abuses of James's administration, — let
us survey his character in relation to his times. He
lived in an epoch when the elements of the English
Constitution were in a state of anarchy. The King
was following that executive instinct which brought the
head of his son to the block. The House of Commons
was following that legislative instinct which eventually
gave it the control of the executive administration.
James talked, and feebly acted, in the spirit of an absolute monarch, looked upon the House of Commons as
only an instrument for getting at the money of his subjects, and when it occupied itself in presenting griev-
ances, instead of voting subsidies, either dissolved it in a
pet or yielded to it in a fright. Had Bacon's nature
been as intense as it was sagacious, had he been a resolute statesman of the good or bad type, this was the

time for him to have anticipated Hampden in the Commons, or **Strafford** in the Council, and given himself, body and soul, to the cause of freedom or the cause of despotism. He did neither; and there is nothing in his writings which would lead us to suppose that he could have done either. The written advice he gave James and Buckingham on the improvement of the law, on church affairs, and on affairs of state, would, if it had been followed, have saved England from the necessity **for** the Long Parliament, Oliver Cromwell, and William of Orange. As it was, he probably prevented more evil than he was made the instrument of committing. But, after counselling wisely, he, like other statesmen of his time, consented to act against his own advice. **He lent** the aid of his professional skill to the court, **yet rather** as a lawyer who obeys a client than as a statesman responsible to his country. And the mischief was, that his mind, like all comprehensive minds, was so fertile in those reasons which convert what is abstractly wrong into what is relatively right, that he could easily find maxims of state to justify the attorney-general in doing what the statesman *in* the attorney-general condemned, especially as the practice of these maxims enabled the attorney-general to keep his office and to hope for a higher one. This was largely the custom with all English public men down to the time when " parliamentary government " was thoroughly established.   Besides, Bacon's attention was scattered over too many objects to allow of an all-excluding devotion to one.   He could not be a Hampden or a Strafford, because he was Bacon. Accomplished as a courtier, politician, orator, lawyer, jurist, statesman, man of letters, philosopher, with a wide-wandering mind that swept over the domain of positive knowledge only to turn dissatisfied into those vast and lonely tracts of meditation where future sciences and inventions slept in their undiscovered principles, it was impossible that a man thus hundred-eyed should be single-handed.   He also lacked two elements of strength which in that day lent vigor to action by contracting thought and inflaming passion.   He was without political and theological prejudice, and he was without political and theological malignity.

But, it may be asked, if he was too broad for the passions of politics, why did he become a politician at all ?   First, because he was an Englishman, the son of the Keeper of the Great Seal, and had breathed an atmosphere of politics — and of not very scrupulous politics — from his cradle ; second, because, well as he thought he understood nature, he understood human nature far better, and was tempted into affairs by conscious talent ; and third, because he was poor, dependent, had immense needs, and saw that poli-

tics had led his father and uncle to wealth and power. And, **coming to the** heart of the matter, if it be asked why a mind of such grandeur and comprehensiveness should sacrifice its integrity for such wealth **as** office could give, and such titles as James could bestow, we can answer the question intelligently only by looking at wealth and titles through Bacon's eyes. His conscience was weakened by that which gives such splendor and attractiveness to his writings, — his imagination. He was a philosopher, but a philosopher in whose character imagination was co-ordinated with reason. This imagination was not merely a quality of his intellect, but an element **of** his nature: and as, through its instinctive workings, he was not content to send **out his** thoughts stoically **bare** of adornment, or limping **and** ragged in cynic squalor, but clothed them in purple **and** gold, and made them move in majestic cadences: so also, through his imagination, he saw, in external pomp and affluence and high place, something that corresponded **to** his own inward opulence and autocracy of intellect; recognized in them the superb and fitting adjuncts and symbols of his internal greatness; and, investing them with a glory not their own, felt that in them the great Bacon was clothed in outward circumstance, that the invisible person was made palpable to the senses, embodied and expressed to all eyes as the man

> Whom a wise king and Nature chose
> Lord Chancellor of both their Laws."

So strong was this illusion, that, when hurled from power and hunted by creditors, he refused to raise money by cutting down the woods of his estate. "I will not," he said, "be stripped of my fine feathers." He had so completely ensouled the accompaniments and "compliment extern" of greatness, that he felt, in losing them, as if portions of the outgrowth of his being had been rudely lopped.

But a day of reckoning was at hand, which was to dissipate all this visionary splendor, and show the hollowness of all accomplishments when unaccompanied by simple integrity. Bacon had idly drifted with the stream of abuses, until at last he partook of them. It is to his credit, that, in 1621, he strenuously advised the calling of the Parliament by which he was impeached. The representatives of the people met in a furious mood, and exhibited a menacing attitude towards the court; and the King, thoroughly cowed, made haste to give up to their vengeful justice the culprits at whom they aimed. Bacon was impeached for corruption in his high office, and, in indescribable agony and abasement of spirit, was compelled by the King to plead guilty to the charges, of a large portion of which he was certainly innocent. The great Chancellor has ever since been imaged to the honest English imagination as a man with **his head** high up **in** the heaven of contemplation, seemingly absorbed in sublime meditations, while his hand is held stealthily out to receive a bribe ! **On** the degree of his moral guilt it is difficult at this time to decide. The probability seems to be that, in accordance with a general custom, he and his dependents received presents from the suitors in his court. The presents were given to influence his decision of **cases.** He — at once profuse and poor — took presents from both **parties,** and then decided according to the law. He **was** exposed by those who, having given money, were exasperated at receiving "killing decrees" in return, — who found that Bacon did not **sell** injustice, but justice. He was sentenced to pay a fine of £ 40,000 ; **to** be imprisoned in the Tower during the King's pleasure; to be forever incapable of holding any public office, place, or employment ; and forbidden to sit in Parliament or come within the verge of the Court. Bacon **seems** himself to have considered that a notorious abuse, in which other chancellors had participated, was reformed in his punishment. He is reported to have said, afterwards, in conversation, " I was the justest judge that was in England these fifty years ; but it was the justest censure in Parliament that was these two hundred years." The courts of Russia are now notoriously corrupt ; in some future time, when the nation imperatively demands a reformation of the judicial tribunals, some great Russian, famous as a thinker and man of letters as well as judge, will, though comparatively innocent, be selected as a victim, and the whole system be rendered infamous in his condemnation.

Bacon lived five years after his disgrace ; and, during these years, though plagued by creditors and vexed by domestic disquiet, he prosecuted his literary and scientific labors with singular vigor and success. In revising old works, in producing new, and in projecting even greater ones than he produced, he displayed an energy and opulence of mind wonderful even in him. He died on the 9th of April, 1626, in consequence of a cold caught in trying an experiment to ascertain if flesh might not be preserved in snow as well as salt ; and his consolation in his last hours was, that the " experiment succeeded excellently well." There are two testimonials to him, after he was hurled from power and place, which convey a vivid idea of the benignant stateliness of his personal presence, — of the impression he made on those contemporaries who were at once his intimates and subordinates, and who, in the most familiar intercourse, felt and honored the easy dignity with which his greatness was worn. " My conceit of his person," says Ben Jonson, " was never increased towards

him by his place or honors; but I have and do **rever-**
ence him for the greatness that **was** only proper to himself; **in that** he seemed to me ever, by his **work, one
of** the greatest men, and most worthy **of admiration,**
that had been in many ages. In his adversity, **I ever**
prayed that God would give him strength; for greatness
he could not want." And Dr. Rawley, his **domestic**
chaplain, **who saw him** as he appeared in the **most**
familiar relations **of** his home, **remarks, with** quaint
veneration, "**I** have been induced to think that, if ever
there were a beam of knowledge derived from God upon
any man in these modern times, it was upon him."

II.

WE propose in this chapter to give some account of Bacon's writings; and the first place in such an account belongs to his philosophical works relating to the interpretation of nature.

As Bacon, from his boyhood, was a thinker living in the thick of affairs, with a discursive reason held in check by the pressure of palpable facts, he equally escaped the narrowness of the secluded student and the narrowness of the practical man of the world. It was therefore but natural that, early in his collegiate life, he should feel a contempt for the objects and the methods of the philosophy current among the scholars of his time. The true object of philosophy must be either to increase our knowledge or add to our power. The ancient and scholastic systems seemed to him to have failed in both. They had not discovered truths, they had not invented arts. Admitting that the highest use of knowledge was the pure joy it afforded the intellect, and that its lowest use was its ministration to the practical wants of man, it seemed to him evident that their

method led as little to knowledge that enriched the mind
as to knowledge that gave cunning to the hands. Aiming at self-culture by self-inspection, rather than by in-
spection of nature, they had neglected, he thought, the
great world of God for the little world of man; **so that
at last** it seemed as if the peculiar distinction of knowledge consisted in knowing that nothing could be **known.**
But the question might arise, Was not the barrenness
of their results due to the selfish littleness, rather than
the disinterested elevation, of their aim? Introduce into
philosophy a philanthropic motive, make man the thinker
aid man the laborer, unite contemplation with a practical purpose, and discard the idea that knowledge was
intended for the exclusive gratification of a few **selected**
spirits, and philosophy would then increase in largeness
and elevation as much as it would increase in usefulness; for if such a revolution **in its** spirit, object, and
method could be made, it would continually furnish new
truths for the intellect to contemplate, from the impetus
given to the discovery of new truths by the perception
that they could be applied to relieve human necessities.
If it were objected that philosophy could not stoop from
her ethical and spiritual heights to the drudgery of investigating natural laws, it might be answered, that what
God had condescended to create it surely was not ignoble in man to examine; " for that which is deserving

of existence is deserving **of** knowledge, the image of existence." If philosophers had a higher notion of their dignity, Francis Bacon did not share it; and, accordingly, early in life he occupied his mind in devising a method of investigating the secrets of nature **in** order to wield her powers.

The conception was one of the noblest that ever entered the mind of man; but was it accomplished? **As** Bacon's name seems to be stereotyped in popular and scientific speech as the " Father of the Inductive Sciences," and as all the charity refused to his life has been heaped upon his philosophical labors, it may seem presumptuous to answer this question. in the negative; yet nothing is more certain than that the inductive sciences have *not* followed the method which he invented, and have *not* arrived at the results which he proposed **to** accomplish.

The mistake, as it regards Bacon, has risen principally from confounding induction with the Baconian *method* of induction. If we were to tell our readers that there were great undiscovered laws in nature, and should strongly advise them to examine particular facts with great care, in order through them to reach **the** knowledge of those laws, **we** should recommend the practice of induction; but even if they should heed and **follow the** advice, we much doubt if any scientific discoveries would ensue. Indeed, if Bacon himself could hear the recommendation made, and could adopt the modern mode of spiritual communication, there would be a succession of indignant raps on the editorial table, which, being interpreted, would run thus : " Ladies and gentlemen, the mode of induction recommended to you is radically vicious and incompetent. Truth **cannot be** discovered in that way; but if you will select any **given** matter which requires investigation, **and will follow** the mechanical mode of procedure laid down in my method of induction (Novum Organum, Book II.), you will be able, without any special scientific genius, to hunt the very form and essence of the nature you seek to its last hiding-place, and compel it to yield up its innermost secret. All that is required is common capacity, united with persevering labor and combination of purpose." This is not exactly Bacon's rhetoric; but, as spirits, when **they** leave the body, seem somehow to acquire a certain pinched and poverty-stricken mode of expression, it will do to convey his idea.

Bacon, the philosopher, is therefore to be considered, not as a man who invented and recommended induction, for induction is as old as human nature, — was, in fact, invented by Adam, — and, as practised in Bacon's time, was the mark of his especial scorn; but he is to be considered as one who invented and recommended a **new** *method* of induction, a system of precise rules to guide induction, a new logic, or organ, which was to supersede the Aristotelian logic. He proudly called it his art of inventing sciences. A method of investigation presupposes, of course, some conception of the objects to be investigated ; and of the infinite variety **and** complexity of nature Bacon had no idea. His method proceeds on the notion that all the phenomena of nature are capable of being referred to combinations of certain abstract qualities of matter, — simple natures, which are limited in number if difficult of access. Such are density, rarity, heat, cold, color, levity, **tenuity,** weight, and the like. These **are** the alphabet of nature ; and, as all words result from the combination **of a few letters,** so all phenomena result from the combination **of a few elements.** What is gold, for example, but the co-ordination of certain qualities, such **as** greatness of weight, closeness **of parts,** fixation, softness, etc. ? Now, if the causes of these simple natures were known, they might be combined by **man** into the same or a similar substance ; " for," he says, " if anybody can make a metal which has all these properties, let men dispute whether it be gold or no." But these qualities are not ultimate ; they are the effects **of causes, and a** knowledge of the causes will enable us to superinduce the effects. The connection between philosophy and practice is this, that what

' in contemplation stands for cause, in operation stands for means **or** instrument; for we know by causes and operate by means." The object of philosophy, therefore, is the investigation of the formal causes of the primary qualities of matter, of those causes which are always present when the qualities are present, always absent when the qualities are absent, increase with their increase, and decrease with their decrease. Facts, then, are the stairs by which we mount into the region of essences; and, grasping and directing these, we can compel nature to create new facts, as truly natural as those she spontaneously produces, for art simply gives its own direction to her working.

From this exposition it will be seen how little foundation there is for Dugald Stewart's remark, that Bacon avoided the fundamental error of the ancients, according to whom "philosophy is the science of causes"; and also for the assertion of Comte and his school, that Bacon was the father of positive science. There is nothing more repugnant to a positivist than the introduction into science of causes and essences; yet it was after these that Bacon aimed. "The spirit of man," **he says,** "is as the lamp of God, wherewith he searcheth **the** *inwardness* of all secrets." The word he uses is " Form," but Form with him is both cause and essence, an immanent cause, a cause that creates a permanent

quality. If he sometimes uses Form as synonymous
with Law, the sense in which he understands Law is not
merely the mode in which a force operates, but the
force itself. Indeed, there is reason to suppose that,
much as he decries Plato, he was still willing to use
Form as identical with Idea, in the Platonic sense of
Idea; for in an aphorism in which he severely condemns
the projection of human conceits upon natural objects,
he remarks that "there is no small difference between
the idols of the human mind and the ideas of the Divine Mind, that is to say, between certain idle dogmas
and the real stamp and impression of created objects as
they are found in Nature." Coleridge had perhaps
this aphorism in mind when he called Bacon the British
Plato.

The object of Bacon's philosophy, then, is the investigation of the forms of simple natures; his method is
the path the understanding must pursue in order to
arrive at this object. This method is a most ingenious
but cumbrous machinery for collecting, tabling, sifting,
testing, and rejecting facts of observation and experiment which have any relation to the nature sought. It
begins with inclusion and proceeds by exclusion. It has
affirmative tables, negative tables, tables of comparison,
tables of exclusion, tables of prerogative instances.
From the mass of individual facts originally collected

everything is eliminated, until nothing is left but **the** form or cause which is sought. The field of induction is confined, as it were, within a triangular space, at the base of which are the facts obtained by observation and experiment. From these the investigator proceeds inwards, by comparison and exclusion, constantly narrowing the field as he advances, until at last, all non-essentials being rejected, nothing is left but the pure form.

Nobody can read the details of this method, as given at length in the second book of the Novum Organum, without admiration for the prodigious constructive power of Bacon's mind. The twenty-seven tables of prerogative instances, or "the comparative value of facts **as** means of investigation," would alone be sufficient to prove the comprehensiveness of his intellect and its capacity of ideal classification. But still the method is **a splendid,** unrealized, and we may add, incompleted, dream. **He** never himself discovered anything by its use. Nobody since his time has discovered anything by its use. And the reason is plain. Apart from its positive defects, there is this general criticism to be made, that a true method must be **a** generalization from **the** mental processes which *have been* followed in discovery and invention; it cannot precede them. If Bacon really had devised the method which succeeding men of science slavishly followed, he would deserve more than the most extravagant panegyrics he has received. Aristotle is famous as a critic for generalizing the rules of epic and dramatic poetry from the practice of Homer and the Greek tragedians ; what fame would not be his, if his rules had preceded Homer and the Greek dramatists ? Yet Macaulay, and many others who have criticised **Bacon,** while pretending to depreciate all rules as useless, still say that Bacon's analysis of the inductive method is **a true** and good analysis, and that the method has since his time been instinctively followed by all successful investigators of nature, — as if Bacon had not constructed his inductive rules from a deep-rooted distrust of men's inductive instincts. **But it is** plain to everybody who has read Comte and Mill and Whewell, that the method of discovery is still a debatable question ; and, with **all** our immense superiority to the age of Bacon in the possession of facts on which to build a method, we have settled as yet on no philosophy of the objects or the processes of science. There are many disputed methods, but no accepted method ; the anarchy of opinions here corresponds to the anarchy in metaphysics ; and the establishment **of a** philosophy of discovery and invention must wait the establishment of a philosophy of the mind which discovers **and** invents.

But we know enough to give the **reasons of Bacon's failure.** The defects of his method can be demonstrated from the separate judgments of his warmest eulogists. First, Bacon was no mathematician, and Playfair admits that " in all physical inquiries where mathematical reasoning has been employed, after **a** few principles have been established by experience, a vast multitude of truths, equally certain with the principles themselves, have been *deduced* from them by the mere application of geometry and algebra." Bacon's prevision, then, did not extend to the foresight of the great part that mathematical science was to perform in the interpretation of nature. Second, Sir John Herschel, who follows Playfair in making Bacon the father of experimental philosophy, still gives a deadly blow to Bacon's celebrated tables of prerogative instances, considered as *real* aids to the understanding, when he admits that the same sagacity which enables an inquirer to assign an instance or observation to its proper class, enables him, without that process, to recognize its proper value. Third, Sir James Mackintosh, who claims for Bacon, that, if he did not himself make discoveries, he taught mankind the *method* by which discoveries are made, and who asserts that the physical sciences owe all that they are or ever will be to Bacon's method and spirit, refers to the 104th aphorism of the first book of the Novum Organum, as containing the condensed essence of his philosophy. This aphorism affirms that the path to the most general truths is a series of ascending inductive steps ; that the lowest generalizations must first be established, then the middle principles, then the highest. It is curious that Mackintosh should praise a philosopher of facts for announcing a theory which facts have disproved. The merest glance at the history of the sciences shows that the opposite principle is rather the true one ; that the most general principles have been first reached. Mill can excuse Bacon for this blunder only by saying that he could not have fallen into it if there had existed in his time a single deductive science, such as mechanics, astronomy, optics, acoustics, etc., now are. Of course he could not ; but the fact remains that he did not foresee the course, or prescribe the true method, of science, and that he did not even appreciate the way in which his contemporaries, Kepler and Galileo, were building up sciences by processes different from his own. It is amazing, however, that Mackintosh — with his knowledge of the discovery of the law of gravitation, the most universal of all natural laws, as an obvious contradiction of the theory — should have adopted Bacon's error.

Fourth, Bacon's method of exclusion, the one element of his system which gave it originality, proceeds, as John Stuart Mill has pointed out, on the assumption that a phenomenon can have but one cause ; and is therefore not applicable to coexistences, as to successions, of phenomena.

Fifth, Bacon's method, though it proceeds on a conception of nature which is an hypothesis exploded, and though it is itself an hypothesis which has proved sterile, still does not admit of hypotheses as guides to investigation. The last and ablest editor of his philosophical works, Mr. Ellis, concedes the practical inutility of his method on this ground, that the process by which scientific truths have been established " involves an element to which nothing corresponds in Bacon's tables of comparison and exclusion ; namely, the application to the facts of observation of a principle of arrangement, an idea, existing in the mind of the discoverer antecedently to the act of induction."

Indeed, Bacon's method was disproved by his own contemporaries. Kepler tried twenty guesses on the orbit of Mars, and the last fitted the facts. Galileo deduced important principles from assumptions, and then brought them to the test of experiment. Gilbert's hypothesis, that " the earth is a great natural magnet with two poles," is now more than an hypothesis. The Novum Organum contains a fling at the argument from final causes ; and, the very year it was published, Harvey, the friend and physician of Bacon, by reasoning on the final cause of the valves in the veins, discovered the circulation of the blood. All these men had the scientific instinct and scientific genius that Bacon lacked.

They made no antithesis between the anticipation of nature and the interpretation of nature, but they anticipated in order to interpret. It is not the disuse of hypotheses, but the testing of hypotheses by facts, and the willingness to give them up when experience decides against them, which characterizes the scientific mind.

Sixth, Bacon, though he aimed to institute a philosophy of observation, and gave rules for observing, was not himself a sharp and accurate observer of nature, — did not possess, as has often been remarked, acuteness in proportion to his comprehensiveness. His Natural History, his History of Life and Death, of Density and Rarity, and the like, all prove a mental defect disqualifying him for the business. His eye roved when it should have been patiently fixed. He caught at resemblances by the instinct of his wide-ranging intellect, and this peculiarity, constantly indulged, impaired his power of distinguishing differences. He spread his mind over a space so large that its full strength was not concentrated on anything. He could not check the discursive action of his intellect and hold it down to the sharp, penetrating, dissecting analysis of single appearances ; and his brain was teeming with too many schemes to allow of that mental fanaticism, that fury of mind, which impelled Kepler to his repeated assaults on the tough problem of the planetary orbits. The same bewildering multiplicity of objects which prevented him from throwing his full force into affairs and taking a decided stand as a statesman, operated likewise to dissipate his energies as an explorer of nature. The analogies, relations, likenesses of things occupied his attention, to the exclusion of a searching examination of the things themselves. As a courtier, lawyer, jurist, politician, statesman, man of science, student of universal knowledge, he has been practically excelled in each **department** by special men, because his intellect was one which refused to be arrested and fixed.

And, in conclusion, the essential defect of the Baconian method consists in its being an invention of genius to dispense with the necessity of genius. It was, **as Mr.** Ellis has well remarked, " a mechanical mode of procedure, pretending **to** lead to absolute certainty of result." It levelled capacities, because the virtue was in the instrument **used,** and not in the person using it. Bacon illustrates the importance of his method by saying that a man of ordinary ability with a pair of compasses can describe a better circle than a man of the greatest genius without such help; that the lame, in the path, outstrip the swift who wander from it ; indeed, the very skill and swiftness of him who runs not in the right direction only increases his aberration. With his view of philosophy, — as the investigation of the forms of a limited number of simple natures, — he thought that, with " the purse of a prince and the assistance of a people," a sufficiently copious natural history might be formed, within a comparatively short period, to furnish the materials for the working of his method; and then the grand instauration of the sciences would be rapidly completed. In this scheme there could, of course, be only one great name, — the name of Bacon. Those who collected the materials, those who applied the method, would be only his clerks. His office was that of Secretary of State for the interpretation of nature; Lord Chancellor of the laws of existence, and Legislator of science; Lord Treasurer of the riches of the universe; the Intellectual Potentate equally of science and art, with no aristocracy round his throne, but with a bureaucracy in its stead, taken from the middle class of intellect and character. There was no place for Harvey and Newton and Halley and Dalton and La Place and Cuvier and Agassiz; for genius was unnecessary: the new logic, the Novum Organum, — Bacon himself, mentally alive in the brains which applied his method, — was all in all. Splendid discoveries would be made, those discoveries would be beneficently applied, but they would be made by clerks and applied by clerks. All these discoveries were latent in the Baconian method, and over all the completed intellectual globe of science, as in the commencement of the Novum Organum, would **be** written, " Francis of Verulam thought thus ! " And if Bacon's method had been really followed by succeeding men of science, this magnificent autocracy of under-standing and imagination would have been justified ; and round the necks of each of them would be a collar, on which would be written, " This person is so and so, ' born thrall ' of Francis of Verulam." That this serene feeling of spiritual superiority, and consciousness of being the founder of a new empire in the world of mind, was *in* Bacon, we know by the general tone of his writings, and the politic contempt with which he speaks of the old autocrats, Aristotle and Plato ; and Harvey, who knew him well, probably intended **to hit** this imperial loftiness, when he described him **as** **" writ-ing** philosophy like a Lord Chancellor." " The guillo-tine governs ! " said Barrère, gayly, when some friend compassionated his perplexities as a practical statesman during the Reign of Terror. " The Method governs ! " would have been the reply of a Baconian underling, had the difficulties of his attempts to penetrate the in-most mysteries of nature been suggested to him.

Thus, by the use of Bacon's own method of exclusion we exclude him from the position due of right to Galileo and Kepler. In the inquiry respecting the father of the inductive sciences, he is not " the nature sought."

What, then, is the cause of his fame among the scientific men of England and France? They certainly have not spent their time in investigating the forms of simple natures; they certainly have not used his method: why have they used his name?

In answer to this question, it may be said that Bacon, participating in the intellectual movement of the higher minds of his age, recognized the paramount importance of observation and experiment in the investigation of nature; and it has since been found convenient to adopt, as the father and founder of the physical sciences, one whose name lends to them so much literary prestige, and who was undoubtedly one of the broadest, richest, and most imperial of human intellects, if he was not one of the most scientific. Then he is the most eloquent of all discoursers on the philosophy of science, and the general greatness of his mind is evident even in the demonstrable errors of his system. No other writer on the subject is a classic, and Bacon is thus a link connecting men of science with men of letters and men of the world. Whewell, Comte, Mill, Herschel — with more abundant material, with the advantage of generalizing the philosophy of the sciences from their history — are instinctively felt by every reader to be smaller men than Bacon. As thinkers, they appear thin and unfruitful when we consider his fulness of suggestive thought; as writers, they have no pretension **to the** massiveness, splendor, condensation, and regal dignity of his rhetoric. **The** Advancement of Learning, and the first book of the Novum Organum, are full of quotable sentences, in which solid wisdom is clothed in the aptest, most vivid, most imaginative, and most executive expression. If a man of science at the present day wishes for a compact statement in which to embody his scorn of bigotry, of dogmatism, of intellectual conceit, of any of the idols of the human understanding which obstruct its perception of natural truth, it is to Bacon that he goes for an aphorism.

And it is doubtless true that the spirit which animates Bacon's philosophical works is a spirit which inspires effort and infuses **cheer.** It is impossible to say **how far** this spirit has animated inventors and discoverers. But we know, from the enthusiastic admiration expressed for him by men of science who could not have been blind **to the** impotence of his method, that all minds his spirit touched it must have influenced. One principle stands plainly out in his writings, — that the intellect of man, purified from its idols, is competent for the conquest of nature ; and to this glorious task he, above all other men, gave an epical dignity and loftiness. His superb rhetoric is the poetry of physical science. The humblest laborer in that field feels, in reading Bacon, that he himself is **one of a band of heroes**, wielding weapons mightier than those of Achilles and Agamemnon, engaged in a siege nobler than that of Troy; **for, in** so far as he **is** honest and capable, he is " Man, the minister and interpreter of Nature," concerned, " not in the amplification of the power of one man over his country, nor in **the** amplification of the power of that country over other countries, but **in** the amplification of the power and kingdom **of** mankind over the universe."   And, while **Bacon has** thus given an ideal elevation to the pursuit **of** science, he has at the same time pointed out most **distinctly those** diseases of the mind which check or mislead it in the task of interpretation.   As a student of nature, his fame is greater than his deserts ; as a student **of** human nature, he is hardly yet appreciated ; and it is to the greater part of the first book of the Novum Organum — where he deals in general reflections on those mental habits and dispositions which interfere with **pure** intellectual conscientiousness, and where his beneficent spirit and rich imagination lend sweetness and beauty to the homeliest practical wisdom — that the reader impatiently returns, after being wearied with the details of his method given in the second book.   His method was antiquated in his own lifetime ; but it is to be feared **that** centuries hence his analysis of the idols of the human understanding will be as fresh as human vanity **and pride.**

It was not, then, in the knowledge of nature, but in the knowledge of human nature, that Bacon pre-eminently excelled. By this it is not meant that he was a metaphysician in the usual sense of the term, — though his works contain as valuable hints to metaphysicians as to naturalists, — for these hints are on matters at one remove from the central problems of metaphysics. In**deed, for** all those questions which relate to the **nature** of the mind and the mode by which it obtains its ideas, **for all** questions which are addressed to our speculative reason alone, he seems to have felt an aversion almost irrational. They appeared to him to minister to the delight and vain-glory of the thinker without yielding any fruit of wisdom which could be applied to human affairs. " Pragmatical man," he says, " should not go away with an opinion that learning is like a lark, that can mount, and sing, and please herself, and nothing **else** ; but may know that she holdeth as well of the **hawk,** that can soar aloft, and can also descend and strike upon the prey." Not, then, the abstract qualities and powers of the human mind, considered as special objects of investigation independent of individuals, but the combination **of** these into concrete character, **in**terested Bacon. He regarded the machinery in motion ; the human being as he thinks, feels, and lives ; men in their relations with men : and the phenomena presented

in history and life he aimed to investigate as he would
investigate the phenomena of the natural world. This
practical science of human nature, in which the discovery of general laws seems hopeless to every mind
not ample enough to escape being overwhelmed by the
confusion, complication, and immense variety of the details, — and which it will probably take ages to complete,
— this science Bacon palpably advanced. His eminence here is evident from his undisputed superiority to other prominent thinkers in the same department. Hallam justly remarks, that, " if we compare
what may be found in the sixth, seventh, and eighth
books De Augmentis; in the Essays, the History of
Henry VII., and the various short treatises contained in
his " [Bacon's] " works on moral and political wisdom,
and on human nature (from experience of which all such
wisdom is drawn) ; — if we compare these works of Bacon with the rhetoric, ethics, and politics of Aristotle, or
with the histories most celebrated for their deep insight
into civil society and human character, — with Thucydi-
des, Tacitus, Philippe de Commines, Machiavel, Davila,
Hume, — we shall, I think, find that one man may be
compared with all these together."

The most valuable peculiarity of this wisdom is, that
it not merely points out what should be done, but it
points out how it can be done. This is especially true

of all his directions for the culture of the individual mind; the mode by which the passions may be disciplined, and the intellect enriched, enlarged, and strengthened. So with the relations of the individual to his household, to society, to government: he indicates the method by which these relations may be known and the duties they imply performed. In his larger speculations, regarding the philosophy of law, the principles of universal justice, and the organic character of national institutions, he anticipates, by the sweep of his intellect, the ideas of the jurists and historians of the present century. Volumes have been written which are merely expansions of this statement of Bacon, that "there are in nature certain fountains of justice, whence all civil laws are derived but as streams; and like as waters **do take** tinctures and tastes from the soils through which they run, so do civil laws vary according to the regions and governments where they are planted, though they proceed from the same fountain." The Advancement of Learning, afterwards translated and expanded into the Latin treatise **De** Augmentis, is an inexhaustible storehouse of such thoughts, — thoughts which have constituted the capital of later thinkers, but which never appear to so much advantage as in the compact imaginative form in which they were originally expressed.

It is important, however, that, in admitting to the full

Bacon's just claims as a philosopher of human nature, we should avoid the mistake of supposing him to have possessed acuteness in the same degree in which he possessed comprehensiveness. Mackintosh says that he is "probably a single instance of a mind which in philosophizing always reaches the point of elevation whence the whole prospect is commanded, without ever rising to that distance which prevents a distinct perception of every part of it." This judgment is accurate as far as it regards parts as elements of a general view; but in the special view of single parts Bacon has been repeatedly excelled by men whom it would be absurd to compare to him in general wisdom. His mind was contracted to details by effort; it dilated by instinct. It was telescopic rather than microscopic: its observation of men was extensive rather than minute. "Were it not better," he asks, "for a man in a fair room to set up one great light, or branching candlestick of lights, than to go about with a small watch-candle into every corner?" Certainly; but the small watch-candle, in some investigations, is better than the great central lamp; and his genius accordingly does not include the special genius of such observers as La Bruyère, Rochefoucauld, Saint-Simon, Balzac, and Shaftesbury, — the detective police of society, politics, and letters, — men whose intellects were contracted to a sharp, sure,

cat-like peering into the darkest crevices of individual natures, whose eyes dissected what they looked upon, and for whom the slightest circumstance was a key that opened the whole character to their glance. For example : Saint-Simon sees a lady whose seemingly ingenuous diffidence makes her charming to everybody. He peers into her soul, and declares, as the result of his vision, that "modesty is one of her arts." Again, after the death of the son of Louis XIV., the court **was** of course overwhelmed with decorous grief; the new dauphin and dauphiness were especially inconsolable for the loss, and, to all witnesses but one, were weeping copiously. Saint-Simon simply says, "Their eyes were wonderfully dry, but well managed." Bacon might have inferred hypocrisy; **but** he would not have observed the lack of moisture in the eyes amid all the convulsive sobbing and the agonized dips and waves of the handker- **chiefs.** Take another instance. . The Duke of Orleans amazed the court by the diabolical recklessness of his conduct. Saint-Simon alone saw that ordinary vices had no pungency for the Duke; that he must spice licentious- ness with atheism, blasphemy, and incest, in order to de- rive any pleasure from it ; and solves the problem by say- ing that he was " born *blasé*," — that he took up vice at the point at which his ancestors had left it, and had no choice but to carry it to new heights of impudence or to reject it altogether.   Again, — to take an example from a practical politician : Shaftesbury, who played the game of faction with such exquisite subtlety in the reign of Charles II., detected the fact of the secret marriage between the king's **brother** and Anne Hyde by noticing **at** dinner that her mother, Lady Clarendon, could not avoid expressing a faint deference in her manner when she helped her daughter to the meat ; and **on** **this** slight indication he acted as confidently as if he had **learned** the fact by being present at the wedding.

Now neither in his life nor in his writings does Bacon **indicate** that he had studied individuals with this keen attentiveness.   His knowledge of human nature was the result of the tranquil deposit, year after **year**, into his receptive and capacious intellect, of **the** facts of **history** and of his own wide experience of various kinds of life. **These he** pondered, classified, reduced to principles, and embodied in sentences which have ever since been quotable texts for jurists, moralists, historians, and statesmen ; and all the while his own servants were deceiving and plundering him, and his subordinates enriching themselves with bribes taken in his name.   The " small watch-candle " would have **been** valuable to him **here.**

The **work** by which his wisdom has reached the popular **mind is** his collection of Essays.   **As** originally published in 1597, it contained only ten ; in the last edition published in his lifetime, the number was increased to fifty-seven. As they were the sifted result of much observation and meditation on public and private life, he truly could say of their matter, that " it could not be found in **books.**" Their originality can hardly be appreciated at present, for most of their thoughts have been incorporated with the minds which have fed on them, and have been continually reproduced in other volumes. **Yet it** is probable that these short treatises are rarely thoroughly mastered, even by the most careful reader. Dugald Stewart testifies that after reading them for the twentieth **time** he observed something which **had escaped** his attention on the nineteenth. They combine the greatest brevity with the greatest beauty **of expression.** The thoughts follow each other with such rapid ease ; each thought is so truly an addition, and not an expansion of the preceding ; the point of view is so continually changed, **in** order that in one little essay the subject may be considered on all its sides and in all its bearings ; and each sentence is so capable of being developed into an essay, — that the work requires long pauses of reflection, and frequent re-perusal, to be estimated at its full worth. It not merely enriches the mind ; it enlarges it, and teaches it comprehensive habits **of** reflection. The disease of mental narrowness and fanaticism, it insensibly cures, by showing that every subject can be completely apprehended only by viewing it from various points; and a reader of Bacon instinctively meets the fussy or furious declaimer with the objection, "But, sir, there is another side to this matter."

It was one of Bacon's mistakes to believe that he would outlive the English language. Those of his works, therefore, which were not written in Latin he was eager to have translated into that tongue. The "Essays," coming home as they did to "men's business and bosoms," he was persuaded would "last as long as books should last"; and as he thought — to use his own words — "that these modern languages would at some time or other play the bankrupt with books," he employed Ben Jonson and others to translate the Essays into Latin. A Dr. Willmott published, in 1720, a translation of this Latin edition into what he called reformed and fashionable English. We will give a specimen. Bacon, in his Essay on Adversity, says: "Prosperity is the blessing of the Old Testament, adversity is the blessing of the New. . . . . . Yet even in the Old Testament, if you listen to David's harp, you shall hear as many hearse-like airs as carols." Dr. Willmott Englishes the Latin in this wise : "Prosperity belongs to the blessings of the Old Testament, adversity to the beatitudes of the New. . . . . Yet even in the Old **Testament,** if you listen to David's harp, you 'll find more lamentable airs than triumphant ones." This is translation with a vengeance!

Next to the Essays and the Advancement of Learning, the most attractive of Bacon's works is his **Wisdom of the** Ancients. Here his reason and imagination, intermingling or interchanging their processes, work conjointly, and produce a magnificent series of poems, **while** remorselessly analyzing imaginations into ideas. He supposes that, anterior to the Greeks, there were thinkers as wise as Bacon; that the heathen fables are poetical embodiments of secrets and mysteries of policy, philosophy, and religion ; truths folded up in mythological personifications ; "sacred relics," indeed, or " abstracted, rarefied airs of better times, which by tradition from more ancient nations fell into the trumpets and flutes of **the** Grecians." He, of course, finds in these fables what he brings to them, the inductive philosophy and all. The book is a marvel of ingenuity, **and** exhibits **the** astounding analogical power of his mind, both as respects analogies of reason and analogies of fancy. Had Bacon lived in the age of Plato and Aristotle, and written this work, he would have fairly triumphed over those philosophers ; for he would have reconciled ancient philosophy with ancient religion, and made faith in Jupiter and Pan consistent with reason.

But the work in which Bacon is most pleasingly exhibited is his philosophical romance, The New Atlantis. This happy island is a Baconian Utopia, a philosopher's paradise, where the Novum Organum is, in imagination, realized, and utility is carried to its loftiest idealization. In this country the king is good, and the people are good, because everything, even commerce, is subordinated to knowledge. "Truth" here "prints goodness." All sensual and malignant passions, all the ugly deformities of actual life, are sedately expelled from this glorious dream of a kingdom where men live in harmony with each other and with nature, and where observers, discoverers, and inventors are invested with an external pomp and dignity and high place corresponding to their intellectual elevation. Here is a college worthy of the name, Solomon's House, "the end of whose foundation is the knowledge of causes and the secret motions of things, and the enlarging the bounds of human empire to the effecting of all things possible"; and in Solomon's House Bacon's ideas are carried out, and man is in the process of "being restored to the sovereignty of nature." In this fiction, too, the peculiar benevolence of Bacon's spirit is displayed; and perhaps the finest sentence in his writings, certainly the one which best indicates the essential feeling of his soul as he regarded human misery and ignorance, occurs in his description of one of the fathers of Solomon's House. " His countenance," he says, " was as the countenance of one who pities men."

But, it may still be asked, how was it that a man of such large wisdom, with a soul of such pervasive beneficence, was so comparatively weak and pliant in his **life ?** This question touches his intellect no less than his character ; and it must be said that, both in the action of his mind and the actions of his life, there is observable a lack of emotional as well as of moral intensity. He is never impassioned, never borne away by an **overmastering** feeling or purpose. **There is no rush of ideas** and passions in his writings, no direct contact **and** close hug of thought and thing. Serenity, not speed, is his characteristic. Majestic as is the movement of his **intellect,** and far-reaching its glance, it still includes, adjusts, *feels into* the objects it contemplates, rather than darts at them like Shakespeare's or pierces them like Chaucer's. And this intelligence, so wise and so worldly-wise, **so** broad, bright, confident, and **calm,** with **the** moral element pervading **it as an** element of insight rather than as a motive of action, — this was the instrument on which **he** equally relied to advance learning **and** to advance Bacon. As a practical politician, he felt assured of his power to comprehend as a whole, and nicely to discern the separate parts of, the most complicated matter which pressed for judgment and for volition. Exercising insight and foresight on a multitude of facts and contingencies all present to his mind at once, he aimed to evoke order from confusion, to read events in their principles, to seize the salient point which properly determines the judgment, and then to act decisively for his purpose, safely for his reputation and fortune. Marvellous as this process of intelligence is, it is liable both to corrupt and mislead unless the moral sentiment be strong and controlling. The man transforms himself into a sort of earthly Providence, and by intelligence believes himself emancipated from strict integrity. But the intellectual eye, even when capable, like Bacon's, of being dilated at will, is no substitute for conscience, and no device has ever been invented which would do away with the usefulness of simple honesty and blind moral instinct. In the most comprehensive view in politics, something is sure to be left out, and that something is apt to vitiate the sagacity of the whole combination.

Indeed, there is such a thing as being over-wise, in dealing with practical affairs, and the defect of Bacon's intellect is seen the moment we compare it with an intellect like that of Luther. Bacon, with his serene superiority to impulse, and his power of giving his mind at pleasure its close compactness or fan-like spread, could hardly have failed to feel for Luther that compassionate contempt with which men possessing many ideas survey men who are possessed by one; yet it is certain that Luther never could have got entangled in Bacon's errors, for his habit was to cut knots **which** Bacon labored to untie. Men of Luther's stamp never aim to be wise by reach, but by intensity, of intelligence. They catch a vivid glimpse of some awful spiritual fact, in whose light the world dwindles and pales, and then follow its inspiration headlong, paying no heed to the insinuating whispers of prudence, and crashing through the glassy expediencies which obstruct **their path.** Such natures, in the short run, are the most **visionary;** in the long run, the most practical. Bacon has been praised by the most pertinacious revilers of his character for his indifference to the metaphysical and theological controversies which raged around him. They seem not to see that this indifference came from his deficiency in the intense moral and religious feelings out of which those controversies arose. It would have been better for himself had he been more of a fanatic; for such a stretch of intelligence as he possessed could be purchased only at the expense of diffusing the forces of his personality in meditative expansiveness, and of

weakening his power of dealing direct blows on the instinct or intuition of the moment.

But, while this man was without the austerer virtues
of humanity, we must not forget that he was also without its sour and malignant vices ; and he stands almost
alone in literature, as a vast, dispassionate intellect, in
which the sentiment of philanthropy has been refined
and purified into the subtile essence of thought. Without this philanthropy or goodness, he tells us, " man is
but a better kind of vermin " ; and love of mankind, with
Bacon, is not merely the noblest feeling but the highest
reason. This beneficence, thus transformed into intelligence, is not a hard opinion, but a rich and mellow
spirit of humanity, which communicates the life of the
quality it embodies ; and we cannot more fitly conclude
than by quoting the noble sentence in which Bacon, after
pointing out the common mistakes regarding the true end
of knowledge, closes by divorcing it from all selfish egotism and ambition. "Men," he says, "have entered
into a desire of learning and knowledge, sometimes upon
a natural curiosity and inquisitive appetite ; sometimes
to entertain their minds with variety and delight ; sometimes for ornament and reputation ; and sometimes to
enable them to victory of wit and contradiction ; and
most times for lucre and profession ; and seldom sin-
cerely, to give a true account of their gift of reason, to

the benefit and use of man : as if there were sought
in knowledge a couch whereupon to rest a searching and
restless spirit ; or **a** terrace for a wandering and variable mind to walk up and down with a fair prospect ; or a
tower of state, for a proud mind to raise itself upon ; or
a fort or commanding-ground for strife or contention ;
or a shop for profit and sale ; and not a rich storehouse,
for the glory of the Creator and the relief of man's
estate."

HOOKER.

THE life of the "learned and judicious" Mr. Richard Hooker, by Izaak Walton, is one of the most perfect biographies of its kind in literature. But it is biography on its knees; and though it contains some exquisite touches of characterization, it does not, perhaps, convey an adequate impression of the energy and enlargement of the soul whose meekness it so tenderly and reverentially portrays. The individuality of the writer is blended with that of his subject, and much of his representation of Hooker is an unconscious idealization of himself. The intellectual limitations of Walton are felt even while we are most charmed by the sweetness of his spirit, and the mind of the greatest thinker the Church of England has produced is not reflected on the page which celebrates his virtues.

Hooker's life is the record of the upward growth of a human nature into that region of sentiments and ideas where sagacity and sanctity, intelligence and goodness, are but different names for one vital fact. His soul, and the character his soul had organized, — the invisible but intensely and immortally alive part of him, —

was domesticated away up in the heavens, even while
the weak visible frame, which *seemed* to contain it,
walked the earth ; and though in this world thrown
controversially, at least, into the Church Militant, the
Church Militant caught, through him, a gleam **of the**
consecrating radiance, and a glimpse of the heaven-
wide ideas, of the Church Triumphant. There is much
careless talk, in our day, of " spiritual " communication ;
but it must never be forgotten that the condition of real
spiritual communication is height of soul ; and that the
true " mediums " are those rare persons through whom,
as through Hooker, spiritual communications stream, in
the conceptions of purified, spiritualized, celestialized
reason.

Hooker was born in 1553, and was the **son of poor**
parents, better qualified to rejoice in his early piety than
to appreciate his early intelligence. The schoolmaster
to whom the boy was sent, happy in a pupil whose inquisitive and acquisitive intellect was accompanied with
docility of temper, believed him, in the words of Walton, " to be blessed with an inward divine light " ; thought
him a little wonder ; and when his parents expressed
their intention to bind him apprentice to some trade, the
good man spared no efforts until he succeeded in interesting Bishop Jewell in the stripling genius. Hooker,
at the age of fourteen, was sent by Jewell to the Uni-

versity of Oxford ; and after Jewell's death Dr. Sandys, the Bishop of London, became his patron. He partly supported himself at the university **by taking** pupils ; and though these pupils were of his own age, they seem to have regarded their young instructor with as much reverence as they gave to the venerable professors, and a great deal more love. Two of these pupils, Edwin Sandys and George Cranmer, rose to distinction. As a teacher, Hooker communicated not merely the results of study, but the spirit of study ; some radiations from his own soul fell upon the minds he informed ; and the youth fortunate enough to be his pupil might have echoed the grateful eulogy of the poet : —

> " For he was like the sun, **giving me light,**
> Pouring into the caves **of my young brain**
> Knowledge from his bright fountains."

No one, perhaps, was better prepared to enter holy orders than Hooker, when, after fourteen years of the profoundest meditation and the most exhaustive study, he, in his twenty-eighth year, was made deacon and priest. And now came the most unfortunate event of his life ; and it came in consequence of an honor. He was appointed to preach at St. Paul's Cross, a pulpit cross erected in the churchyard of St. Paul's Cathedral, and from which a sermon was preached every Sunday by some eminent divine, before an assemblage composed of the Court, the city magistracy, and a great crowd of **people.** When Hooker arrived in London on Thursday, he was afflicted with so severe a cold that he despaired of being able to use his voice on Sunday. His host was a linen-draper by the name of Churchman; and the wife of this man took such care of her clerical guest, **that** his cold was sufficiently cured to enable him to preach his sermon. Before he could sufficiently express his gratitude, she proposed further to increase her claim upon it. Mrs. Churchman — unlike the rest of her sex — was a match-maker; and she represented to him that he, being of a weak constitution, ought to have a wife who would prove a nurse to him, and thus, by affectionate care, prolong his existence, and make it comfortable. Her benevolence **not** stopping here, she offered **to provide** such a one for him herself, if he thought fit to **marry.** **The** good man, who had, in his sermon, deemed himself capable of arguing the question of two wills in God, "an antecedent and a consequent will, — his first will, that all men should be saved; his second, that those only should be saved who had lived answerable to the degree of grace afforded them," — a subject large enough to convulse the theological world, — the good man listened to Mrs. Churchman with a more serene trustfulness than he would have listened **to an** Archbishop, and gave her power to select such a nurse-wife for him:

he, the thinker and scholar, — who, in the sweep of his mind through human learning, had probably never encountered an intelligence capable of deceiving his own, — falling blandly into the toils of an ignorant, cunning, and low-minded match-maker! This benevolent lady had a daughter, whose manners were vulgar, whose face was unprepossessing, whose temper was irritable and exacting, but who had youth, and romance enough to discriminate between being married and going out to service ; and this was the wife Mrs. Churchman selected, and this **was the** wife gratefully and guilelessly received from her hands by the "judicious Mr. Hooker." Izaak Walton moralizes sweetly and sedately over this transaction, taking the ground that it was providential, and **that** affliction is a divine diet imposed by God on souls that **he loves.** Is this the right way to look at **it?** Everything is providential after it has happened ; but retribution is in the events of providence, as well as chastening. Hooker, in truth, had unconsciously slipped into a sin ; for he had intended a marriage of convenience, and that of the worst sort. He had violated all the providential conditions implied in the sacred relation of marriage. It was a marriage in which there was no mutual affection, no assurance of mutual help, no union of souls ; **and as he** took his wife to be his nurse, what wonder that she preferred the more natural office of

vixen? And though every man and woman who **reads** the account of the manner in which she tormented **him** thinks she deserved to have had some mechanical contrivance attached to her shoulders which should box her ears at every scolding word she uttered, it seems to be overlooked that great *original* injustice was done to her. We take much delight in being the first who has ever said a humane word for the *injudicious* Mrs. Hooker. Married, but not mated, to that angelic intellect and that meek spirit, — taken as a servant more than as a wife, — she felt the degradation of her position keenly; and, there being no possibility of equality between them, she, in spiritual self-defence, established in the household the despotism of caprice and the tyranny of the tongue.

His marriage compelled Hooker to resign his fellowship at Oxford; and he accepted a small parish in the diocese **of** Lincoln. Here, about a year afterwards, he was visited by his two former pupils, Edwin Sandys and George Cranmer. It was sufficient for Mrs. Hooker to know that they were scholars, and that they revered her husband. She accordingly at once set in motion certain petty feminine modes of annoyance, to indicate that her husband was her servant, and that his friends were unwelcome guests. As soon as they were fairly engaged in conversation, recalling and living over the quiet joys of their college life, the amiable lady that Mr. Hooker had married to be his nurse called him sharply to come and rock the cradle. His friends were all but turned out of the house. Cranmer, in parting with him, said: "Good tutor, I am sorry that your lot is fallen in no better ground as to your parsonage; and more sorry that your wife proves not a more comfortable companion, after you have wearied yourself in your restless studies." "My dear George," was Hooker's answer, "if saints have usually a double share in the miseries of this life, I, that am none, ought not to repine at what my wise Creator hath appointed for me, but labor — as indeed I do daily — to submit mine to his will, and possess my soul in patience and peace." Is it not to be supposed that John Calvin, if placed in similar circumstances, would have shown a little more of the ancient Adam? Would it not have been somewhat dangerous for Catherine, wife of Martin Luther, to have screamed to her husband to come and rock the cradle while he was discoursing with Melancthon on the insufficiency of works?

One result of this visit of his pupils was that Sandys, whose father was Archbishop of York, warmly represented to that dignitary of the Church the scandal of allowing such a combination of the saint and sage as Richard Hooker to be buried in a small country parson-

age ; and, the mastership of the Temple falling vacant
at this time, the Archbishop used his influence with the
judges and benchers, and in March, 1585, obtained
the place for Hooker. But this promotion was destined
to give him new disquiets, rather than diminish old ones.
The lecturer who preached the evening sermons at
the Temple was Walter Travers, — an able, learned,
and resolute theologian, who preferred the Presbyterian
form of church-government to the Episcopal, and who,
in his theological belief, agreed with the Puritans. It
soon came to be noted that the sermon by Hooker in
the morning disagreed, both as to doctrine and discipline, with the sermon delivered by his subaltern in the
evening ; and **it** was wittily said that "the forenoon
sermon spake Canterbury and the afternoon Geneva."
This difference soon engaged public attention. Canterbury stepped in, and prohibited Geneva from preaching.
Travers appealed unsuccessfully to the Privy Council,
and then his friends privately printed his petition.
Hooker felt himself compelled to answer it. As the
controversy refers **to** deep mysteries of religion, still
vehemently debated, it would be impertinent to venture
a judgment on the relative merits of the disputants ;
but it may be said that the reasoning of Hooker, when
the discussion does **not** turn on the meaning of authoritative Scripture texts, insinuates itself with more sub-

tile cogency into the natural heart and brain, and is incomparably more human and humane, than the reasoning of his antagonist. A fine intellectual contempt steals out in Hooker's rejoinder to the charges of Travers regarding some minor ceremonies, for which the Puritans, in their natural jealousy of everything that seemed popish, had, perhaps, an irrational horror, and to which the Churchmen were apt to give an equally irrational importance. Hooker quietly refers to " other exceptions, so like these, as but to name I should have thought a greater fault than to commit them." One retort has acquired deserved celebrity : " Your next argument consists of railing and reasons. To your railing I say nothing ; to your reasons I say what follows."

It was unfortunate for Hooker's logic that it was supported by the arm of power. Travers had the great advantage of being persecuted ; and his numerous friends in the Temple found ways to make Hooker so uncomfortable that he wished himself back in his secluded parish, with nobody to torment him but his wife. He was a great controversialist, as far as reason enters into controversies ; but the passions which turn controversies into contentions, and edge arguments with invective, were foreign to his serenely capacious intellect and peaceable disposition. As he brooded over the condition of the Church and the disputes raging within it, he more and more felt the necessity of surveying the whole controversy from a higher ground, in larger relations, and in a more Christian spirit. So far, the dispute raged within, and had not rent, the Church. The Puritans were not dissenters, attacking the Church from without, but reformers, attempting to alter its constitution from within. The idea occurred to Hooker, that a treatise might be written, demonstrating " the power of the Church to make canons for the use of ceremonies, and by law to impose obedience to them, as upon her children," — written with sufficient comprehensiveness of thought and learning to convince the reason of his opponents, and with sufficient comprehensiveness of love to engage their affections. This **idea** ripened into the Ecclesiastical Polity. He began this treatise at the Temple ; but he found that the theological atmosphere of the place, though it stimulated the intellectual, was ungenial to the loving qualities he intended to embody in his treatise ; and he therefore begged the Archbishop to transfer him to some quiet parsonage, where he might think in peace. Accordingly, in 1591, he received the Rectory of Boscum; and afterwards, in 1595, the Queen, who seems to have held him in great respect, presented him with the living of Bourne, where he remained until his death, which occurred in the year 1600, in his forty-sixth year. In 1594 four books of the Ecclesiastical **Polity** were published, and a fifth in 1597; the others not till after his death. **Walton** gives a most **beautiful** picture **of** him in his parsonage, illustrating Hooker's own maxim, "**that** the life **of a pious** clergy-**man is** visible rhetoric." His humility, benevolence, self-denial, devotion to his duties, the innocent **wisdom** which marked his whole intercourse with his parish-ioners, and his fasting and mortifications, are **all set forth in** Walton's blandest diction. The most surprising **item in this** list of perfections is **the last**; for how, with "**the** clownish **and** silly " Mrs. Hooker always snarling **and** snapping **below**, while he **was** looking into the empyrean of ideas from the summits of his intellect, he needed **any more of** the discipline **of mortification, it** would puzzle the **most** resolute ascetic **to tell. That** amiable **lady, as** soon **as she** understood **that** her hus-band was opposed to the Puritans, seems to have joined **them;** spite, and the desire to plague him, appearing to **inspire** her with **an** unwonted interest **in** theology, **though we have no** record of **her** theological genius, **except the** apparently erroneous report that, after Hooker's death, she destroyed or mutilated some of his manuscripts. **In Keble's Preface to his edition of** Hooker's Works will **be found an elaborate** account **of the publication** of the last three books of the Ec-**clesiastical Polity, and an** examination **and** approximate settlement of the question regarding their authenticity and completeness.

Hooker's nature was essentially an intellectual one; and the wonder of his mental biography is the celerity and certainty with which he transmuted knowledge and experience into intelligence. It may be a fancy, but we think it can be detected in an occasional uncharacteristic tartness of expression, that he had carried up **even** Mrs. Hooker into the region of his intellect, and dissolved her termagant tongue into **a fine** spiritual essence of gentle sarcasm. Not only did his vast learn**ing** pass, as successively acquired, from memory into faculty, but the daily beauty of his life left its finest and last result in his brain. **His** patience, humility, **dis**interestedness, self-denial, his pious and humane sentiments, every resistance to temptation, every benevolent **act,** every holy prayer, were by some subtile chemistry turned into thought, and gave his intellect an upward lift, — increasing the range of its vision, and bringing it into closer proximity with great ideas. We cannot read **a** page of his writings, without feeling the presence of this spiritual power in conception, statement, and argument. And this moral excellence, which has thus become moral intelligence, this holiness which is in perfect union with reason, this spirit of love which can not **only feel but** see, gives a softness, richness, sweetness,

and warmth to his thinking, quite as peculiar to it as its
dignity, amplitude, and elevation.

As a result of this deep, silent, and rapid growth of
nature, this holding in his intelligence all the results
of his emotional and moral life, he attaches our sympathies as we follow the stream of his arguments; for we
feel that he has *communed* with all the principles he
communicates, and knows by direct perception the spiritual realities he announces.   His intellect, accordingly,
does not act by intuitive flashes; but "his soul has
sight" of eternal verities, and directs at them a clear,
steady, divining gaze.   He has no lucky thoughts;
everything is earned; **he** knows what he knows, in all
its multitudinous relations, and cannot be surprised by
sudden objections, convicting him of oversight of **even**
the minutest application of any principle he holds in his
calm, strong grasp.   And as a controversialist he has
the immense advantage of descending into the field of
controversy from a height above it, and commanding it,
while his opponents are wrangling with their minds on a
level with it.   The great difficulty in the man of thought
is, to connect his thought with life; and half the literature of theology and morals is therefore mere satire,
simply exhibiting the immense, unbridged, ironic gulf
that yawns, wide as that between Lazarus and Dives,
between truth and duty on the one hand and the actual

affairs and conduct of the world on the other. **But** Hooker, one of the loftiest of thinkers, was also one of the most practical. His shining idea, away up in the heaven of contemplation, sends **its** rays of light and warmth in a thousand directions upon the earth; illuminating palace and cottage; piercing into the crevices and corners of concrete existence; relating the high **with the** low, austere obligation with feeble performance; and showing the obscure tendencies of imperfect institutions to realize divine laws.

This capacious soul was lodged in one of the feeblest of bodies. Physiologists are never weary of telling us that masculine health is necessary to vigor of mind; but the vast mental strength of Hooker was independent of his physical constitution. **His appearance** in the pulpit conveyed no idea of a great man. Small in stature, with a low voice, using no gesture, never moving his person or lifting his eyes from his sermon, he seemed the very embodiment of clerical incapacity and dulness; but soon the thoughtful listener found his mind fascinated by the automaton speaker; a still, devout ecstasy breathed from the pallid lips; the profoundest thought and the most extensive learning found calm expression in the low accents; and, more surprising still, the somewhat rude mother-tongue of Englishmen was heard for the first time from the lips of a master of prose composition, demonstrating its capacity for all the purposes of the most refined and most enlarged philosophic thought. Indeed, the serene might of Hooker's soul is perhaps most obviously perceived in his style, — in the easy power with which he wields and bends to his purpose a language not yet trained into a ready vehicle of philosophic expression. It is doubtful if any English writer since his time has shown equal power in the construction of long sentences, — those sentences in which the thought, and the atmosphere of the thought, and the modifications of the thought, are all included in one sweeping period, which gathers clause after clause as it rolls melodiously on to its foreseen conclusion, having the general gravity and grandeur of its modulated movement pervaded by an inexpressibly sweet undertone of individual sentiment. And his strength is free from every fretful and morbid quality such as commonly taint the performances of a strong mind lodged in a sickly body. It is as serene, wholesome, and comprehensive, as it is powerful.

The Ecclesiastical Polity is the great theological work of the Elizabethan age. Pope Clement having said to Cardinal Allen and Dr. Stapleton, English Roman Catholics at Rome, that he had never met with an English book whose writer deserved the name of author, they replied that a poor, obscure English priest had written **a work on** church polity, which if he should **read would** change his opinion. At the conclusion of the first book, the Pope is said to have delivered this judgment: "There is no learning that this man hath not searched into, nothing too hard for his understanding. This man indeed deserves the name of **an** author; his books will get reverence from age; for there is in them such seeds of eternity, that, if the rest be like this, they shall last until the last fire consume all learning."

But it must be admitted that the rest, however great their merits, are not "like this." The first book of the Ecclesiastical Polity is not only the best, but it is that in which Hooker's mind is most effectually brought **into** relation with all thinking minds, and **that in** virtue **of** which he takes his high place in the history of **literature** and philosophy. The theologians he opposed **insisted** that a definite scheme of church polity was revealed in the Scriptures, and was obligatory on Christians. This, **of** course, reduced the controversy to a **mere** wrangle about the meaning of certain texts; and, as this mode of disputation does not make any call upon the higher mental and spiritual powers, it has always been popular among theologians,— giving everybody a chance in the textual and logical skirmish, and conducing to that anarchy of opinions which is not without its charm to the sternest champion of authority, if he has in

him **the** belligerent instinct. But Hooker, constitution
ally averse to controversy, and looking at it, not as an
end, but a means, had that aching for order which characterizes a peaceable spirit, and that demand for fundamental ideas which characterizes a great mind. **Ac-**
cordingly, in the first book, he mounts above the controversy before entering into it, and surveys the whole
question of law, from the one eternal, Divine Law to the
laws which are in force among men. He makes the
laws which God has written in the reason of man divine
laws, as well as those he has supernaturally revealed
in the Scriptures; and especially he enforces the somewhat startling principle, that law is variable or invaria-
ble, not according to the source from which it emanates,
but according to the matter to which it refers. If the
matter be changeable, be mutable, the law must partici-
pate in the mutability of that which it was designed to
regulate; and this principle, he insists, is independent
of the fact whether the law originated in God or in the
divinely constituted reason of man. There are some
laws which God has written in the reason of man which
are immutable; there are some laws supernaturally
revealed in Scripture which are mutable. In the **first**
case, no circumstance can justify their violation, in the
other, circumstances necessitate a change. **The** bearing
of this principle on the right of the Church of England

to command rules and ceremonies which might not have been commanded by Scripture is plain. Even if the principle were denied by his opponents, it could be properly denied only by being confuted ; and to confute it exacted the lifting up of the controversy into the region of ideas.

But it is not so much in the conception and application of one principle, as in the exhibition of many principles harmoniously related, that Hooker's largeness of comprehension is shown. No other great logician is **so free** from logical fanaticism. His mind gravitates to truth ; and it therefore limits and guards the application of single *truths*, detecting that fine point where many principles unite in forming wisdom, and refusing to be pushed too far in any one direction. He has his hands on the reins of a hundred wild horses, unaccustomed to exercise their strength and fleetness in joint effort ; but **the** moment they feel the might of his meekness, they all sedately obey the directing power which sends them in orderly motion to a common goal. The central idea of his book is **law.** Even God, he contends, " works not only according to his own *will*, but the *counsel* of his own will," according **" to** the *order* which he before all ages hath set down for himself to do all things by." A self-conscious, personal, working, divine **reason is** therefore **at** the heart of things, and infinite *power* and **infinite** *love* are identical **with** infinite *intelligence.* Hooker's breadth of mind is evinced in his refusing, unlike most theologians, to emphasize and detach **any** one of these divine perfections, whether it be power, or love, or intelligence. Intelligence is *in* power and love; power and love are *in* intelligence.

It would be impossible, in our short space, **to trace** the descent of **Hooker's** central idea of law to its **applications** to men and states. The law which the angels **obey, the law** of nature, the law which binds man as an **individual, the law** which binds **him as** member of a politic community, **the law which binds him as a member** of a religious **community,** the **law which** binds **nations** in their mutual relations, — all are **exhibited with** a force and clearness **of** vision, **a** mastery **of ethical** and political philosophy, **a** power **of** dealing with relative as well as **absolute** truth, and a sagacity of practical observation, which are remarkable both in their **separate** excellence and their exquisite combination. **To this** comprehensive treatise Agassiz the naturalist, Story the jurist, Webster the statesman, Garrison the reformer, could all go for principles, and for applications of principles. He appreciates, beyond any other thinker who has taken his stand on the Higher Law, but who **still believes in** the binding force **of** the laws of **men, the difficulty of making an individual, to whom** that **Law**

is revealed through reason, a member of **a politic or re-**
ligious *community ;* and he admits that the best men,
individually, are often those who are apt to be most unmanageable in their relations to state and church. The
argument he addresses to such minds, though it may not
be conclusive, is probably the least unsatisfactory that
· has ever been framed ; for it is presented in connection
with all that he has previously said in regard to the
binding force of the divine law.

Of this divine law, — the law which angels obey ; the
law of love ; the law which binds in virtue of its power
to allure and attract, and which weds obligation to ecstasy, — of this law he thus speaks in language which
seems touched with a consecrating radiance : —

"But now that we may lift up our eyes (as it were)
from the footstool to the throne of God, and, leaving
these natural, consider a little the state of heavenly and
divine creatures : touching angels, which are spirits im-
material and intellectual, the glorious inhabitants of
those sacred palaces, where nothing but light and
blessed immortality, no shadow of matter for tears, dis-
contentments, griefs, and uncomfortable passions to work
upon, but all joy, tranquillity, and peace, even for ever
and ever doth dwell : as in number and order they are
huge, mighty, and royal armies, so likewise in perfec-
tion of obedience unto that law, which the Highest,

whom **they** adore, love, and imitate, **hath** imposed upon them, such observants they are thereof, that our Saviour himself, being to set down the perfect idea of **that** which we are to pray and **wish for on earth, did not** teach to pray and wish for more than only that here it might be with us as with them it is in **heaven. God,** which moveth mere natural agents as an efficient **only,** doth otherwise move intellectual creatures, and especially **his** holy angels : for, beholding the face of God, in admiration of so great excellency they all adore him ; and, being rapt with the love of his beauty, they cleave inseparably forever unto him.   Desire to resemble him in goodness maketh them unweariable, and even insatiable, in their longing to do by all means all manner of **good unto** all the creatures of God, but especially unto the children of men`: in the countenance of whose nature, looking downward, they behold themselves beneath themselves ; even as upward, in God, beneath whom themselves are, they see that character which is nowhere but in them-selves and us resembled. . . . . Angelical actions may, therefore, be reduced unto these three general kinds : first, most delectable love, arising from the visible apprehension of the purity, glory, and beauty of God, **in-**visible saving only to spirits that are pure ; secondly, adoration, grounded upon the evidence of the greatness of God, on whom they **see how** all things depend ; thirdly, imitation, bred by the presence of his exemplary goodness, who ceaseth not before them daily to fill heaven **and** earth with the rich treasures of most free and undeserved grace."

And though the concluding passage of the first book of the Ecclesiastical Polity has been a thousand times quoted, it would be unjust to Hooker not here to cite the sentence which most perfectly embodies his soul: —

" Wherefore, that here we may briefly end : of law there can be no less acknowledged, than that her seat is the bosom of God, her voice the harmony of the world : all things in heaven and earth do her homage, the very least as feeling her care, and the greatest as not exempted from her power ; **both angels** and men **and** creatures of what condition soever, though each in different sort and manner, yet all with uniform consent, **admiring** her as the mother of their peace and their joy."

In concluding these essays on the Literature of the **Age** of Elizabeth, let us pass rapidly in review the writers to whom they have referred. And first for the dramatists, whose works — in our day on the dissecting-tables of criticism, but in their own all alive with intellect and passion — made the theatres of Elizabeth and James rock and ring with the clamors or plaudits of a mob too excited to be analytic. Of these professors of the **science** of human nature, we have attempted to portray **the fiery** imagination that flames through the fustian and animal fierceness of Marlowe; the bluff arrogance of the outspoken Jonson, with his solid understanding, caustic humor, delicate fancy, and undeviating belief in Ben; the close observation and teeming mother-**wit** which found vent in the limpid verse of Heywood; Middleton's sardonic sagacity, and Marston's envenomed **satire;** the suffering, and the soaring and singing cheer, the beggary and the benignity, so quaintly united in Dekkar's vagrant life **and sunny** genius; Webster's bewildering terror, and Chapman's haughty aspiration; the subtile sentiment of Beaumont; the fertile, flashing, and ebullient spirit of Fletcher; **the easy dignity of** Massinger's thinking, and the sonorous majesty of **his** style; the fastidious **elegance** and melting tenderness of Ford; and the one-souled, " myriad-minded " Shakespeare, who is **so** unmistakably beyond them all.

Then, recurring to the undramatic poets, we have endeavored to catch a glimpse of the fairy-land of Spenser's celestialized imagination; and lightly to touch on the characteristics of the poets who preceded and followed him; on the sternly serious and unjoyous **creativeness of** Sackville; the meditative fulness and tender fancy of " well-languaged " Daniel; the enthusiastic expansiveness of description, and pure, bright, and vigorous diction of Drayton ; the sententious sharpness of Hall ; the clear imaginative insight and dialectic felicity of Davies ; the metaphysical voluptuousness and witty unreason of Donne ; the genial, thoughtful, well-proportioned soul of Wotton ; the fantastic devoutness of Herbert; and the coarsely frenzied commonplaces **of** Warner,

> " Who stood
> Up to the chin in the Pierian " — mud!

Again, in Sidney we have striven to portray genius and goodness as expressed in behavior ; in Raleigh, genius **and** audacity as expressed in insatiable, though somewhat equivocal, activity of arm and brain ; in Bacon, the beneficence and the autocracy of an intellect whose comprehensiveness needs no celebration ; **and** in Hooker, the passage of holiness into intelligence, **and** the spirit of love into the power of reason.

And, in attempting to delineate so many diverse individualities, we have been painfully conscious of another **and** more difficult audience than that we address. The imperial intellects, — **the** Bacons, Hookers, Shakespeares, **and** Spensers, the men who on earth are as much alive now as they were two hundred and fifty years ago, — are, in their assured intellectual dominion, blandly careless of the judgments of individuals ; but there is a large class of writers whose genius we have considered, who have well-nigh passed away from the protecting admiration and affectionate memory of general readers. As we, more or less roughly, handled these, as we felt the pulse of life throbbing in every time-stained and dust-covered volume, — dust out of which Man was originally made, and to which Man, as author, is commonly so sure to return, — the books resumed their original form of men, became personal forces, to resent impeachments of their honor, or misconceptions of their genius ; and a troop of Spirits stalked from -the neglected pages to confront their irreverent critic. There they were, — ominous or contemptuous judges of the person who assumed to be their judge : on the faces of some, sarcastic denial ; on others, tender reproaches ; on others, benevolent pity ; on others, serenely beautiful indifference or disdain. " Who taught you," their looks seemed to say, " to deliver dogmatic judgments on us ? What know you of our birth, culture, passions, temptations, struggles, motives, two hundred years ago ? What right have you, to blame ? What qualifications have you, to praise ? Let us abide in our earthly oblivion, — in our immortal life. It is sufficient that our works demonstrated on earth the inextinguishable vitality of the Soul that glowed within us ; and, for the rest, we have long passed to the only infallible — the Almighty — critic and judge of works and of men ! "